On the Fence

Chance City Series, Book Two

Robin Deeter

Table of Contents

Other books by Robin Deeter

Chance City Series

The Paha Sapa Saga

Make sure to sign up at my website, www.robindeeter.com to receive email alerts about new releases, contests, news about upcoming works, and contests.

ROBIN DEETER

DEDICATION

This book is dedicated to Essie Michael, who constantly inspires me with her love, loyalty, and generosity (not to mention giving me a good boot in the rear when I need it).

A special thank you to Hunter Stetson, who gave me permission to use his name for a character in the series.

CHAPTER ONE

The Greyhound streaked down an alley between two buildings in hot pursuit of its prey; a pickpocket whom Det. Cyrus Decker and Deputy Brock Guthrie had been trying to catch for two weeks. Their co-worker, Deputy Ellie Jeffries, had dressed up as an old lady that day and the crook had taken the bait.

Cy, as he was called by most people, whistled to his dog, Slink, and the Greyhound moved even faster, easily catching up to the thief. He cut to the right and nipped at the pickpocket's heels, tripping the man, who went down hard. Rolling over, the man was instantly covered with doggie kisses as Slink wagged his tail excitedly.

Laughing, the man pushed Slink aside and attempted to run again, but he halted when he came face-to-face with another dog. The huge German Shepherd-Husky mix didn't share Slink's view that this was playtime. Instead, he bared his sharp fangs and let out a low, rumbling growl, making it clear that he was very serious about the pickpocket remaining still.

At a different whistle from Cy, Slink backed off and sat down.

Brock, a broad shouldered, blond man, came up behind

the other dog with a big grin on his face. "Good boy, Burt," he said.

Burt didn't pay him any mind, intent on doing his job. He didn't let down his guard for a second and barked when the robber moved. Brock stepped around Burt and hauled the guy to his feet.

"Guess what, jackass? You're under arrest for theft," Brock said as Cy reached them.

Cy gave Burt a hand signal. Burt sat down, but he kept a watchful eye on the criminal, whom Brock was handcuffing.

The crook sneered at them. "Using dogs. Isn't that cheating or something?"

Cy grinned. "No, that's called good police work."

Brock jerked his head in Cy's direction. "We don't agree on a whole lot, but he's right. Let's go."

Loud panting drew their attention to the mouth of the alley. A black Pug raced towards them, his tongue protruding from his open mouth as he ran.

"Told you he'd find us," Cy said.

Brock smirked at him. "Don't be so damn cocky."

"I'm not. I just know my dogs, that's all," Cy said. "Good boy, Pudge."

Pudge danced around a little and then bit the crook on the ankle.

"Ow! What did he do that for?" the guy said, sidestepping the little dog.

Cy and Brock laughed.

"For good measure," Cy said. "Knock it off, Pudge."

Pudge sneezed an affirmative response. Cy praised the other dogs and gave all of them a little piece of wasna. His Uncle Cotton, a Comanche man, still made the Indian staple and Cy always kept it on hand as a reward for his dogs.

As they walked out to the main street, Pudge ran ahead of them, performing pirouettes on his hind legs.

Brock grinned. "He's really putting on a good show."

Cy grunted. "Yeah, but he's not getting any more treats right now. Pudge, knock it off."

Pudge dropped to all fours and silently regarded them with his big, dark eyes.

"Don't look at me like that. You just had a treat," Cy said.

Pudge growled his disagreement.

Cy pointed at him. "No backtalk."

Brock hid a smile when Pudge turned his back to them and trotted away. Pudge was smart enough to know that when someone smiled or laughed at him that they weren't serious about a command that had just been given. Although he didn't like Cy very much, Brock loved Cy's dogs and he never interfered with their training. Therefore, he listened to what Cy told him about his training methods and followed them.

He was surprised to see a smile tugging at Cy's mouth, too.

Cy shrugged at his look, his dark eyes twinkling. "I'm just as susceptible to how cute they are as you. I just hide it better, that's all."

Brock shook his head and marched their prisoner forward.

Sitting at his desk a short time later, Brock worked on a report on the apprehension of the pickpocket, but he was distracted by images of a gorgeous dark-haired beauty with exotic brown eyes and soft lips. Cy's sister, Daphne, drew his eyes every time she was around and his thoughts were on her much of the time.

Her beauty, intelligence, and kindness called to him. She'd made her feelings for him very clear when she'd kissed him in September. It was almost November and the memory of that kiss hadn't dimmed in Brock's mind one little bit. She'd accused him of being racist, and he knew that she was right, but his hatred for the Comanche had been deeply ingrained in him by the murder of his beloved grandfather by some Comanche braves. As a child, he'd witnessed the attack and he'd never gotten over it.

That hatred was one of the reasons he barely tolerated Cy. He also didn't care for Cy much because their boss, Sheriff Rob Anderson, thought that the department needed someone like Cy on their staff, as though Brock and the other deputies weren't doing a good enough job. Brock also didn't like the way Cy seemed to think that he was clear to issue orders to the deputies.

All of this served to fuel the animosity between the two men. However, since they'd made a truce in September, it hadn't been as strong. They were slowly learning how to work together even though they still butted heads on a daily basis. Brock had developed a grudging respect for Cy and Cy gave Brock credit for his solid investigative and excellent photography skills.

Brock sighed and forced his mind back to his report, propping his feet up on his desk and getting down to business. Ellie Jeffries came in the door as he finished up. He smiled at the petite brunette.

"Well, I see that you're back to your normal self," he commented.

Ellie nodded. "And glad of it. I don't know how actors stay in those getups all night. I was glad to get that wig off, too. It might be cold out, but I was hotter than blazes in it."

Brock grinned. "But you did make a very pretty old lady."

Ellie laughed and hung up her woolen coat. "Thanks. I'm just glad you caught the guy. I didn't want to have to keep dressing up like that."

Brock put his report in a file folder and got up. "I'm glad we got him, too. He's not cooperating much, though. Walt Gaines is supposed to stop by to talk to him."

Ellie groaned. "Oh, no. Not Walt."

Brock chuckled. "What's the matter? Don't wanna see the man who's in love with you?"

Ellie wanted to punch Brock. "No, I don't. How many times do I have to tell him that I'm not interested?"

Crossing to a filing cabinet, Brock said, "I'm guessing a whole heap more. What's so wrong with Walt? He seems like a nice enough fella."

"Too nice," Ellie said. "I can't make him mad. I've tried."

Brock put the file away and gave her a dubious look. "So you prefer bad-tempered men?"

Ellie flopped down in her chair. "Of course not."

Brock sat down on a corner of her desk. "You're pining for me, aren't you?"

Ellie laughed at his teasing. "Yes, Brock. You found me out. No, there's only one woman pining over you, and she's related to your arch enemy."

Frowning, Brock moved away from her desk and put on his coat.

"What's the matter, Brock? Don't like the truth?" Ellie asked. "You know you're a horse's ass for not callin' on her. Happiness is right at your fingertips, but you won't take a risk, will you?"

Brock jammed on his hat and said, "I'm going out on patrol."

He went out the door, but didn't get very far before an idea occurred to him. Going back inside, he strode over to Ellie's desk.

"Yeah?" She eyed him quizzically.

"I'll tell you what, I'll call on Daphne if you let Walt take you out. If I have to take a risk, so do you," Brock said.

Ellie thought about it. She liked Daphne and she thought that her and Brock would be good together if Brock could get over his aversion to Indians. Going out with Walt was a small price to pay if it meant that she could help two people take a chance on love.

5

She stuck her hand out. "Done. Shake on it."

Brock's eyebrows shot up. He'd expected her to refuse. However, there was no way to back out of the deal that he'd proposed, so he shook her hand. "Done."

Showing much more confidence than he felt, he went out the door again, cursing his pride and big mouth.

~~*~~

"Well, there comes one of our fine deputies," Sandy Hopper, owner of the Chowhound Saloon quipped.

Brock smiled. "Hi, Sandy. How's business?"

She poured him a beer and sat it on the bar. "Booming, which you already know."

Sitting on a stool, Brock said, "Yeah. I do. How's Betty doing? She feel any better?"

Sandy's brown eyes filled with concern over the mention of one of her saloon girls. "Not really. Damn flu doesn't want to let go."

Brock frowned as he took a sip of beer. "I guess it's stronger this year. You be careful so you don't get it."

Sandy nodded. "I got a strong constitution. Don't worry about me. So when are you gonna get smart and let me take you in the back?"

Brock laughed. "Sandy, I don't think I could handle a woman like you."

"A woman like me? What's that mean?"

He leaned forward and lowered his voice conspiratorially. "As I hear it, you like to saddle your men and put the spurs to them."

Sandy gave a delighted laugh. "You heard right, honey!"

Grinning, Brock said, "See? I knew it wasn't just a rumor. I'll bet you keep Jim busy."

She gave him a saucy wink. "Whatever makes you think that?"

"Call it a hunch," Brock said. "What's for lunch?"

"Pot roast."

"Sounds good," Brock said. "Let me ask you a question."

Sandy nodded. "Okay. Shoot."

Brock looked around the place as he thought about how to frame the question. While the Chowhound was actually a very attractive establishment, it wasn't showy. Oak wainscoting ran halfway up the walls, and gold-and-cream wallpaper filled the space between it and the ceiling, which consisted of large, polished oak beams.

A large fireplace stood on the outside wall while a small stage was situated on the opposite side of the room. Sandy kept the barroom clean along with the bar area itself. Although she wore trousers and blouses in lieu of dresses and skirts, Sandy was a fastidious person, who often chastised patrons for being too messy.

The private rooms where her girls entertained men were also clean. The girls who rented the rooms were required to keep them that way. Everyone knew about the operation, including Chance City's law enforcement staff, but they viewed it as the lesser of two evils, the worst evil being a bunch of overly amorous drunk men wandering the streets looking for company.

Sandy and her companion, Jim, ran a fairly orderly saloon and took good care of their girls, including making them see the doctor on a regular basis and giving them decent food to eat. Without Sandy and Jim, many of the girls who worked for them wouldn't have a roof over their heads or any money. Sheriff Rob Anderson wasn't blind concerning the Chowhound, but a lot of important council members and other officials frequented it and attempting to put it out of business wouldn't get him or his staff anywhere except fired.

"I ain't gettin' any younger, Brock. What's your question?" Sandy asked.

"Am I crazy for wanting to see Daphne even though Cy and I hate each other?"

Sandy was well aware of the contentious relationship between the two men. Of course, there wasn't much that she didn't know about what happened around the city. She and Benny McFarlend, owner of Big Benny's Saloon, had an unofficial partnership and they shared information about patrons. All of the law enforcement staff in Chance City frequented both establishments, so the bar owners often knew what the sheriff's department was working on.

Rather than working against Rob and his employees, the friendships that existed between them benefited them because both bar owners often parted with information that helped apprehend criminals. This enabled the sheriff's department to keep the crime rate down.

Sandy said, "Well, I don't think you're crazy, but you're gonna have to decide whether courting her is worth putting up with Cy's crap or not. The other thing you'd better think about is whether or not you could ever live with Cy. Oh, and then there's the fact that you hate the Comanche. Daphne's part Comanche. And lastly, the rest of Cy's family hates you, except Cotton, but there aren't too many people Cotton hates. All of this boils down to how badly you wanna see her."

Brock took another swig of beer. "I can't get her out of my head, so I guess pretty bad."

Sandy nodded sagely. "You know, any man who's interested in Daphne has to understand that she's not gonna move out of her family's home. Are you going to be able to live under the same roof as Cy? I know one man who wouldn't care where he lived as long as he could be with her."

Brock's thoughtful expression darkened into a scowl. "You mean Benny. I know that he's sweet on her."

"You hit the nail on the head. He flirts with her, but he's been a gentleman and hasn't gotten serious about pursuing her because he knows that she's been waiting for you to make a move," Sandy said. "He's not gonna wait forever, though. So you'd better think hard on this, but hurry up and make up your mind. I'll be back with your lunch."

Brock nodded as Sandy walked away, his mind already working on the situation.

ROBIN DEETER

CHAPTER TWO

Ellie was nothing if not efficient. When faced with a problem, she met it head-on instead of going out around it. Sometimes this involved using deception and her feminine wiles and other times it meant throwing her position as a deputy around. Brock wasn't the only one who was having second thoughts about the deal that they'd made. Her reluctance annoyed her, though, and she told herself that she was being silly.

The defense attorney was kind, intelligent, and even-tempered. He was fairly nice to look at, too, but in a shabby, aw-shucks sort of way. She'd heard that he became a completely different person in court, but she'd never seen him in that capacity. Ellie couldn't really say why she was averse to having Walt call on her, but something about him bothered her.

So when he walked in with his big, battered briefcase and a smile on his face, she frowned a little. If he noticed, Walt didn't show it.

"Hello, Miss Ellie," he said in his quiet Irish accent.

"Hi, Walt. Your client is ready for you," she said. "It's pretty cut-and-dried, though."

"Say no more," Walt said, his hazel eyes twinkling

behind his glasses. "I never like to have a preconceived notion about a client."

Ellie nodded. "All right. I'll bring him into the visiting room."

Walt watched her walking away, taking in her fine, petite form in the trousers she wore. Taking a deep breath, he forced his mind back to the matter at hand and went into the visiting room. Ellie entered with his client just as he was sitting down.

"Here he is. Good luck," she said. "He won't talk."

Walt smiled. "Thanks."

He knew that would change as soon as she left the room. It always did with criminals. True to form, she'd no sooner gotten out the door before the crook leaned forward and whispered that he didn't do it. Walt nodded, pretended to take notes, and made sympathetic noises, but he'd made up his mind about the client's guilt after the first few sentences out of the man's mouth.

Walt was happy to let the man go on about his poor family and bad upbringing, things that had no bearing on the case. After twenty minutes, Walt informed the thief that he had all of the information he needed and that he'd see him on the day of the trial, which was set for the next week. They shook hands and Walt tapped on the door for Ellie to come get the prisoner.

Usually Walt would have stuck around a little to invite Ellie to dinner, but he was somewhat distracted that day. As she came out of the cell area down the hall, Walt gave her a friendly wave and headed for the door.

Ellie was tempted to just let him go so she didn't have to deal with him, but a deal was a deal and she'd rather get her part of it over with.

"Walt, wait!" she called.

Surprised, Walt turned around quickly, almost dropping his briefcase. "Did ya need somethin' then?"

Ellie was normally very confident around men, but not when it came to Walt. She ran her eyes over his tall form and up to his bright hazel eyes. His dark brown hair was always tussled, giving him a slightly harried look and he rarely looked like he'd shaven. It was hard to get a fix on his build because his clothes were rumpled and loose on him.

"Well, I was thinking about your last dinner invitation and thought, what the heck? What could it hurt?" she responded, cringing inwardly at the brusque statement. "That didn't come out right. What I meant was that I'd very much like to dine with you."

Walt smiled. "Well, this is a pleasant surprise. A *very* pleasant one. When does it suit ya?" It was hard to contain his excitement, but he managed it.

"How about tomorrow tonight? Is that too short notice?" she asked.

"Not at all. Will seven be all right?"

"That'll be fine," she said.

Walt nodded. "Good. I'll come for ya then. I know where ya live."

Ellie blinked a couple of times. "You do?"

"Aye. I know where all of the law enforcement staff live. I never know when I might need one of ya," Walt said. "Well, have a good day. I'm lookin' forward to our evenin'."

Ellie forced herself to say, "Me, too. See ya then."

Walt waited until he was well away from the sheriff's office before allowing himself to grin like an idiot.

When Brock got back to the sheriff's office, he was dismayed to find that Ellie had already made good on her promise to let Walt take her out.

"Your turn," she said, smiling overly-sweetly at him as he sat down at his desk.

He frowned. "Shut up. I'm working on it. I can't help it that I didn't see Daphne yet. So how is old Gainsey?"

Ellie said, "He's not old. Huh. Come to think of it, I don't know how old he is. I'm guessing about thirty or thereabouts. Do you know how old he is?"

Brock laughed. "No, but I'm not surprised. No one knows a whole lot about him. I guess he's lived around here about five years or so."

"How'd he become a lawyer?" Ellie asked.

"You'll have to ask him because I have no idea," Brock said. "I'll be interested to hear about how things went. Where's Cy?"

"In his office," Ellie said. "He's brooding about the Clifford case. Best to let him be. You know how he gets when he's like that."

Brock let out a short hum of understanding and took out a small notepad. He quickly wrote something on it, ripped it off, and pulled out an envelope from a desk drawer. Tucking the paper inside it, he sealed it shut, and wrote on it. Ellie was a very curious person and tried to see what he was writing, but her desk was too far away from his.

Looking up, Brock caught her watching him. "I'll be right back, Miss Busybody," he said.

"Just a little hint?" Ellie coaxed.

"Nope," Brock said, grinning before he went through the kitchen and out the back door.

Pudge sat on Cy's desk, looking out the window, his big, dark eyes taking in the scene outside it. Cy smiled at the intense look on the pug's face as he sketched him. Drawing often helped Cy work through tough cases and Pudge was always a willing model.

Suddenly Pudge yipped and jumped off the desk, scattering papers and knocking Cy's cup of coffee over in his haste to get to the door. Pudge barked and pranced while Cy swore and rushed to mop up the mess before the coffee destroyed too many papers.

The door to the old shed that Cy had confiscated opened and Brock came inside, shutting the door quickly against the brisk wind. A scratch at the door made Brock back up and reopen the door. Slink and Burt crowded into what Brock had dubbed the Dog House.

Cy looked at Brock. "What?"

This was how he normally greeted Brock.

Brock looked at Slink. "I see that Rob's wife made Slink another sweater."

Slink nudged Brock's hand, wanting to be petted. Cy grunted as his gaze traveled disapprovingly over the gray and white garment.

"I keep telling her that he's fine without it, but she has it in her head that he's too skinny to be able to keep warm," Cy said.

"Well, to be fair, the poor dog doesn't have very thick fur," Brock said. "What's the harm in him wearing a sweater?"

"The problem is that it makes it easier for someone to get a hold of him and hurt him," Cy said. "And it also increases the risk of him getting caught on something. I don't want him to get used to wearing one because he's gonna want to do it all the time. If we're out in the field and he has one on, I'm not gonna have time to stop and take it off."

Brock accepted a kiss on his cheek from Slink. "Oh. I never thought about that."

Cy said, "The first rule to working with dogs is always minimizing the danger to them. That's why I'm the only one who feeds them. If they get used to accepting food from other people, it makes it easy for them to be poisoned."

"Okay, okay," Brock said. "I didn't come out here for a dog training lesson. Give this to Daphne."

Cy took the envelope, read his sister's name, and narrowed his eyes at Brock. "What is it?"

"It's a note. Don't read it," Brock said. "Any breakthroughs on the Clifford case?"

Cy sat down in his chair and motioned to the other one. "Might as well walk through it together and see what we come up with."

Putting on the professional persona he used around Cy, Brock sat and prepared for a round of the back and forth brainstorming that he and Cy had developed. They might not like each other much personally, but they worked well professionally. By the time a half an hour had passed, they'd come up with another couple of leads to check into.

When Brock got up to leave, Cy tapped the envelope Brock had given him. "Am I gonna like this?"

Brock's face relaxed into a devilish grin. "Nope."

Cy wanted to throw a knife at Brock's back as he quickly left his office.

~~*~~

Daphne washed the supper dishes while her cousin, Johnny, dried. He usually offered and she was glad because he provided a good diversion from her sometimes depressing thoughts.

"I can't believe we had two calves born on the same day," he said as she handed him another dish to dry. "One Hereford and one Longhorn. And our Holstein pair will be here next week, too. Things are moving along. Leigh's a genius."

Daphne laughed. "If I didn't know better, I'd say you had a crush on her the way you go on about her."

Johnny's blue eyes sparkled even as he blushed. "Naw, but she is a beautiful woman. Cy's a lucky man. I just appreciate her smarts, that's all. Plus, she's so nice."

"Yes, Leigh is a good woman and the smartest thing Cy ever did was marrying her," Daphne said, ignoring the pinprick of jealously to her heart.

"Yep," Johnny said.

Daphne said, "When we're done here, I want you to try on those shirts I made for you."

"Okay. I'll give you money for the material," Johnny said.

"That's not necessary," Daphne said.

Johnny said, "Yeah, it is. I got some money now since I've been making some stuff for folks and material ain't cheap. I don't want you and Cy to keep buying stuff for me. It ain't right."

"Johnny, you know that we haven't minded. You've had a hard time of it. Besides, you built that beautiful arch for the driveway and you've been making all kinds of repairs around here. The porch looks great, by the way," Daphne said.

He shrugged. "It's the least I could do since you and Cy have been so good to me. But it's time for me to start making my own way. A man has to be able to stand on his own two feet, Daphne."

Daphne smiled. She'd never tell him since men didn't like to be called adorable, but he was. With his messy blond hair, bright blue eyes, and dimples, Johnny was the sort of man that many girls went for. He was always respectful of women and did anything he was asked without complaint.

Over the year that he'd been with her and Cy, he'd filled out more and lost some of his boyishness. His face was a little more chiseled and his shoulders broader. But he'd kept his sweet, affable personality.

"I'm very proud of you for working so hard," Daphne said.

"Thanks."

The rapid pitter-patter of dog paws sounded on the stairs and their collie pup, Queenie came barreling into the kitchen, barking up a storm. She went to the door, pawing at it.

Johnny said, "Cy must be home. She only goes crazy like that when him and the rest come along."

Daphne dried her hands and opened the kitchen door. Queenie ran outside, making a beeline for the barn. It wasn't too long before her brother strode in the door.

"Hi," he said. "How are you guys?"

"We're fine," Daphne said. "You look tired."

"No more than usual," he said. "Here. This is for you."

Daphne took the envelope he handed her. She read annoyance and curiosity in his expression before reading her name on the front of it.

"Who is it from?" she asked.

Cy's expression darkened. "Brock."

Hope flashed in Daphne's heart, but she kept calm as she opened the envelope and took out the note.

Daphne,

I can't get you out of my mind. Will you join me for dinner tomorrow night? Let Cy know your answer. If it's yes, I'll pick you up tomorrow night at seven unless an emergency comes up. I'll pray real hard that it doesn't.

Brock

Daphne couldn't stop the big smile that lit up her face. "He wants to have dinner tomorrow night." She put a hand to her forehead. "I don't believe it. After all this time."

Cy grunted and hung up his coat and hat.

Daphne said, "I don't care if you like it or not, Cy. Don't begrudge me happiness."

Cy faced her again. "I'm not. I just don't want you to get hurt. I don't understand why he wants to see you since you're part Comanche. He's always hated us because of our heritage."

"Maybe he's coming around," Daphne said. "I'm a grown woman, Cy. I'm willing to take a chance."

Cy arched a brow, conveying his doubt. "I just don't understand what you see in him. Can you answer me that?"

Daphne met his gaze. "I think there's a lot more to Brock than what you see."

"I see too much of him," Cy said. "Now I have to see him outside of work, too."

Johnny frowned. "This isn't about you, Cy. This is about something that makes Daphne happy. Besides, it's her business if she wants to be courted by Brock."

Cy's eyes widened. Johnny didn't normally take sides when he and Daphne argued. "Do you like Brock?"

Johnny shrugged. "I don't know him well enough to know if I do or not. Just because you don't get along with him doesn't mean that other people don't."

Cy knew he wasn't going to change Daphne's mind about seeing Brock, so he dropped the subject in favor of a much more pleasant one. "Where's my wife?"

"At Cotton's," Daphne said.

"It's dark out," Cy responded, stepping over to the sink to wash up.

Daphne chuckled. "Your wife will be fine. She can handle herself just fine. Now sit down and eat your supper."

Cy opened the door and let out a sharp whistle. The dogs soon ran in the door, greeting Daphne and Johnny. Cy got out their food bowls and divvied out the scraps that Daphne had put into a larger bowl for them.

He snapped his fingers. "Sit!"

All four canines dropped their haunches to the floor.

"Stay."

Cy lined the bowls up by the far wall and walked away. However, he didn't give them permission to eat just yet. He waited until he'd washed his hands again.

"Go ahead," he said.

The dogs leaped for their bowls, downing half their meal before Cy had barely begun his own. Queenie finished hers and then stared at Pudge, who stood next to her. The Pug glanced at her and she whined. Cy watched with a smile as Pudge took out a piece of chicken from his bowl, put it on the floor, and nudged it over to her. Queenie gobbled it up and gave Pudge's ear a couple licks of thanks.

Johnny laughed. "Pudge is a ladies' man. One of these days we'll have little Pollies or Cugs. What would you call them?"

"Ugly," Cy said.

Daphne hit his shoulder. "That's not nice."

"But it's true," Cy said. "Can you imagine a long-haired Pudge or a short Collie?"

Daphne laughed as she imagined that. "I'm not sure what you'd use a dog like that for, but knowing you, you'd find something."

Cy grinned. "Well, we're not gonna find out. I'll find a suitable stud Collie when the time is right."

Johnny said, "You'd better make sure Pudge isn't around when that other dog is. He'll fight for his lady."

Though Pudge was small, he was solid muscle and fearless around other animals. He'd chased horses, dogs, cats, and once had even gone after a coyote. His size didn't deter him from fighting any perceived enemy.

Johnny said, "Well, I'll see you in the morning. I'm gonna go work on that sign I'm making for Mr. Skyler. I told him I'd have it for him by the end of the week."

Daphne said, "Don't be up too late."

"Yes, ma'am," Johnny said. "Goodnight."

Cy lifted his hand in response as his cousin went out the door. Daphne said, "Goodnight. I'm going to bed a little early. Tell Brock that I said yes."

Knowing it was useless to try to change her mind, Cy said, "Okay. Goodnight."

Daphne took the note Brock had sent and went upstairs, her happiness too strong to be dimmed by Cy's disapproval.

CHAPTER THREE

Leigh put her horse, Cutter, away and gave him a little bit of sweet feed as a treat before going into the house. It was dark downstairs and she figured that Daphne had already gone to bed. Cy's horse was in the barn, so she knew that he was home. She hung up her coat and hat and took off her boots before mounting the stairs.

Just as she passed the washroom, someone grabbed her from behind, clamping a hand over her mouth and pulling her roughly against them.

"Do I need to be jealous of you and Cotton?" Cy growled into her ear.

His warm breath grazed her skin and her pulse jumped in response. She shook her head, smiling against his palm. Then his free hand traveled up over her midriff to cup her breast and she gasped. Heat pooled inside and she swallowed a moan.

Cy laughed softly, kissed her cheek, and released her. "I'm glad to hear that."

He practically dragged her into their room, quickly shutting the door. Leigh saw that he'd been reading one of his law journals. He was always reading up on new investigative and forensic techniques. She also noted that he was shirtless, revealing his muscular torso and arms.

She looped her arms around his neck, pressing a kiss to his lips. "Hello, Detective."

His short beard and mustache were pleasantly scratchy. She hadn't been sure at first that she would like him with a beard, but she had to admit that he looked good with one. Cy had told her that he usually grew one for the winter. Unlike his cousins, who seemed to have inherited more Comanche traits than he had, Cy was able to grow a beard and his chest was covered in a fine matting of short, dark hair.

"Hello, honey. Did you have a good day?" he asked.

"Two calves were born and they're healthy, so I'd call that a good day."

Cy leaned forward, buried his face against her neck, and inhaled her scent. She smelled of horses, hay, and Leigh; a combination that drove him crazy. "Good. We need healthy calves. Which kinds?"

"Hereford and Longhorn."

When Cy's teeth scored the sensitive skin near her ear, Leigh couldn't hold back a moan. His hands traveled down her back to her rear end, giving it a playful squeeze.

She squealed a little and he laughed.

"I keep telling you that that tickles," she said smiling into his dark eyes.

"And I keep telling you that I like hearing you make that sound, so that's why I do it," he said.

The heat in his gaze made her body temperature rise. "Shut up," she said, pressing her mouth to his.

Cy chuckled against her lips and then sucked in a breath when he felt Leigh's fingers skim over his stomach before going to his trouser buttons. She took advantage and deepened the kiss. He tasted of beer and some sort of dessert. These weren't two flavors that normally went together, but Leigh had discovered that anything tasted good when it came to Cy.

While she worked on his pants, he unbuttoned her

blouse. He broke off their kissing so that he could see what he uncovered as he parted the garment.

"You're so beautiful," he said, his gaze traveling over her. "I have to be the luckiest man on Earth."

Leigh's cheeks flushed and she smiled. "Well, I'm pretty lucky, too. Are you gonna stare all night or actually do something?"

Cy laughed at her brusque question because it was just Leigh's way of deflecting the shyness his compliments always caused. His wife was a passionate lover, but his words of appreciation brought out Leigh's bashful side. In answer to her question, he quickly helped her off with the rest of her garments.

Then he buried his hands in her honey-brown hair and gave her an urgent kiss, their naked bodies coming into contact. Leigh moaned as she felt his rapidly stiffening member rub against her stomach. She slid her hands down his powerful chest to take him in her palm. Everything about her husband was beautiful, including that part of him. Her first husband had been a generous, fun lover, but making love with Cy was so different. He was more demanding, but she felt his love for her in every kiss and touch.

He picked her up and laid her on the bed, his expression intense as he lay down next to her. Leigh sighed and closed her eyes as Cy's hands roamed over her. He cupped a breast and closed his mouth around her nipple, drawing it deep into his mouth. Leigh arched her back and squeezed his bicep.

Cy loved the way Leigh sounded and tasted. No other woman had ever excited him the way she did. She was everything wrapped up in the most delicious package. Intelligent, kind, strong, and so beautiful that it made him ache with longing. He controlled himself for as long as possible before his restraint snapped and he couldn't wait any longer.

Leigh's ardor had reached the same pitch as his and she

welcomed him into her arms and inside her body. His movements were sure and measured, falling into a graceful rhythm that swiftly took her to the brink. She marveled at the way he always timed it right, taking them over the edge into bliss together. It broke over her and she was helpless to do anything but hang onto him as it flowed through them.

She gladly took his weight as the ecstasy ebbed, caressing his broad shoulders as their breathing and heartbeats slowed from a gallop to a walk. As with every time they made love, Leigh prayed that she'd made a baby with the man she loved. Then she kissed his cheek and smiled, knowing what was coming next.

Before they'd gotten married, Cy had told her that he became chatty after lovemaking, but she hadn't believed it about her normally reticent man. He'd proved her wrong. It was as though the physical release also set free all of the things he'd thought that day, pouring out in a steady stream as they lay together.

Cy carefully rolled away from Leigh, bringing her with him so that he could hold her.

He blew out a breath. "Damn, Leigh. You're incredible."

She kissed his chest. "You're not so bad yourself, Detective."

"I'm glad to hear it."

Leigh smiled when he kissed he forehead and then he grunted a little. "Oh, boy. I know that sound. What's wrong?"

"Brock asked Daphne to dinner."

Leigh gasped and raised her head to meet his gaze. "He didn't!"

Cy's jaw clenched for a moment. "I wish he hadn't."

"That's great!" Leigh said.

"Whose side are you on?" Cy groused.

Leigh smiled. "Hers. She's been hoping so hard. I'm happy for her."

"It's a disaster waiting to happen," Cy said. "He can't stand anything to do with Indians and Daphne's part Comanche. Plus, he hates our family. Yep, he's gonna break her heart and then I'm gonna have to break his face."

"You don't know that. Besides, it's Daphne's heart and if she wants to take a risk then no one has any business interfering, Cy," Leigh said. "Love can do wonderful things. Maybe he'll see that just because Indians did something horrible when he was a kid that it doesn't mean that *all* Indians are bad."

The way Cy shifted conveyed his doubt.

"Cy, you listen to me. Don't you go sticking your nose in this," Leigh said.

"How am I supposed to do that? I work with him and she's my sister! I love her and I don't want to see her get hurt," Cy said.

"Neither do I, but you can't fight her battles for her. Besides, you want her to be happy, don't you?"

He grunted in affirmation.

"Then if Brock makes her happy, you're going to have to find a way to accept it."

Cy scowled at her. "You know, it's really annoying when you're so reasonable. I hate it when you're right, too."

Leigh laughed and slid on top of him. "I'll take your mind off how annoying I am."

He smiled when she bit his earlobe. "I don't wanna."

Her giggle made him grin. "Liar."

Cy wrapped his arms around her, unable to resist his wife's charms. "Okay, but you'd better make it worth my while."

"Shut up," she said against his mouth. "By the time I'm done with you, you won't be able to walk."

"Promises, promises."

She kissed him and made good on that promise.

ROBIN DEETER

CHAPTER FOUR

As he rode up to Silver's Mercantile the next day, Johnny's heart sank at the sight of the Silver triplets standing outside. He'd come to buy some nails and sandpaper. For a moment he considered going on by and stopping back later, but he was pressed for time and didn't have all day to mess around.

The triplets were all beautiful young women with dark hair and blue eyes, and they never lacked for male attention. The trouble was that all of them were sweet on Johnny and he hated to try to pick between them and cause discord between the siblings. Sometimes it was exhausting trying to tactfully turn down their advances without ruffling feathers.

Steeling himself against what was coming, Johnny dismounted and tied his horse to the hitching post outside the store and approached it. He respectfully removed his hat as he neared the sisters. Their pretty faces lit up when they caught sight of him. He was glad that they all wore different dresses under their black cloaks, but he still had trouble telling them apart.

"Well, there's that handsome Johnny," one of them said.

Hoping he was right, Johnny said, "Thanks, Heidi. You're all looking pretty today, not that you don't every day, of course."

Heidi smiled. "Aren't you the flatterer? What brings you to our store?"

Her sister, Joanie piped up. "Yes, is there something we can help you find?"

The prospect of being escorted throughout the store by the three of them was a daunting one. "No, no. That's not necessary. I'm just here to buy some nails and sandpaper. I appreciate your kind offer, though."

"If you do need anything, anything at all, you just let me know," Georgia, the third and boldest sister said, her meaning plain as day.

Johnny pretended not to catch it. "Much obliged. Well, I'd best get to it and get back to work."

"So soon?" Heidi said. "I was wondering if you'd like to come to tea after church on Sunday."

Georgia said, "Johnny doesn't go to church, Heidi."

"That doesn't mean that he can't come after it," Heidi said.

Joanie eyed Johnny. "You could come and sit by me."

Oh, good Lord. Johnny said, "Well, I appreciate the invite, but I just can't."

"Why not?" Joanie asked, giving him a come-hither look.

He swallowed hard. If only there were just one of them. Finally fed up, Johnny squared his shoulders and said, "Ladies, the truth is that I just can't make up my mind between you all and I don't expect I'll ever be able to do that. You're all just too beautiful and have such sweet dispositions that it makes it real hard for a man to choose. It's real plain how much you all think of me and I'm truly honored, but even if I could just pick one of you, I'd hate to cause strife between you."

The sisters pouted, but they appreciated his honesty.

"You're a true gentleman, Johnny," Heidi said.

Georgia sighed then brightened. "I know! You could spend some time alone with each one of us and then decide who you like best. And we wouldn't get mad if we weren't the one you picked. We might not like it, but we wouldn't hold it against one another, would we, girls?"

Heidi and Joanie hastily agreed.

"So you come after church on Sunday to have dinner with us and then you and I can spend a little time together," Georgia said. "I go first because I'm the one who thought of the idea."

Johnny's shoulders slumped. He should have kept his mouth shut and just gone on his way. "Well, you'd better check with your folks about it. I don't think they'll like that idea too much."

Heidi said, "Don't worry about that. We can handle Pa."

That's what I'm afraid of. "Um, well, I'm sorry, ladies, I just—"

"Johnny!"

Johnny was never so glad to hear his best friend's voice as he was right then. He turned to see Ray Stratton riding up to the store.

"There you are!" Ray said, jumping down from his horse. "Ladies," he said, touching the brim of his expensive hat. "I hope you don't mind if I borrow my buddy here. I have important business to discuss with him."

Ignoring the sisters' protests, Ray hauled Johnny into the store with him.

"That was rude, but God bless you," Johnny said.

Ray grinned, his gray eyes gleaming. "Saved you in the nick of time, huh?"

Johnny nodded. "You don't know the half of it. They've cooked up some cockamamie idea about me spending time with each of them so I could make up my mind which one I like the best."

Ray laughed. "You oughta just take them all at once,

Johnny. Then you could make a decision and save some time in the process. That's what I'd do."

Johnny colored at Ray's ribald remark. "You might be able to do that, but I can't. I wasn't raised that way."

"You gotta quit that good boy stuff, Johnny. That's one of the reasons they like you so much," Ray said. "You need to go see one of Sandy's girls and tell everyone about it. They're husband hunting and you've been deemed suitable by their father."

Johnny gaped at him. "I have?"

Ray rolled his eyes. "Why else do you think he lets them stand around and talk with you, even when it's only you and one of them?"

Johnny had never thought about it. "He doesn't let other fellas?"

"No. Watch this," Ray said.

Johnny watched him go out the door and engage the triplets in conversation. They giggled at whatever he said to them. Knowing Ray, it was most likely something scandalous. In a couple of minutes, Shane Silver went to the door and told the girls to go on home. Ray bid them good day and then came back in the store again.

"Told you," Ray said. "You really need to pay more attention to gossip, Johnny."

"I don't like gossip and I'm not gonna go see one of Sandy's girls. I don't got anything against them, but that's not the kind of girl I'm looking for," Johnny said.

Ray said, "You're not looking for any girl at all. Why is that?"

Johnny moved off down the aisle to where the nails were. "Because I ain't set up for a wife yet, Ray. I live in a bunkhouse. That ain't no place for a woman. Once I have a house of my own, then I'll find someone."

Ray scratched his chin. "Who says you have to get married right away? Why don't you just have some fun?"

Johnny turned to Ray, his blue eyes meeting Ray's, his expression stern. "I'll tell you why. Ma and Pa 'had some fun' and had to get married because of me. He made her miserable every day and I hate that I'm the reason that she was bound to that son of a bitch. I'll mourn Ma until the day I die, but I'm glad that Pa's dead and I hope he burns in Hell.

"So, I'm gonna work hard and make a decent living before I settle down. I want to take care of a woman the way she deserves to be. I know that you don't understand that, but I'm asking you to respect it, Ray."

Ray ran a hand through his black hair and blew out a breath. "You never told me that before. I'm sorry. I'll quit pestering you about women."

"Thanks. Now, look, come up to Cotton's tonight, but right now I gotta get back to the ranch," Johnny said. "Okay?"

Ray nodded. "Sure. See ya then."

Johnny gave him a tight smile and walked down the aisle, trying to ignore the futile anger in his heart.

~~*~~

"You look beautiful," Leigh said.

She'd helped Daphne choose her evening ensemble for her evening with Brock.

"I'm scared to death," Daphne said. "Scared to death that he won't show up, scared that he will and I'll make a fool of myself. What if Cy's right and this is a huge mistake?"

Leigh said, "I felt the same way about coming here, but sometimes taking a risk is worth it. Besides, you've waited long enough to have the chance to get to know Brock better. Don't listen to Cy. You know how men are. Both of them will come around."

Daphne smoothed down the deep blue muslin dress she wore and looked at her hair again in the mirror. "I hope so. Cy is so stubborn. I'd forgotten that about him while he was away. I sure got reminded in a hurry."

Leigh said, "I know, but he's got a good heart. Don't worry. I'll do what I can to make him see reason."

Daphne said, "Thanks, but don't be surprised if I cuff him upside the head once in a while."

Leigh laughed. "That'll be entertaining."

"He'd better not make trouble for Brock when he comes for me or I'll skip the cuffing and just whack him with a frying pan."

They laughed and Daphne blew out the lamp in her room. When they descended the stairs, Leigh made the dogs go lie down so that they didn't get hair all over Daphne's dress. Cy and Johnny were finishing up the supper dishes when they came into the kitchen.

"Wow! You look like a dream!" Johnny told her.

Daphne smiled. "You think so?"

Johnny nodded as he dried a dish. "I sure do. He won't be able to take his eyes off you."

Cy wiped his hands on a towel and turned around so he could see Daphne. "Johnny's right, sis. You look beautiful. I hope that you have a wonderful time tonight."

Daphne blinked a couple of times. "You do?"

Cy said, "Look, I know that Brock and I don't get along, but that doesn't mean that I don't want you to be happy. And as much as I can't stand him, if he makes you happy, well, I won't stand in your way. He'd better treat you right, though, or I'll kill him. That's all the more I'll say about it."

Daphne went to him and kissed his cheek. "Thank you."

The dogs barked, announcing that someone was there. Daphne felt a little faint now that the moment had come for her to spend time with Brock alone. Her mouth went dry and her heart fluttered inside her chest. When someone knocked on the kitchen door, she almost jumped.

Johnny rushed to answer it and Cy shot him an annoyed glance over being beaten to the punch. The kid had the speed of a jackrabbit sometimes.

Johnny pulled the door open. "Hi, Brock. Come on in. Your lady awaits you."

Even Cy smiled at his funny greeting.

Brock stepped into the kitchen and Daphne felt even fainter at the sight of him in a fine, black overcoat. She'd only ever seen him in one of his sack coats and older clothes. He was infinitely more handsome in his evening attire. He'd attractively combed his blond hair and shaved.

"Thanks, Johnny," he said, his intense blue eyes going immediately to Daphne.

Her deep brown hair that ended just below her ears gleamed like mahogany and her large, dark eyes were exotic and hypnotizing. The blue dress gave a hint of cleavage and molded to Daphne's lush curves. Desire ran through Brock's veins as his eyes traveled over her.

Cy barely kept from glowering at Brock as he greeted him. "I see that no disasters came up."

Brock smiled, playing along. They'd already had a heated argument about Daphne at work and they'd finally decided that they both knew where each other stood and that they wouldn't do anything to upset Daphne that evening.

"No, but even if something does come up, don't come looking for me," Brock said. "I'm going to be too busy dining with this gorgeous woman."

Daphne blushed, but her eyes never left his as he came to stand before her. "Thank you. You look very handsome."

"Thanks. Are you ready?" Brock asked.

"Yes," Daphne said.

Brock held out his hand for the wrap she held. When she gave it to him, he draped it over her shoulders, taking the opportunity to touch her lightly as he placed it. Cy was glad to see that Brock was being a gentleman even if he did think that Brock took a little longer than necessary.

Johnny surprised everyone when he stepped right up to

Brock and said, "Now look here, you have her home at a decent hour and you better be a gentleman tonight. Cause if I hear you weren't, I'll make you sorry. Do we understand each other?"

Brock arched an eyebrow at Johnny. "We do."

Satisfied, Johnny smiled and kissed Daphne's cheek. "Have a nice time. See you all in the morning."

So saying, Johnny put on his coat and left. Leigh was the first one to let out a snort of laughter, followed by Daphne. Cy tried to fight it, but watching Johnny take Brock to task had been comical. He let out a laugh and Brock stared at him for a moment before breaking into laughter. Brock hadn't ever heard Cy really laugh before and it was a little shocking to know that the detective was capable of it.

When their mirth had subsided, Brock offered an arm to Daphne. "Shall we?"

"Yes," she said.

Leigh and Cy wished them a good time and they left the house. Brock helped Daphne into the buggy he'd brought and spread a heavy wool blanket over her lap.

"Thank you," she said.

He smiled and Daphne couldn't look away from his vibrant blue eyes. Then he moved away and she could breathe again. Unlike the day she'd kissed him, she felt unsure and shy around him. She'd been attracted to him for so long that being with him now was overwhelming.

Brock settled on the seat next to her, acutely aware of her close proximity. Glancing at her, he caught her looking at him and he thought there'd never been a more beautiful woman. He longed to kiss her, but it wasn't the right time or place.

"Okay. Here we go."

Once they were underway, Daphne said, "Brock, I don't want to talk about Cy tonight. I just want to have a nice time and avoid any unpleasantness."

Brock agreed. "Fine by me. I see him enough. I don't

want to talk about him, either. I'm much more interested in you."

"I'm glad to hear that. I have to ask you something and I want you to be honest."

He said, "Of course I'll be honest. Go ahead."

Daphne fiddled with the handle of her purse a little. "Are you able to deal with the fact that I'm part Comanche given how you feel about them?"

Brock said, "I've been thinking hard about that. You were right the day you came to the office. It's been a long time since those Indians attacked us, and in my brain, I know that none of you had anything to do with that. But in my heart, it's hard to remember that. I'm working on it, though. But where you're concerned, you're just a beautiful woman who happens to have Comanche heritage. I only think good things about you, Daphne."

Happiness surged through her. "I'm so relieved to hear you say that. When you come to our powwows you can join right in."

Shocked, Brock could only stare at her. Daphne burst into laughter and he realized that she'd been joking. He laughed with her then.

"You should have seen the look on your face!" she said, holding her stomach.

"I can see I'm gonna have to watch out for you," Brock said, smiling. "Are you always this tricky?"

Her eyes twinkled in the moonlight. "You'll just have to wait and see."

Brock hadn't realized that Daphne had such a playful personality. "Are you sure you and Cy are related? You sure don't act like it."

Daphne said, "Cy has always been more serious than me. He has a good sense of humor, but hides it well."

"I'll take your word for it. That's enough about him, though. How's Cotton these days? Still got women lining up outside his tipi?" he asked.

Daphne shook his head. "He'll never change. I love

him, though. He's always there when I need him. When anyone needs him, really."

Brock said, "He's one Indian I've always liked."

Daphne's eyes widened. "Really? I didn't know that you knew him so well."

"He comes to Benny's and we play pool," Brock said. "I don't know how anyone couldn't like him, Indian or not. There are just people in this world that you like right away and he's one of them." Then he turned his gaze on her. "You must have inherited that from him."

Daphne's smile turned shy again. "You didn't feel that way about me. Stop teasing me."

"Oh, yes, I did. I tried not to, but I couldn't help it. You were so pretty and sweet. What man wouldn't be attracted to you?"

Daphne said, "I should've kissed you a long time ago. Then you would have called on me sooner."

Brock smiled. "I wouldn't have minded that a bit. Kissing pretty women is never a hardship." He cringed inside at his stupid remark.

Daphne stifled the hard stab of jealousy that knifed through her. Arching an eyebrow at him, she said, "I know that you have a way with the ladies, Brock. I've heard that you're very popular, so don't think I'm not aware of it. But I'll tell you this; if things become serious between us and you cheat on me, I still have enough Comanche blood in me to know how to scalp someone. Keep that in mind."

All traces of humor were gone from her expression and Brock believed that she meant it. "You're right, Daphne. I've never been committed to a woman, but I've never led anyone on, either. I don't know where things with us will lead, but since the day you kissed me, you've been the only woman I've thought about."

Daphne's heart filled with joy. "Really?"

"Yeah. It's true, I swear," Brock said seriously. "I don't think you're gonna have anything to worry about, but should I have anything to worry about? As I understand it, there are several fellas around who've taken a shine to you. You told me that yourself."

She smiled. "You mean Benny, don't you?"

"Yeah, but he's not the only competition, Daphne," Brock said.

Giving him a coy look, she said, "I don't know what you're talking about."

He grinned. "You know exactly what I'm talking about."

"Maybe, I do. As long as you behave, you won't have anything to worry about, either," she said.

"Aha! Your bossy side is coming out. Now I *know* that you're related to Cy," Brock said.

Daphne playfully smacked his arm and, just like that, all traces of her nerves fled as they laughed together. As the horse trotted into the city, the night suddenly felt alive with magic and possibility. Daphne prayed that it would continue, hoping with all of her heart that her dreams would come true.

CHAPTER FIVE

Ellie pulled her door open when Walt knocked and stood blinking up at him, thinking at first that a strange man stood on her porch.

"Good evenin', Miss Ellie," Walt said, smiling.

"Good evening," she said, still surprised.

Although he still wore his glasses, his appearance was completely different than Ellie was used to. He wore a beautiful charcoal gray suit with a light paisley gray vest, white shirt, and a black tie. His dark hair had been tamed and he was clean-shaven. His chiseled, angular facial features were very attractive and the suit revealed that Walt was a very fit male.

A knowing smile curved Walt's mouth. "I've shocked ya a wee bit, haven't I?"

"You certainly have," she said. "I don't even know what to say. You should look that good every day." *Why am I suddenly putting my foot in my mouth around him?* "I mean, you look very handsome."

Her flustered state amused him. "Well, I have my reasons for that. If ya play yer cards right, I might share them with ya."

Ellie's brows came together. His statement aroused her

curiosity. "What's that mean?"

Walt didn't answer as his eyes traveled slowly over her lithe, petite form and he felt a tug of desire in his loins. "Ye look lovely, lass."

His hot gaze and the appreciation in his soft, nicely timbered voice made her breath quicken. Ellie felt like a gazelle being pursued by a hazel-eyed lion. That unsettled feeling came back and yet she suddenly found Walt fascinating. Her statement to Brock about Walt being too nice rose in her mind and she knew that her previous impression of Walt had been completely off the mark. He seemed vaguely threatening, but instead of feeling afraid, excitement sparked within her.

"I'm glad you think so," she said.

"Are ya ready then?"

"Oh. Yes. I'll just get my cloak," she said.

Walt waited while she retrieved it and locked her front door after she came out onto the porch.

"Do ya mind walkin'?" he asked. "I spend all day cooped up in buildings so it's nice to be out in the fresh air and stretch my legs."

"No. I don't mind," she said, taking the arm he offered her.

They descended the porch steps to the street and Walt looked back at her house. "Ye've a nice little place."

"Thank you. I like it. Ma and Pa don't like me living alone, but I wanted to be independent. Plus, with my job, I didn't want to be disturbing them by coming home at all hours of the day and night," Ellie said.

"Well, that's very considerate of ya. How'd ya convince yer father to let ya become a deputy and move away from home?"

"I had to fight him tooth-and-nail about it all, but he finally realized that I was going to do it no matter what. My cousin is a deputy in Oklahoma City. When he and I were growing up, we followed all of the famous lawmen in the newspapers. It's all I've ever wanted to do. I learned how to fight and all about the job. When the position opened up, I marched right into Rob's office and told him that I was the best person for the job."

Walt grinned. "What did he say to that?"

Ellie said, "He laughed because he thought that I was joking, but when I he saw that I was serious, he went ahead and interviewed me. A few days later, he came to my house to offer me the job. Pa about had a conniption, but Rob promised to watch out for me and Pa settled down. Once I had enough money saved up, I moved out. I love Pa, but he's always trying to protect me."

Walt said, "All good fathers try to protect their daughters, Ellie."

"I know, but when those daughters grow up, they can decide things for themselves. Women aren't stupid, Walt," Ellie said.

"No one would ever accuse ya of bein' stupid, least of all me," Walt said. "Yer an intelligent, beautiful woman, and I appreciate ya as such."

"Thanks. So what made you become a lawyer?" Ellie asked.

"I'm from a long line of barristers, and I followed in my father and grandfather's footsteps," he said nonchalantly. "My father is actually British, but we lived in Ireland until we came to America when I was seventeen. That's why my accent isn't as pronounced as some Irishmen. I've lost it a little."

"Do your parents live in Chance City?" she asked.

"They don't," Walt said. "They live in Chicago. I followed a lass here, but things didn't work out."

"Why not?" Ellie asked as they turned the corner onto Main Street.

"Well, ya see, I don't like sharin' my women with other men," Walt said.

"Oh! I'm so sorry about that," Ellie said.

"Thanks, but I think she did me a favor."

"Why do you say that?"

"Because I met the prettiest deputy ya ever did see and she hasn't been out of my mind much," Walt said, winking at her.

Ellie blushed. "Why did you keep asking me to dinner after I turned you down a couple of times?"

"Haven't ya heard? Us Irish are stubborn and I knew that I'd wear ya down. I figured if I annoyed ya enough, you'd give in just to get me off yer back." He laughed at the guilty expression on her face. "But ya see, I intend to sweep ya off yer feet, Ellie, and by the time I'm done, ye'll never want to get me off yer back."

A shiver ran through Ellie, but it had nothing to do with the cold. It was caused by the glint of something dark that flashed in his eyes for a brief moment. Then it was gone and he smiled, his face the one of a man happy to be with a special lady.

That little glimmer of something dark should've deterred her from wanting to spend the evening with Walt, but instead, she felt drawn to him and her interest in him grew. She had the feeling that there was much more to Walt than she'd ever imagined and that getting to know him might be the most exciting thing she'd ever do.

~~*~~

By the time dinner was over, Daphne felt even more as though she were in a dream. Brock was attentive, witty, and kept her entertained throughout the evening. Several people stopped by their table and Brock introduced her to them. He was popular with a lot of people and he was a social person, which often helped him in his career.

Once they'd eaten their dessert, they departed the restaurant, getting back in his buggy.

"It got colder," Brock remarked. "I'll get you home so that you can get in where it's warm."

Daphne said, "Don't worry about me. I have this blanket and it was so warm in the restaurant that the air feels good."

"Okay. I had a good time tonight," Brock said.

"Me, too."

Brock smiled at her. "Good enough that you'd want to do it again?"

Daphne pretended to mull it over. "I guess so."

"Don't sound so thrilled."

She batted her eyelashes at him. "I mean, yes, Deputy Guthrie, I'd love to have dinner with you again!"

He laughed. "All right. Don't overdo it."

"You're a hard man to please," Daphne said.

Their light-hearted banter continued as he drove her home. About halfway there, they heard horses come up behind them. Brock moved over to make sure the riders had plenty of room to get out around them, but they stayed behind Brock's buggy. A prickle of warning broke out over Brock's shoulders.

Daphne felt Brock stiffen beside her and she glanced back at the riders. There were four of them and they were very focused on her. She put a hand on Brock's leg, squeezing it anxiously. He took her hand and gave her a reassuring smile. A couple of the riders moved up alongside the buggy.

"Evenin', Deputy," one of them said. "You and the little Comanche having a good time?"

Brock bristled at the disdain in the man's voice. "I'd appreciate it if you didn't talk about Miss Decker that way. Don't be making trouble, either. I don't want to have to arrest you and ruin my nice night."

The man smiled as he scratched his scruffy chin. "Well, aren't you the gentleman? I heard that you don't got time for Injuns, but here you are with one. Must be because she's a woman. Their women sure are pretty, so I can't blame you."

Brock wanted to punch the guy in the face, but he also wanted to kick his own ass. His well-known hatred of Indians was coming back to bite him in a big way.

"Not that it's any of your business," Brock said, "But a man is allowed to change his mind about something. You're in the presence of a lady and I'm sure your ma taught you to respect a woman. Now, leave us be, fellas. Goodnight."

He clucked to their horse, moving it into a faster trot, but the riders stuck with them. That feeling of impending doom wash over Brock again, but he did his best to appear as though he was ignoring their unwanted escorts. His first concern was keeping Daphne safe and he hoped that the group of men would give up their game and move on.

However, that wasn't the case. One of them rode over in front of their horse, stopping it.

Brock said, "Fellas, you don't want to do this."

"Oh, I think we do," the same man said. "Get out, Guthrie."

Keeping a cool head, Brock said, "No. I'm not getting out. Here's what's gonna happen; you're gonna get the hell out of here while you still can."

The leader said, "There are four of us and only one of you. What are you going to do to stop us?"

Turning his eyes on each man in turn, Brock said, "You don't want to find out. Now, just go on your way."

"Get out of the buggy," the leader repeated. "We don't want you. We want the squaw."

Anger filled Daphne at his use of the derogatory term. She lifted her chin proudly and gazed back at the man with contempt in her eyes.

"Boy, look at how bold she is," he said. "This is gonna be fun."

"Yes, it'll be fun to slit your throat," Daphne said. "Us Comanche women are good with knives."

Brock didn't interfere. Admiration for her grew inside him. She was creating a diversion, giving him time to come up with a plan. It seemed as though she'd learned a few things from Cy and the men in her family.

The men guffawed over her remarks.

"Is that right?" another man asked.

Daphne smiled sweetly at him even though she trembled inside. "It'll be a pleasure to spill your blood. After all, that's what us Comanche do best."

Brock glanced at her with wide eyes over the way she spoke. It was time to end this now. Surreptitiously, Brock drew his gun while Daphne kept baiting their foes. She said more and more outrageous things until the men laughed uproariously. That's when Brock made his move.

"Run," he said to Daphne in a low voice so only she could hear him. "Run as fast as you can."

Swiftly, Brock brought his gun up, firing a shot at the leader. The bullet hit him dead center in the chest, blowing him off his horse before the others registered what had happened. Brock fired again, winging one of the other men.

"Daphne, run!" Brock commanded.

The buggy moved as he took aim again. One of the other thugs fired at him, but his aim was off. Another shot rang out, but it came from behind Brock. He was shocked to see one of the three remaining men grab his leg. The shot could only have come from Daphne. She must be carrying a gun, Brock thought. The two injured men, spurred their horses into action, thundering away into the night.

Brock drew a bead on the last man. "Hold it right there. Get off that horse. Now!"

He got down and held his hands up in the air.

Keeping a close eye on the guy, Brock got out of the buggy. "On the ground, hands behind your back. You're under arrest."

Out of the corner of his eye, Brock saw Daphne move forward, holding her gun on the man, too. Once the thug had laid down, Brock handcuffed him and turned to Daphne.

"You okay?"

She nodded. "Yes."

They were in a conundrum. Brock needed to get the living prisoner and the dead one back to town, but he didn't want to leave Daphne alone. Although the injured men had ridden off, they could still be waiting for them somewhere along the road in either direction. If they saw Daphne alone, they might go after her.

"Daphne, I know that you're scared, but I gotta take them to town. If I put the dead guy in the buggy, can you drive it to town while I ride along with this guy?" he asked.

Daphne didn't want to ride with the dead body, but she saw the wisdom in his idea. Besides, the dead man couldn't hurt her and she refused to give in to fear.

"I can do it," she said.

Brock was proud of her. Even though he saw fear in her expression, she was being brave.

"Good. What's your name?" he asked the remaining criminal.

"Toby Perkins, sir."

His voice wasn't the mature voice of a man. Brock hadn't been able to tell in the dark, but it sounded as though Toby was a teenager.

"How old are you, son?" he asked.

"Sixteen."

"What are you doing with that bunch?" Brock asked. "Never mind. There'll be time enough for explanations back at the jail. Daphne, keep your gun on him while I get the other guy in the buggy."

"He's just a boy," Daphne said.

Brock said, "A boy who was with a gang of men who were up to no good. He makes a false move, you shoot him."

Daphne didn't like it, but Brock was right. Toby might be a boy, but he'd been involved in something very adult. She had no way to know if he could be trusted.

"All right. I will," she said firmly.

Toby stood very still while Brock put the deceased man in the buggy.

"All right," Brock said. "I got him, Daphne. I'll ride alongside the buggy. Let's go."

Daphne got in the buggy, doing the best she could to ignore the dead man beside her. He smelled of sweat, dirt, and blood. Picking up the reins, she clucked to the horse and put it into a trot, wanting to get to the office as quickly as possible.

"Get a move on, Toby," Brock said after he'd mounted. "Behave yourself. I've already killed one man tonight. I've got no problem killing another. Understand?"

Toby nodded. "Yes, sir."

Then he turned around and started jogging by the buggy horse with Brock following close behind.

CHAPTER SIX

One of the night deputies, Wheezer, sat with Daphne while Brock and the other night deputy, Aaron, took care of getting the deceased goon to the undertaker's.

Wheezer's heart went out to Daphne. She wasn't used to being involved in dangerous situations. He admired the way she'd handled herself. Even though she'd been scared, she'd still had the presence of mind to help Brock get them out of trouble. She was still being brave. Even though she was pale under her slightly bronze skin tone, she sat straight in her chair, her eyes dry as she sipped coffee.

The older, colored man said, "When Brock's done, he'll get you home safe. I'll have Aaron ride with you just to make sure everything's all right, but those other two are most likely long gone. They'll need to see a doctor."

Daphne gave him a small smile. "Thank you."

"You want some more coffee?" Wheezer asked kindly.

"No," Daphne said. "Wheezer do you ever hate who you are?"

Wheezer gave her a quizzical look. "What do you mean?"

"Do you ever hate being black? Sometimes I hate being

49

part Comanche because of the way people think about us. I know that sounds terrible, but it's true. Those men came after us tonight because they wanted *me*," Daphne said. "Why are white men so fascinated by Indian women? Why do they think that they can just take what they want from us and that we'll take it?"

Wheezer sighed. He had no easy answer for her. "Near as I can tell, people of different races either seem to be real interested in people of another one, and not for good reasons a lot of the time. I don't hate being colored. The good Lord made me this way for a reason, same as he made you part Comanche for a reason."

Daphne put her coffee cup on Wheezer's desk. "And what reason is that?"

"We're strong people, Daphne, and we can show other people, not just whites, that we're good and decent. We can show them that we don't deserve to be made slaves or that we're bloodthirsty savages. We're human, just the same as they are. That's what we're here for, honey," he said. "So no matter what other people say about us or do to us, we gotta show them that we're not gonna let that stop us from livin' our lives." He chuckled. "I think you showed those men that you weren't just gonna let them do what they wanted to."

"I guess so," she said, trying to stop the trembling in her hands by clasping them together in her lap. "I've never shot anyone before. I know that he wanted to hurt me, but I still feel guilty."

Wheezer grunted. "I don't like shooting people, either, but sometimes there's just no way around it. I felt the same way the first time I shot a fella, so I understand. I hope you never have to do it again, but you don't have anything to feel guilty about."

Daphne nodded and fell silent.

Brock and Aaron came back.

"C'mon, Daphne, I'll take you home," Brock said.

She rose stiffly.

"You should take Aaron with you," Wheezer said. "I can handle things here."

Brock said, "We'll be fine. There won't be any more trouble."

Aaron, a man somewhere in his thirties, said, "You better hope not. Cy will skin you alive if anything happens to her."

Brock said, "I'm not afraid of Cy. C'mon, Daphne."

He put an arm around her and led her outside. The weather had deteriorated rapidly. Icy pellets bounced off every surface and had whitened the road. Traveling out to the Decker ranch wouldn't be a good idea.

"Daphne, how about you stay with Ellie tonight? If we try to get to your ranch tonight, we'll be soaked the skin. The road won't be safe, either," Brock said.

Daphne said, "I think you're right. I could just stay at the hotel. No need to bother Ellie."

Brock said, "She won't mind. Knowing that you're not alone will make me feel better, too."

Daphne didn't relish being alone, so she gave in. "All right, if you're sure she won't mind."

"She won't. I promise," Brock said.

Daphne let Brock put her in the buggy. As they drove to Ellie's house, Daphne kept her tears inside, not wanting to appear weak. When they arrived at Ellie's, Brock helped her up onto the porch since the footing had grown slippery by then.

"I'm sorry," Daphne said.

Brock stopped the hand he'd about to knock on the door with in midair. "What about?"

"For our evening being ruined," she said. "Everything was so wonderful until they showed up."

Putting a hand on her shoulder, Brock said, "It's not your fault, Daphne. You didn't cause the situation."

"Yes, I did. It's because of who I am, what I am. People hate us because of our heritage. We're just filthy Indians and people think they can treat us like dirt, like we don't deserve respect," Daphne said.

The stress of the evening was getting to her and she couldn't contain her feelings anymore.

Splotches of color appeared on Brock's face as shame burned in his stomach. How many times had he said such things about Indians? How often had he said that Indians were little better than animals and that the world would be a better place without them? Too many to count.

But he didn't feel that way about Daphne. She was a good, beautiful woman, who just happened to be part Comanche. She'd never done anything bad to anyone and she hadn't deserved to be treated with disrespect or hate. As he stared down into her tear-brightened eyes, Brock felt a shift in his heart.

Pulling her against him, Brock stroked a hand down over her sleet-dampened hair. "You didn't deserve what happened tonight and you've never deserved all of the cruelty you've had to face. You're a special woman, Daphne."

Daphne leaned against him, letting him comfort her. She closed her eyes and let out her sorrow in quiet sobs. Brock held her tighter and kissed her forehead.

"Shh, it's okay, Daphne. You're safe now. Everything will be all right," he murmured.

Daphne swallowed another sob and regained control of her emotions. She pushed away from him, wiping away her tears with her gloves. "No, it won't. I can't see you anymore, Brock. This will keep happening and given how you feel about Indians, you'll get tired of dealing with it."

"Daphne, I know what happened was bad, but it doesn't have anything to do with things between you and me," Brock said. "I thought we settled the whole Comanche thing."

"That was before four men came after us because they wanted to rape a Comanche woman!" Daphne's voice rose. "It won't be the only time something like this comes up, Brock."

Brock's expression tightened. "I'm not gonna let anyone interfere in our relationship, Daphne. It's just getting started and I don't want to stop seeing you. Don't *you* let anyone come between us, either. We waited too long to just give up because of some dumbasses. Besides, we showed them that they'd better not mess with us. I killed one, shot another, and you shot one. I didn't know you carried a gun and could shoot."

A smile played around her lips. "I can shoot, but not all that well."

"Looked to me like you can shoot pretty good."

Daphne's smile grew. "I was aiming for his head."

Brock grinned and then laughed. "Well, just aim for his leg the next time and you'll probably get his head."

A fit of giggles overcame Daphne then, another release of the strain she'd been under. Brock hugged her again and they laughed together. The front door opened and Ellie, brandishing a revolver, confronted them. She'd heard their voices because her bedroom was right above the kitchen.

"Brock? Daphne?" she queried. "What's wrong?"

"Daphne needs to stay here tonight. We'll explain," Brock said.

"C'mon in out of the cold," Ellie said, standing back to give them room to pass by her.

Once they were inside, Ellie shut and locked the door, and led them to her kitchen.

"Have a seat. I'll get some coffee going and you can tell me what's going on," Ellie said.

Brock took Daphne's wrap from her and hung it on a hook by the kitchen door. He was a regular guest at Ellie's and he knew where things were kept. Then he hung up his own coat and sat at the table with Daphne.

She looked around Ellie's little kitchen, liking the pretty floral curtains and noting how clean Ellie kept things. Colorful braided rugs covered the floor under the table and chairs and the space in front of the sink. Ellie finished making the coffee and sat down in an empty chair.

"Okay, now what happened?"

They explained the situation to Ellie and she grew angry.

When they finished, Ellie patted Daphne's arm. "My kind of woman. Don't take no shit from anyone. They all got what they deserved."

Brock hid a smile over Daphne's surprised expression. "You have to remember that Ellie's a deputy, Daphne. We're used to shooting people and Ellie sort of likes it."

Ellie nodded. "If they deserve it, I sure do. They had no business coming after you like that. Men like that only understand one thing; violence. Unfortunately, it's the only thing that gets through to them. Especially where women are concerned. Women can't be too careful and having a gun on you was a good idea, Daphne. Keep carrying it."

Daphne said, "Pa always insisted that Ma and I carry one, even if it was just a little derringer. Cy bought me my revolver when he came home after he was fired. I never had to use it before."

Ellie patted her arm again. "I hope you never have to again, but at least you know that you can."

Brock finished his coffee and winked at Daphne. "I think she needs some target practice, though. She meant to take off the guy's head but shot a hole in his leg instead."

Ellie tried not to laugh but lost the battle. Daphne and Brock laughed, too, and Daphne finally understood why gallows humor helped. Finding something funny about death and carnage helped ease the emotional toll on a person. It wasn't right in a way, but sometimes it kept military and law enforcement staff sane. Daphne also found that there was something life affirming in laughing in the face of death or danger.

Brock stood up and stretched. "Daphne, you're in good hands. I'll take you home in the morning. Try to get some rest."

Ellie said, "You could sleep on the sofa, Brock. It's terrible out there."

Brock said, "Nah. I gotta get the horse home. Old Dewey is out there in this. I put his blanket on, but still. I'll be back in the morning."

Ellie and Daphne rose as well.

Ellie said, "I'll be in the parlor, Daphne."

Brock silently thanked Ellie for her discretion. Before Daphne could protest, he wrapped his arms around her and pressed his lips to hers. After a moment's resistance, Daphne relaxed, leaning into him while she slid her arms around his neck. She opened her mouth and Brock's tongue delved inside to dance with hers. She couldn't get close enough to him and pressed harder against his chest. Then she remembered where they were and broke away from Brock. His gaze held hers, desire in his sky blue eyes.

"You listen to me, Daphne. Nothing or no one is gonna keep me from you," he said in a low, throaty voice. "You hear me? So you just get that idea of not seeing me out of your mind. I'm not taking no for an answer."

It was hard to answer him for the tide of passion flowing through her body. She nodded a little. "All right."

He pressed a quick kiss to her mouth. "I'll be back in a few hours."

She nodded again and he went out the door. After a few moments, Daphne regained her wits and walked into the parlor. Ellie sat on the sofa.

"All squared away?" she asked.

"Yes," Daphne answered.

"I'll show you the guest room. It's small, but comfortable," Ellie said, leading her upstairs.

Daphne yawned as exhaustion set in. "I'm sure it's very nice."

Ellie went into the room and lit a candle on a small bedside table. "Well, it ain't much, but it's cozy."

She moved out so that Daphne could get in. When Ellie had said that it was small, she hadn't been kidding, Daphne saw. The room was just big enough for a small bed, nightstand, and a little chest of drawers, which stood behind the door, preventing it from opening all the way.

"We call this the Tiny Room," Ellie said.

Daphne said, "I can see why. We?"

"Me and the boys. Rob named it that after he stayed over after poker one night," Ellie said.

Daphne's eyebrows rose. "Rob spent the night?"

Ellie laughed. "We play poker a couple times a week and every so often, one of the fellas gets too drunk to make it home. They stay in here."

"But you're not married. You're here alone with them?"

"Yep. They know better to try anything funny, not that any of them would, anyway. I keep my gun right by my bed and when I aim for someone's head, I hit it. I'll be right back with a nightgown for you."

With that, Ellie left her, going down the hall to her own room. Daphne shut the door and took off her dress. Ellie knocked on the door and Daphne opened it.

"Here you go," she said.

"Thank you for everything, Ellie," Daphne said.

"You're welcome," Ellie said. "Sleep well."

She withdrew from the room. Daphne changed, pulled the bedcovers down, and slipped into the little bed. The little room seemed to have a loving atmosphere and Daphne did indeed feel cozy as she grew warm. She blew out the candle on the nightstand and was soon asleep.

CHAPTER SEVEN

"C'mon in, Cy," Brock called out when someone pounded on his front door.

It opened and slammed shut.

"Where's my sister?" Cy demanded, striding into the kitchen.

"At Ellie's," Brock said. "Sit down and I'll tell you why."

"I'll stand," Cy said. "Why is she at Ellie's?"

"I take it you didn't stop by the office," Brock said.

Cy cocked his head.

Brock told Cy the story and the dark fire in Cy's eyes made Brock a little uneasy. Even when he and Brock had argued and come to blows, he'd never seen the expression of pure fury that settled on Cy's face.

"So I took her to Ellie's for the night and now I'll take her home. I was just about ready to leave when you showed up," Brock said.

"I'll take her home," Cy said.

Brock said, "No. I told her I'd be back for her, so I'm gonna take her just like I planned."

"I was afraid of something like this happening," Cy said. "People aren't going to accept the two of you."

"Because I'm white?"

"Because everyone knows that you hate Indians," Cy said. "Now all of a sudden you're out with an Indian woman? That's gonna draw all kinds of attention, Brock."

"I understand—"

"No, you don't!" Cy interjected. "You have no idea what we go through! The way people have always looked at us. How many times I had to defend Daphne at school. How many times we've been called filthy Injuns. Been spit on, beaten up, or shunned because of the blood that runs through our veins. You've had an easy life, Brock. Your grandfather may have been murdered by Comanche, but other than that, you've had everything that anyone could want."

The images of Daphne enduring that kind of abuse as a little girl horrified Brock. No child deserved that, but especially a young girl. Brock would kill anyone who treated his siblings or children that way. Cy's anger was well founded, and Brock didn't make light of it.

"You're right, Cy. I don't know what any of that is like, but last night I got a tiny taste of what she's been through—what you've all had to deal with," Brock said. "Over the last couple of months, I've been doing a lot thinking about some of the things she said to me the day you found us at work."

Cy shifted on his feet slightly and raised an eyebrow. Brock almost laughed. Like Leigh, he was learning how to read Cy's body language. The detective wanted him to continue.

"I've always prided myself on being intelligent and using common sense, but when I really got thinking about the situation, I saw that I've been letting emotion cloud my judgment for a long time. Other than being a pain in my ass, you've never done anything bad to me or to anyone around here.

"Neither has Daphne. Now, your cousins have a way of getting in trouble. They don't usually start it, but you gotta admit that they're good at baiting people, Cy," Brock said.

Cy smiled a little and nodded.

"I've always liked Cotton, though. I don't know anyone who doesn't like him," Brock said.

"That's true," Cy said. "I don't think Cotton has an enemy within a hundred-mile radius."

Brock said, "You and I aren't ever gonna see eye-to-eye on a lot of things, but where your sister is concerned, we agree. She deserves to be happy and to not be harassed. I'm gonna keep seeing her, so you and I are gonna have to figure out a way to get along. The rest of your family, too."

Cy let out a sarcastic laugh. "So you're telling me that you're suddenly an Indian lover?"

Brock said, "No. I wouldn't go that far, but I'm starting to see that I've been putting the blame for my grandfather's death on people who don't deserve it. I'm a deputy and I only arrest the guilty parties. I've been putting that logic to use while I've been thinking about all of this. You and your family had no involvement in Grandpa's murder, so I shouldn't hold you accountable for that just because of your heritage.

"I can't stand you most of the time, but that doesn't have anything to do with you being part Comanche anymore. Now I just hate you because you act like your shit doesn't stink because you used to work for Pinkerton."

Cy smiled. "I know you hate that Rob hired me. Look, the truth is that I actually respect your work ethic. I always have. You're as good an investigator as a lot of the detectives I worked with at Pinkerton, and you're an excellent photographer. But your attitude rubs me the wrong way. You're cocky, you purposely aggravate me at every turn, and make my job as miserable as possible.

"I know that you're hoping that I'll quit, but I won't. I'd love to so that I don't have to deal with you, but our family needs the money I'm making to help improve the ranch. If it wasn't for Leigh, we'd most likely lose the place. So you can keep being a jerk, but I'm not going anywhere."

Brock said, "Well, you're no picnic to be around, either. You're right. I do want you to quit. We've been doing just fine without you. It irks the hell out of me that Rob thought we needed someone like you."

Cy shook his head. "So you're taking that out on *me*? I have no idea why Rob kept coming after me so hard. I didn't ask to be brought in on cases. I left that life behind and I just wanted to be left alone, but you know Rob. Once he gets an idea in his head, he doesn't quit. Things got even worse for us financially, so when he offered that last time, I took him up on it."

Brock said, "I didn't know that things had gotten that bad."

"Don't worry about it. I'm only telling you so that you understand that my reasons for accepting the job have nothing to do with you," Cy said. "I have a family to take care of, and I live up to my responsibilities."

Brock completely understood that. He narrowed his eyes at Cy. "That may be, but you're still conceited."

"Me? I think it's the other way around."

"No, it's not. You try to order me around like you're my superior, but you're not. I don't give a crap if Rob gave you a fancy title, you're no better than me," Brock said. "He never told any of us that you were over us, so as far as I'm concerned, we're equals."

Looking at things from Brock's point of view, Cy knew that he'd feel the same way. During his time with Pinkerton, he'd dealt with contacts and other detectives off and on, but no one steady. He'd gotten so used to working on his own that he'd forgotten what it was like to work as a team.

"All right. You got a point," Cy conceded. "I'll try to watch that, but I'm not gonna take your crap."

"And I'm not gonna take yours." Brock gave him a

half-smile. "It might be easier if we each dished out a little less."

Cy nodded. "Might be."

"Okay. I'm going to go take your sister home," Brock said.

"Fine. See you at work. I'll let Rob know where you are," Cy said.

He left as abruptly as he'd come, leaving Brock to shake his head and smile.

~~*~~

Daphne felt at loose ends at Ellie's because she had nothing to do. She was too used to being up early to make breakfast for her family and then start in on all of her other work. So sitting at Ellie's table while the deputy made and served breakfast felt completely wrong.

Ellie was a talkative person and she kept up a running conversation as they ate, mostly about work. Daphne paid attention, but she also wondered if Brock would really come to take her home. She worried that he'd changed his mind overnight about continuing to see her.

Maybe he'd decided that he didn't want to be bothered after all. However, she prided herself on being strong and tried not to jump to conclusions.

She didn't realize that her feelings were so transparent until Ellie said, "Don't worry. He'll be here. Brock always does what he says he will."

Daphne smiled a little. "I can't help it. I'd given up hope that he'd ever want to see me, and it was such a surprise when he asked me to dinner. We had a wonderful time last night until that happened."

Ellie took their plates to the sink. "And now you think that he won't want anything to do with you."

"Yes. He said he still wants to see me, but maybe he changed his mind."

Ellie said, "He still wants to see you. Trust me. You're

all he's thought about for the last couple of months. There's no way that he changed his mind."

Daphne's eyes lit with happiness. "He's been thinking about me?"

"That's right. I'm glad he finally came to his senses. You're a good woman and any man would be lucky to have you."

"Thank you, Ellie," Daphne said.

A knock sounded on the kitchen door and Daphne's heartbeat broke into a trot when Ellie admitted Brock inside.

He immediately looked at Daphne, giving her a smile. "Good morning. Did you sleep well?"

She rose from her chair. "Like a baby. The Tiny Room is so cozy."

"Yeah. I've spent a few nights in there after I got too drunk to drive home. Don't pass that around. People would be scandalized." Brock's smile said that he didn't really care if they would be or not.

Ellie said, "It's none of their business, but keeping it under our hats is a good idea anyway."

Daphne said, "My lips are sealed."

She thanked Ellie as Brock helped her with her wrap and then they got in Brock's buggy.

"See ya at work, Jabs," Brock said to Ellie as they pulled away from her house.

Ellie raised a hand to him and closed the kitchen door again.

As they rode through town, Brock asked, "How are you holding up?"

"I'm fine. Much better than last night. I'm sor—"

Brock put a hand over hers. "Don't do that, Daphne. There's nothing for you to be sorry about. The fault was all theirs. And I owe you a big apology, too."

Her forehead puckered. "What for? You saved me."

"Not about last night." He fidgeted with the reins a little. "I'm sorry for being so hard on your family. You were right about the things you said to me that day in the sheriff's office. I've been taking out my anger and grief on people who don't deserve it, you included. I let it blind me to the facts, which are that not all Indians are bad, just like not all white people are bad.

"I think part of it is that there are times when I see the braves who killed him in my mind when I look at Indians now. That's not rational and I'm usually rational about anything else. You opened my eyes, Daphne, because I was attracted to you despite you being part Comanche. I began to see that I really didn't think about that fact. You were just a very beautiful woman who I wanted to get to know better."

Daphne couldn't believe what she was hearing. Brock's tense posture conveyed his discomfort with the subject, but he was bravely forging ahead to explain his feelings.

"What made you decide to ask me to dinner after all this time?"

Brock gave her a sheepish smile. "Ellie. She told me that I needed to get off my rear and do something about the situation. She was right. So here I am. Doing something about it. Cy and I sort of reached an agreement about things this morning when he came looking for you."

Daphne groaned and put a hand to her forehead. "I knew he'd search for me. Sorry about that."

"It's okay. I'm glad he's a good brother," Brock said. "Look, I don't know what the future is gonna hold for us, Daphne, but when I decide to do something, I do it, if at all possible. So, since I want to get to know you better, that means I have to get to know your family, too."

Daphne cringed. "Oh, Brock. They hate you."

Brock laughed. "I know and I'm not fond of them, either, but maybe I can come to an agreement with them, too. Besides, I already like Cotton. Maybe I'll get to like them, too."

He and Daphne exchanged doubtful looks and burst into laughter.

"Okay, maybe not like. Tolerate. I'm willing to try, anyhow," Brock said.

Daphne met his gaze. "This is a big step for you. Are you sure you're ready?"

Brock said, "I've wasted enough time, Daphne. It's time to sink or swim and I'm gonna try like hell to swim."

"All right. I'll try to help keep you afloat," Daphne said.

He briefly took her hand and smiled before turning back to the road.

~~*~~

When Brock drove up to the Decker's house, Johnny and Leigh came out of the house right away. Johnny angrily marched toward the buggy.

"Are you all right, Daphne?" he asked, glaring at Brock.

"I'm fine, Johnny," Daphne said.

"Shame on you, Brock," Johnny said. "I thought you were a good man."

Daphne said, "Johnny, Brock didn't do anything wrong. I'll explain everything, but Brock has to get to work."

Johnny looked back and forth between her and Brock. "So you didn't … I mean … everything is okay?"

He colored as he helped Daphne down from the buggy and Brock had to clench his jaw to keep from smiling.

"Everything is fine, Johnny," Daphne assured him.

"All right."

Brock said, "I promise that I treated Daphne right, Johnny."

After regarding him for a moment, Johnny nodded, seemingly satisfied.

Brock nodded at Leigh. "I'll bet Cy took off out of here this morning like a bat out of Hell."

Leigh smiled. "He sure did. He slammed the kitchen door shut so hard I thought it was gonna come off the hinges."

Brock chuckled. "He came in my front door the same way."

"Sorry about that," Leigh said. "But we were all real worried."

Brock looped the reins over the buggy brake and hopped out. "Well, let's go in the house and we'll tell you what happened."

When they'd finished telling their tale, Johnny hugged Daphne. "I'm so glad you're all right. You sure were brave."

"Thank you," she said.

Leigh echoed his sentiments.

Brock said, "I have to get to work."

Daphne said, "I'll walk you out."

Brock said goodbye to Leigh, and Johnny and Daphne followed him out to the buggy.

"Thank you for everything," Daphne said.

"Don't mention it. How about we give this another try tomorrow night?" he asked.

Her smile made his heartbeat jump a little. "I'd really like that."

"Me, too. Same time?"

"Yes."

Brock gave her a brief kiss, not caring if anyone saw. "See you tomorrow night."

Daphne nodded. "Have a good day. Stay safe."

Brock got in his buggy, touched the brim of his hat, and drove away. Daphne watched until he was gone and then went to change and freshen up so she could start her day.

CHAPTER EIGHT

When Brock arrived at the sheriff's office, Rob called him into his office.

"Daphne okay?" he asked.

"Yeah. She's a strong woman," Brock said. "It's not every woman who would have done what she did."

Rob nodded. "I agree. Glad that the both of you are all right." He fidgeted with his shirtsleeve. "You gonna see her again?"

Brock smiled. "You're nosy, Rob."

"Not nosy, just curious."

"Yeah, I'm gonna see her again."

"Glad to hear it. Now I don't have to yell at you for being a moron," Rob said. "You'd be an idiot not to."

"You're right about that. Well, I'd better get to work before my boss fires me," Brock quipped.

"That's right. Hop to, boy," Rob said, standing up. "I have a meeting with the town council."

"Better you than me," Brock said.

Rob grunted and left for his meeting while Brock went to his desk. Sitting down, he noticed Ellie staring off into space, a pencil poised over a tablet.

He snapped his fingers. "Ellie. Hey!"

Ellie jerked and looked at him. "What? Did you say something?"

"What the heck were you thinking about?"

Her cheeks turned pink. "Walt."

With everything that had happened the night before, he'd forgotten that Ellie had gone to dinner with the lawyer.

"Really? So how was your evening with Gainsey? Pretty good if you were daydreaming that much."

Ellie frowned. "It's not like that. He's odd."

"Odd? How?"

"Well, he showed up all spruced up. I didn't recognize him at first. He wore an expensive suit and he actually combed his hair and shaved. I have to say that he's a handsome man," Ellie said.

Brock shrugged. "That doesn't sound strange. Most men try to look nice when they go out with a lady."

"True, but he's sort of secretive and I couldn't get much personal information out of him at dinner. He was fun and all, but we didn't talk about anything important," she said. "There's just something off about him."

"Are you going to see him again?" Brock asked.

"Yeah. He invited me to dinner tonight at his house. I confess that I'm really curious to see where he lives," Ellie said.

Brock crossed his arms over his chest. "Do you think he's dangerous? Is it a good idea for you to go there alone?"

Ellie said, "We won't be alone. He said that a married couple he's friends with will be there."

The office door opened and the subject of their discussion walked through it.

"Hello," Walt said, smiling. "There's the fair Ellie and our Brock."

Ellie noted that he hadn't shaved, but at least his clothes weren't all that rumpled. "Here we are."

Her cool tone intrigued Brock, but Walt didn't seem to

notice it.

"What can we do for you, Walt?" Brock asked.

Walt adjusted his glasses. "I've come to see young Toby."

Ellie's eyes widened. "You have?"

"I have."

"How did you know he was here? He was just arrested last night," Ellie said.

Walt gave her a smile and her pulse jumped a little. "Let's just say that a little birdie told me."

Brock scowled at him. "This little birdie wouldn't happen to be one of the guys that came after me and Daphne last night, would it? Because if you're aiding and abetting a criminal I'll have to arrest you. Besides, he's guilty, Walt. I should know since I was there."

Walt narrowed his eyes a little. "And just what is he guilty of? Did he fire a weapon? Did he even *have* a weapon? Bein' with a bunch of ruffians doesn't mean he's guilty of anything."

Brock was taken aback by Walt's sudden change in demeanor. He'd gone from the affable lawyer to the shrewd, skilled attorney in a matter of seconds. Walt was right, though. When he'd arrested Toby, the boy hadn't had a weapon.

Walt pressed his advantage. "Someone has to look out for the boy. The poor lad has no one now since you killed his brother, Brock."

Brock paled. "That was his brother? He never mentioned that. He wouldn't tell us anything."

"Well, who could blame him? Ye'd just killed his brother right in front of him. He's scared to death about what's gonna happen to him. Why dontcha release him to me? He's committed no crime," Walt said.

"That we know of," Brock said.

Walt stepped closer, his hazel eyes turning a shade cooler. "Well, now, his past crimes, if there are any, aren't any concern to ya. Nothin' can be proved nor disproved, so that has no bearin' on the current situation."

Ellie was transfixed by the way Walt adroitly got around Brock's argument. She said, "That may be, but he probably knows where those other two would hole up. He has information about wanted criminals."

Walt smiled. "Are ya proposin' a deal? Hmm? He tells ya what he knows and ya let him go?"

Ellie said, "We don't have that power. You'll have to talk to Reese about it, Walt."

"So he's aware of the situation then?"

"That's right," she said.

Walt said, "I see. Well, how about lettin' me see the boy?"

Brock said, "Sure. C'mon."

"Ellie, I'm lookin' forward to tonight." Walt gave her a smile and followed Brock, not waiting for her to respond.

Rob had come back while they'd been talking. He waited until the two men were out of earshot to say, "Ellie, I can't tell you what to do on your free time, but be careful where Walt's concerned."

She gave him a startled look. "Why? What's wrong with him?"

Rob said, "Nothing's wrong with him, exactly. He can be possessive, so you need to make it clear that you're not gonna put up with that sort of thing."

"Of course, I won't," Ellie agreed.

Rob nodded approvingly. "Good. Where's Cy?"

"Out on patrol," she said.

"Okay. I forgot something I need. I'll be back as soon as I can. I hope it's not a long meeting."

Ellie said goodbye to him and went back to work.

~~*~~

"It's not funny!"

Cotton and Ray laughed as Johnny finished relaying his dilemma to them as they sat around the fire at Cotton's place.

Ray said, "Oh, yes, it is."

Johnny put his head in his hands. "What the heck am I gonna do? How am I supposed to choose between three beautiful women who are identical?"

Cotton took pity on the young man. "If you don't want a woman in your life, you're going to have to make that very clear to them."

"I have! I told them I wouldn't get married until I was better situated. It's like I can't say anything wrong, though," Johnny lamented. "It just makes them want me more? Why me?"

Cotton chuckled. "Because you're a good man who happens to be charming and handsome. Men like that can be hard to find."

Ray bridled at his pointed look. "What? I'm a good guy."

"I didn't say you weren't, but women don't consider you marriage material," Cotton responded.

"They don't think you are, either," Ray shot back.

Cotton said, "I know and that's the way I like it. I am free, like the wind and stars. Like the storm, I can choose which direction I go and what I do. But you? You're young and someday you're going to want to find a woman to love and have children with."

Ray said, "Not anytime soon. Maybe never."

Johnny snorted. "I should say not. You don't even have a permanent home. How would you take care of a wife and kids?"

Ray had fine clothing, expensive guns, and other valuable possessions, but they weren't all kept in the same place. He had a bunch of friends and family he stayed with and he stashed his stuff here and there. A restless soul, he didn't cotton to the idea of being in one place too long.

"And that's just the way I like it. Maybe that'll change some day and maybe it won't," Ray said. "But I'm fine in the meantime."

Cotton said, "A man should know what he wants, but he is also defined by his past behavior and changing someone's perception of you later on can be hard."

Ray frowned. "We were talking about Johnny. Why are you lecturing me? You're in no position to talk."

Cotton took no offense. His midnight eyes filled with humor. "I'm not lecturing you. I am merely bringing something to your attention that you may not have thought about. As for me, that sort of life is over for me. I loved my wife and our children, but after they died, I was too heartbroken to think about marriage again.

"That's my choice and I searched my soul long and hard over it. I was offered other women, but I refused them, knowing that I could never love them. Some men don't care about that, but I'm perhaps more tender-hearted than them."

Ray grinned rakishly. "I'd say that you have a lot of love to give women. A man after my own heart."

Johnny shook his head. "Cotton, don't you want someone as a companion? Don't you get lonely?"

"Not really. Every so often, I do, but for the most part, I'm content just as I am. Ray is right: I rarely lack for company," Cotton replied.

Johnny bit back the critical words that threatened to escape his mouth. It was his frustration over the Silver sisters situation that made him grouchy. He heaved a sigh. "Well, I'm glad you fellas are content, but none of this is helping me. I can't be rude to them, but I can't seem to make them understand that I'm not interested."

Ray said, "I keep telling you to just go see one of Sandy's girls and then brag about it. Their father wouldn't let you within ten feet of them. Problem solved."

With a laugh, Cotton said, "While that's true, it would also damage Johnny's good reputation, which I'm sure he'd like to keep."

Ray took a gulp of whiskey. "Okay, so tell them that you started seeing someone."

"But I haven't," Johnny said. "People are gonna want to see the girl I'm supposed to be seeing."

"It's not a bad idea," Cotton said.

Johnny looked at him like he'd lost his mind. "Are you going senile? I'm not seeing any girl."

"But you could pretend to," Cotton said.

"You mean lie? I'm not doing that."

Cotton chuckled. "You won't be lying. I know just the girl who would be happy to pretend to be seeing you. For the right price."

Johnny shook his head. "I'm not seeing a prostitute."

"She's not," Cotton said. "Dory is a nice young lady. I know her mother."

Ray laughed. "I'll bet you know her real well."

Johnny threw a stone at him. It bounced off Ray's forehead, making Cotton laugh.

"Ouch! Knock it off!" Ray complained.

"Then how about you show some respect?" Johnny reprimanded him.

Cotton said, "I'll talk to Dory for you so she understands that this is just a job."

"I haven't agreed to it," Johnny protested.

Ray asked, "You want to get rid of the Silver sisters, don't you?"

Johnny groaned. "Yes."

"Then it is settled," Cotton said. "I'll talk to Dory and have her come see you tomorrow."

Johnny gave Cotton a curious look. "What's she look like? Is she pretty?"

"She's a very pretty girl. Red hair, blue eyes. She's shy, but very nice," Cotton said.

"Okay. I don't believe I'm goin' along with this. I just hope it works," Johnny said, rising from the log on which he'd been sitting. "Well, tomorrow comes early, so I'd better get to bed. Thanks for supper, Cotton."

"Anytime."

Ray left with Johnny, the two young men clowning

around as they went. Cotton put out the outside fire and went to bed. He wasn't sure how long he'd been asleep when he heard his tipi flap open and shut. His hand curled around the knife he kept near his sleeping pallet, but when he opened his eyes, he saw that a weapon wasn't needed.

He smiled as the girl came to the sleeping pallet and sank down on her knees by his side. Wordlessly, she stretched out by him and he covered them with his blanket. Inside, hot rage burned in Cotton's heart, but he hid it from Dory. Her presence in his tipi meant that her drunk of a father was at it again.

She snuggled up to him and Cotton put an arm around her. There was nothing sexual about the embrace. At eighteen, Dory was a complete innocent and, although Cotton was known for his philandering ways, he had a certain moral code concerning women. Girls Dory's age didn't interest him romantically.

He'd met Dory about a year ago when she'd burst into his camp, on the run from her father. She'd begged Cotton to hide her and he'd given her refuge in his tipi. When her father had come along, Cotton had lied, saying that no girl had come through his camp. Cotton hadn't felt guilty about the deception in the least.

If Maynard Klingerman had tried to get in Cotton's tipi, he wouldn't have gotten home that night. Cotton would have gutted him like a felled deer. For the most part, Cotton was a friendly, easygoing person, but he wasn't so far out of touch with his Comanche heritage that he'd forgotten how to kill and inflict great injury. Maynard had called Cotton a bunch of nasty names and had gone on his way.

That night, Cotton had kept Dory with him, afraid that if she went home while Maynard was still awake that there would be more trouble for her. He'd become her refuge and he'd told her to come to him whenever she needed him, which had been a lot more often lately. As he comforted Dory, Cotton's thoughts turned black. Murder sounded good right then.

Once her trembling subsided, Dory said, "I'm sorry, Cotton. I don't mean to keep bothering you. I don't have anywhere else to go."

"You never bother me, Dory," Cotton said. "I'm happy to help you."

"Thank you," she said.

"How would you like to make some money?" he asked.

"You mean work?" she asked, raising up on an elbow.

Her eyes sparkled in the light from the low-burning embers in Cotton's fire.

"Yes. It's easy work," Cotton said. "I want you to let my nephew court you."

Her mouth dropped open. "I'm no whore!"

He laughed. "I know that. Johnny is a very respectful young man with strict morals. He would never take advantage of you. Now, here's what I want you to do…"

CHAPTER NINE

Daphne hummed as she made breakfast the next morning. She couldn't wait to see Brock that night, hoping that nothing would spoil their evening this time. Leigh came into the kitchen from outside, a pail of milk in her hand.

"I'll put this down in the cellar," she said. "Do you need anything from down there, Daphne?"

"No, thanks. Cold out?"

Leigh made a derisive sound. "This is mild compared to what I'm used to. It'll be an easy winter if it stays like this."

"Yes, I imagine that Massachusetts is much colder," Daphne said.

"You'd imagine right," Leigh said, going down into the cellar.

Daphne chuckled and turned back to the sausage in the frying pan. Her mind drifted to the handsome deputy she'd be going out with that evening. Brock hadn't said what they were going to do, but she didn't much care as long as she was with him.

Johnny came in the door and hung up his coat. "Morning, Daphne. Something smells good."

She accepted his kiss on her cheek and said, "Sausage and pancakes."

"My favorite," he said, grinning. "Can I help with something?"

"No. Just wash up and sit down."

"Yes, ma'am."

Leigh came up from the cellar and said, "That's it! We're getting a cat!"

Daphne's shoulders dropped. "Oh, no."

"Yep. Got into the flour bin again, damn it." Leigh's green eyes spat fire. "I don't care what my husband says, having four dogs don't make a bit of difference because they're not always here. Besides, they don't go down to the cellar and that's where those mice are. If we had some barn cats, we wouldn't have as many mice on the whole place. I'm gonna ask David or Daniel if they have any kittens at their ranch. I'll take as many as they've got. Two for in the house and the rest for the barn."

Johnny's eyes grew big. "Won't the dogs eat them?"

"No. They're well trained and we'll make sure they leave the cats alone. We can't keep having our flour and stuff ruined by mice. Things are too expensive," Leigh replied as she washed up.

Daphne couldn't wait to see the sparks fly between Cy and his feisty wife. When it came to the ranch work, Leigh ruled with an iron fist.

No sooner did Cy come in the door with another pail of milk than Johnny said, "We're getting cats, Cy."

Johnny often jumped the gun when it came to relaying information that other people would've preferred to have imparted. Leigh frowned while Daphne's lips twitched as she tried to hide a smile.

"No, we're not," Cy said.

"Leigh says we are," Johnny said.

Cy's eyes found Leigh's. "We've talked about this."

Leigh put her hands on her hips. "We're getting cats. The mice got into the flour again and, I don't know about you, but I don't want to eat stuff that might have mice poop in it. Besides it's too expensive to keep replacing it."

With a sound of disgust, Daphne sat down the bowl of the pancake batter she'd been mixing. "No pancakes. I used that flour to make this batter."

Johnny said, "I don't want no mice poop pancakes."

Leigh gave Cy a hard look. "We're getting a mama cat and some kittens and that's final."

Cy didn't want mice poop pancakes, either, and the mice were getting out of hand. "Okay. Fine. We'll get cats."

Leigh nodded. "After breakfast, I'll take a crate over to David's and get some."

Daphne said, "Well, we still have sausage and I'll make some eggs."

"Dang mice," Johnny said. "I could practically taste those pancakes."

Cy said, "I'll bring home new flour tonight."

They were about halfway through breakfast when someone knocked on the front door. Daphne answered it and saw a young woman standing on the porch.

"May I help you?" she asked.

"I hope so, ma'am. I'm looking for Johnny. Is he here?"

Daphne's eyebrows shot up. It was the first time that a girl had come there asking for her cousin. "Yes, he's here. Come in. And you would be?"

"Dory Klingerman, ma'am."

Daphne led her into the kitchen. "Johnny, you have a visitor."

Johnny took one look at Dory and shot to his feet. "Hello, ma'am. You must be Dory."

Dory smiled at him. "That's right. Cotton sent me to talk to you about making a cradle for a friend of mine."

He held out a hand to her. "It's a pleasure to meet you."

Johnny's heart hammered in his chest as they shook

hands. He'd never seen such a pretty girl before.

"Likewise," Dory said.

Johnny introduced her to everyone and said, "Come on out to my woodshop and we'll talk about what sort of design you want."

"Okay."

Johnny donned his coat and hat and ushered her out the door.

Cy chuckled. "Did you see his face? I'd say that Cupid struck. He turned almost as red as the barn."

Leigh said, "She's a pretty girl and she seems nice."

Daphne said, "I wonder how she knows Cotton. You don't think…?"

Cy shook his head. "Cotton wouldn't want a woman that young. He's a ladies' man, but he does have a line that he won't cross. No, she knows him some other way."

"Uh oh," Leigh said. "Your detective mind just started working on that."

Cy said, "Can't help being curious."

"Curious as a cat," Daphne said.

"Shut up. Cats," Cy muttered.

Leigh and Daphne laughed at him as they finished their breakfast.

~~*~~

"I can't believe you're courting an Injun woman."

Brock's lips pursed as he finished with his tie that night. Looking at his father, Doug, he said, "Pa, we've talked about this. Don't talk about Daphne like that. She's a good woman, no matter her heritage. You're gonna have to get used to it, because I'm not going to stop seeing her."

Doug sighed. "I thought you hated them."

"I never hated Daphne."

"What about that lousy brother of hers?"

Brock said, "We've come to an understanding about some things, Pa. We're both trying for Daphne's sake.

Can't you try for mine? What happened to Grandpa had nothing to do with them."

Doug made a dismissive gesture. "One Indian's just like the next. You can't trust them, Brock. You wait. No good will come of this."

Brock said, "Is that why you play cards with Cotton all the time?"

Doug grinned. "Now, that is one Injun I like. Too bad they're not all like that."

Brock gave Doug a level look. "Daphne is Cotton's niece, Pa. That should carry a little weight with you."

Doug's face fell. "Oh. I keep forgetting about that. Well, she might be all right. We'll see. Those other ones? Forget it. David Lone Wolf is just that; a wolf in sheep's clothing. The prices him and those heathen boys charge for horses is downright robbery."

Not in the mood to hear his father's ranting, Brock said, "I gotta go, Pa. I'll see you in the morning."

He made good his escape, leaving even though it was a little early. Driving the buggy along, he let his mind drift to much more pleasant things. Daphne's lovely face rose in his mind. Everything about her enchanted him. Her luminous, dark eyes and shiny cap of mahogany hair drew his eyes and he'd barely been able to look away from her when they'd been out to dinner.

Turning up the lane of Sundance Ranch, Brock heard dogs barking and was met by all four canines. Burt jumped up in the buggy and Brock had to ward off his sloppy kisses.

"Get out of here," Brock said. "Out!"

Burt whined and jumped out again as they arrived at the house. The dogs trailed him to the door and it opened just as he lifted his hand to knock.

"C'mon in, Brock," Cy said. "Daphne will be down shortly."

"I'm a little early," Brock said, following him into the parlor.

He'd never been beyond the kitchen before and he was curious to see what the rest of the house was like. As they entered the parlor the dogs set up a racket. Brock saw a large yellow tabby cat curled up on the sofa by Leigh.

"I didn't know you had cats," Brock said.

Cy's expression darkened. "We just got some today. Mice problems."

Leigh laughed. "He hates the idea of a cat in the barn, much less the house."

Cy quieted the dogs and sat down in one of the chairs. "Have a seat."

Brock sat down by the cat and held out a hand to it. "We have cats. Three, in fact."

"No wonder I can't stand you," Cy said.

"Brock!" Leigh admonished. "Shame on you."

"Don't worry about it," Brock said.

Leigh said, "I'll bet you don't have any mice, do you?"

"Here and there, but they're great mousers. Mice don't last long if they're dumb enough to come inside," Brock said, scratching the tabby's ears. "This cat's pretty calm for being in a new place with dogs."

"Maybe it's half-dead," Cy said hopefully.

Leigh said, "Stop it! Daniel said that she's very friendly with their dogs, so she's used to them."

"Stupid dogs," Cy muttered.

A calico kitten came out from underneath the sofa, its little back arched and its fur standing out all over. Pudge got down on his belly and crawled towards it. The kitten growled and hissed while the pug rolled over and whined.

Cy said, "Pudge! Knock it off. Don't submit to a cat!"

Pudge rolled back over, but kept inching closer. Then he raised a paw to it. The kitten backed away, growling louder. Pudge got up and bowed down, barking and then running away, classic doggie behavior for "come play with me". The kitten didn't respond, but the mama cat got down off the couch and walked right up to Pudge, rubbing her head against the little dog.

Ecstatic to have made friends with the new family member, Pudge licked the cat's ears and ran rapid circuits around the room. Even Cy laughed at his antics as the cat sat down and calmly washed her paw while Pudge acted like a puppy. The kitten had ducked back under the sofa. The mama cat jumped up on Cy's lap and Brock cracked up at the disgusted look on Cy's face.

The cat was oblivious to Cy's feelings and draped herself across his legs, purring loudly.

"Now what am I supposed to do?" he asked.

Leigh giggled. "You could try petting her."

Cy shot her a dark look before briefly running his fingers over her back. The cat turned her face to his hand and started washing it.

"I think she likes you," Brock said. "Stupid cat."

Leigh let loose with a laugh as Daphne came into the room. Brock stood up, the cat forgotten as he took in Daphne's beauty. He liked the deep wine dress on her as much has he had the blue one.

"You look beautiful," he said.

Daphne blushed. "Thank you."

"You're welcome. Ready?"

She said goodnight to Cy and Leigh and they embarked on their second night out.

CHAPTER TEN

Nothing went wrong that night. Brock took her to a different restaurant and then they stopped at Benny's for a little dancing. He knew that his brother, Aaron, had been going to play there that night. They'd laughed off and on during dinner at Cy's reaction to having cats and learned more about each other.

As soon as they went inside the saloon, fiddle and piano music greeted their ears. Daphne saw a man in a wheelchair playing the piano and smiled. Carter "Wheels" Ellis was a much-loved figure in Chance City. His fingers moved deftly over the keys, confidently hitting the right notes. Aaron Guthrie, younger than Brock by one year, stood close to the piano, sawing a lively tune on his fiddle.

Although his eyes were the same blue as Brock's, he had their mother's dark hair. He was too busy playing to notice that Brock had arrived.

"Well, there's a fine lass if ever I saw one," Benny said in his best Irish accent as Daphne and Brock approached the bar.

"Hello, Benny. How are you tonight?"

"Better now that you're here." His green eyes twinkled. The open admiration in his gaze made Brock's stomach clench with jealousy.

"We came to do some dancing," Brock told him, putting a hand on Daphne's shoulder.

He and Benny stared at each other for a few moments before the bartender nodded. "Well, you're in luck since Aaron and Wheels are at it. You gonna play?"

"No. I don't have my guitar with me," Brock said. "Another time."

"Okay. What are you drinkin'?"

Daphne said, "I'll have a sarsaparilla, please."

"Beer," Brock said.

Benny poured their drinks and they found a table as the song ended. The crowd clapped and cheered while Aaron bowed and Wheels saluted them. Seeing his big brother, Aaron made his way over to their table, Wheels close behind him. Aaron pulled out a chair and Wheels moved into the empty space beside Daphne.

"Hello, pretty lady," he said. "How's the Indian princess tonight?"

Brock wanted to punch him until Daphne laughed. Apparently she knew Wheels and didn't mind his teasing.

"I'm fine. How's the handsomest man on two wheels?"

"Finer than frog hair split four ways. Gonna dance with me later?" he asked.

"Of course," she said.

Brock frowned. "Not tonight, Wheels. I'm gonna be keeping her busy."

Daphne said, "Don't speak for me, Brock. I always dance with Wheels."

"Yeah, Deputy, she always dances with me," Wheels said.

Brock didn't want to watch Daphne sit on Wheels' lap. It wasn't proper, but Wheels coaxed women into doing it. In the past, Brock had laughed as much as anyone else over it, but now that he was seeing Daphne, the idea of her sitting on any other man's lap but his angered him.

Brock said, "I didn't know that you came here so

much, Daphne."

"I come off and on with Cy and our cousins when I need to blow off a little steam," she said.

Aaron watched the exchange with amusement. He didn't share his father and brother's deep-seeded hatred of Indians and had nothing against the Decker or Lone Wolf families. His brother's jealousy towards Wheels was funny, considering they were such close friends.

Wheels said, "It's been a while. I've been missin' my favorite dancin' partner."

"And I've been missing my favorite Mississippi boy," she said, patting his arm.

Aaron saw Brock's eyes narrow. "Brock, I brought your guitar just in case you showed up. How about we play a song and give Wheels a break?"

Brock almost refused, but he didn't want to look like a jealous jackass, so he said, "All right. Have fun."

Wheels let out a whoop and rolled out to the dance floor. Brock warmed up a little bit and then he and Aaron played a fast song. Daphne sat on Wheels' lap and laughed when he started spinning nimbly around on the chair.

He'd been injured in the army and sent home, unable to walk after suffering spinal damage when his horse had been shot out from under him. Although initially devastated, he hadn't allowed himself to wallow long, figuring that at least he was able to draw breath and be with his family.

His father, Vern, a brilliant inventor, who did ingenious things with metal and all sorts of machinery, had helped design a special chair using bicycle wheels and a custom-made seat that let Wheels move around more freely than a regular wheelchair would have.

Wheels had spent hours practicing speeding along, turning quickly, and spinning. As a result, his upper body had grown powerful and he could maneuver around people and objects with ease. He'd always loved dancing and still did, even though he'd had to modify the way he went about it.

Brock watched Wheels and Daphne spin around on the dance floor and stifled his jealously. How could he begrudge his buddy some happiness? Although popular with the women, none of them were interested in seriously seeing Wheels. Brock had never asked Wheels, but he often wondered if things below the belt worked or not. It was a sensitive subject that Brock had no intention of bringing up.

As his fingers moved over the strings, Brock enjoyed listening to Daphne laugh and seeing her eyes lit up with happiness. Wheels spun and she held on tight, squealing over the speed at which they moved. Wheels laughed and spun in the other direction. The regulars at Benny's always encouraged him to dance, amazed at the things he could do in his chair. They clapped and cheered him on.

When the song ended, Wheels brought Daphne over to the stage.

"Here's your lady, Deputy. All in one piece."

Daphne chuckled and kissed his cheek. "Thanks for the wonderful dance."

"You're welcome, sweetheart. Back to the piano I go."

He wheeled over to the piano and struck up a drinking song. Benny sang along from behind the bar, his baritone voice blending with Wheels' tenor. Brock twirled Daphne around as he sang along.

Daphne loved his smooth tenor voice and his smile as he held her and they moved around the floor. The heat of his palm at the small of her back made her tingle and the desire in his eyes made her pulse race. When the music shifted into a slower rhythm, Brock pulled her a little closer and she inhaled his slightly musky cologne. It tantalized her senses and his gaze captured hers.

Holding Daphne felt so right, so incredible and Brock's acute awareness of her beauty sent desire singing through his body. From her shiny, mahogany hair to her feet she was gorgeous and his hunger for her intensified as they danced.

After a few more songs, Aaron and Wheels announced that they were done for the night, which caused a lot of grumbling and groans of protest. Daphne and Brock took their leave soon after since he had to be up early for work.

Settling in the buggy, Daphne said, "Thank you for such a wonderful time. I've never heard you sing or play before. You're very good."

Brock smiled. "Thanks. Aaron, Nora, and me inherited Ma's musical ability. She sings and plays piano. We play at home a lot."

"That's really nice."

"Yeah. You're a really good dancer."

"All Indians are good dancers," she teased him. "Didn't you know that?"

He laughed. "No, I didn't, but then again, I have to confess that I really don't know a whole lot about them. I've never wanted to learn, but being with you makes me want to. I want to know you better and since that's a part of you, I really should."

She cocked her head at him a little. "I'm impressed, Deputy. You seem to be overcoming some of your hatred."

"I'm trying." His expression had turned bashful. "Uh, Cy told me about all of the stuff you guys went through as kids. It really opened my eyes. If people treated my family like that, I'd be pissed off and hate them, too. You guys were just kids and hadn't hurt anyone. Kids shouldn't be treated like that, no matter what race they are."

Daphne laid her hand on his arm, touched by his remarks. "Thank you for seeing that. I know that this has to be hard for you, changing your perception of me and my heritage. I'm not saying that the Comanche didn't kill a lot of people. My ancestors were a very war-like people, but a lot of times they had reason to be. But my family has been peaceful for a long time. Other than my cousins and Cy getting in bar fights, we haven't hurt anyone."

Brock took her hand and kissed the back of it. "You're right. It's hard, but I'm beginning to see how biased my thinking has been. Be patient with me, okay?"

She smiled and nodded and Brock couldn't wait any longer to kiss her. They were far enough from town that they were alone on the road. He stopped the buggy.

Daphne gave him a confused look. "What are you doing?"

He replied by cupping her face and brushing his lips against hers. She surprised him by grasping his coat and pulling him closer. Thrusting a hand into her silky hair, he took what she offered him, delving his tongue into her mouth. When she moaned and wrapped her arms around his midsection, he deepened the kiss further. She tasted sweet from the sarsaparilla she'd drank and her lips were incredibly soft.

Fire swept through Daphne as Brock plundered her mouth. She responded ardently to him, sliding even closer as he growled and slid a hand under her cloak, caressing her back. She'd kissed men in the past, but they'd never stirred her senses the way Brock did. His lips were warm and firm and she couldn't get enough of him.

Brock almost moved his hand around to cup her breast, but caught himself and drew back from her, his breathing ragged. Her passion-filled expression didn't make it easy to restrain himself.

In a husky voice, he said, "I'd better get you home."

Daphne nodded a little. "Yes, that's probably a good idea."

Putting distance between them, Brock took up the reins again, and they moved on down the road. They held hands, though, unwilling to stop touching altogether. Daphne couldn't believe that she was riding by Brock's side after having dreamed of being with him for long.

He squeezed her hand. "Penny for your thoughts?"

Her smile made his heartbeat throb again. "I'm just very happy, that's all."

Putting an arm around her shoulders, he pulled her against his side and kissed her temple. "Me, too, sweetheart."

Daphne blinked away the tears his term of endearment created. They didn't talk much the rest of the way home. Words weren't necessary because their hearts did the talking for them.

ROBIN DEETER

CHAPTER ELEVEN

The next night, Johnny burst into Cy's house, looking for his cousin. Cy and Leigh sat at the kitchen table going over their books.

"How many times do I have to tell you not to bang the door?" Cy complained.

"Sorry. I can't get my tie tied. Can you do it?" Johnny asked. "I'm taking Dory out and I'm nervous as a goat pooping peach pits."

Leigh grinned. "You like this girl, huh?"

Johnny shook his head as Cy worked on the tie. "I think I'm in love."

"Love?" Cy gave him a doubtful look. "You've only spent an hour or so with her. There's no way you can love her."

Johnny met his gaze. "You never heard of love at first sight? Well, trust me, it exists. I can't get her out of my mind. Those big blue eyes of hers and she's so sweet and—"

"You're infatuated," Cy interjected. "That's normal. You have to take your time and get to know her."

Johnny's gesture included both Cy and Leigh. "You two didn't. It only took a couple of weeks for you to get married."

Leigh said, "That was a different situation, Johnny. I came here purposely to marry Cy. Dory isn't a mail order bride, though. There's no expectation of marriage. Cy's right. Enjoy getting to know Dory. Have some fun and see what happens."

Cy finished tying Johnny's tie. "There you go. You look good. Other than that one funeral, I don't think I've ever seen you in a suit. I see you had your ears lowered, too."

Johnny smoothed down the back of his hair even though it was already neat. "Yeah. I wanna look my best. I've never called on a lady before. I'm about ready to jump out of my skin."

With a grin, Leigh said, "Easy, there. It'll be all right. You're a good-looking fella and you're fun and respectful. Just the sort of man most women like."

"Thanks. I better get going. I don't wanna be late," Johnny said.

"Have fun," Leigh said.

"I reckon I will." Johnny gave them a big grin and hurried out the door.

~~*~~

Johnny whistled as he drove along, keeping the horse at a trot. He'd been pleasantly surprised to learn that Dory didn't live very far from Sundance Ranch. Finding Dory's house proved easy and it wasn't long before he reached her home. He took a breath, hopped out of the buggy, and jogged over to the house.

Just as he stepped onto the porch of the plain white clapboard house, he heard yelling from within the house. Suddenly the front door was yanked open and a surly looking man with dark hair rushed towards Johnny. He brandished a revolver, which he pointed at Johnny's head.

"You need to leave. Dory ain't going anywhere with no Comanche lover."

Johnny's voice stuck in his throat for a moment. "Sir, my family are good people. So am I. Please lower the gun, sir. I mean no harm."

"Sure you don't. You just wanna get her alone and knock her up. I won't have it!"

The smell of booze was strong on the man and Johnny realized that he wasn't dealing with a man who was in his right mind.

Splotches of color broke out on his face. "No, sir, you're wrong. I have too much respect for women to ever treat Dory that way. I promise."

Dory's father sneered at him. "Sure, sure. If you ain't outta here in the next ten seconds, I'm gonna shoot your sorry hide full of holes, boy. Now get!"

Dory grabbed her father's shoulder. "Pa! Leave him alone. He's a good man."

He turned around and gave her a hard shove. Johnny couldn't see behind him, but he heard Dory fall to the floor.

"Now, see here! There ain't no cause to treat a woman like that!" Johnny protested.

He moved toward the drunk man, who focused his attention on Johnny again and raised the gun.

"Stop right there!"

Johnny's temper simmered. "Shame on you for hurting a woman. Dory, you all right?"

"I'm fine."

"I said get out of here!"

Johnny wasn't about to leave Dory and her mother there with the violent man. "Sir, if you could lower the gun, we could talk this out like—"

The gun went off and Johnny was blown off his feet as the bullet ripped into his body. Fire spread through his chest, limiting his ability to breathe. Right before his head smacked off the porch floor, rendering him unconscious, Johnny heard Dory scream. Then he sank down into oblivion.

~~*~~

Dory ran along the trail she knew well, her breathing coming in harsh gasps as she moved at top speed. As Cotton's clearing loomed ahead, she started screaming his name as loud as she could. Exiting the woods, Dory saw that cross sticks had been placed outside his tipi, indicating that he had company. She didn't care.

"Cotton! Come quick! It's Johnny! Please!" she screamed.

Cotton threw the tipi flap open, rushing out in only his breechcloth and leggings. "What happened?"

"Pa shot him! I got away. I don't know if he's alive."

Cotton didn't ask questions. "Go to the ranch and have Cy go to your house. Stay at the ranch until someone comes for you."

Dory's blue eyes swam with tears. "But, Ma is—"

Cotton put his hands on her shoulders. "I'll take care of Noreen. Go!"

She took off down the trail that led to Sundance Ranch and Cotton retrieved his shirt and weapons, telling his lady friend what had occurred. Then he ran into the woods, intent on saving his nephew and Noreen even if it meant murdering Maynard.

~~*~~

Arriving at the Klingerman residence, Cotton crept carefully towards the house. All was quiet, but he saw Johnny lying prone on the porch. On silent feet, he ran for the porch, keeping a sharp eye out for Maynard. Reaching Johnny's side, Cotton shook him a little, but Johnny didn't move. Leaning down, Cotton listened to see if Johnny was still breathing.

When he heard air moving faintly in and out of Johnny's mouth, he felt slightly faint with relief.

Unbuttoning Johnny's coat, Cotton was dismayed by the amount of blood that had soaked through his shirt. Still staying alert to his surroundings, Cotton stepped off the porch and scooped up a handful of dirt. He spat in it several times and then pressed the damp mass to the bullet hole in Johnny's chest.

There was nothing else he could do for Johnny until help arrived, but he had to make sure the Noreen was safe. Stealthily, he opened the front door and crept through it. He heard quiet weeping and followed the sound. He found Noreen sitting against a wall in the parlor.

She saw him and started crying harder.

"Is he here?" Cotton whispered.

"No. He left. Said he wasn't gonna hang for killing an Indian lover," Noreen said. "Where's Dory?"

"At my nephew's ranch. Help is on the way," Cotton said, helping her up.

He guided her to a chair.

"How is Johnny?"

Cotton's stomach lurched. "Alive, but I don't know if he'll survive."

Noreen put her face in her hands and sobbed.

"Noreen, I hate to leave you, but I have to get Johnny to town. Take this." He pressed a pistol into her hand. "If Maynard comes back, shoot to kill. Do you understand?"

Noreen nodded. Cotton ran out to the porch, carefully scooped Johnny up, and took him to the buggy. Lying him gently across the seat, Cotton covered Johnny with a blanket and then hopped up in the buggy.

He had to stand since the buggy was only a two seater, but since he possessed excellent balance, Cotton had no trouble staying upright as he drove the horse away from the Klingerman house. Slapping the reins against the horse's rump, he urged it into a canter, asking the Great Spirit to give the horse's hooves wings and to give his nephew the strength to hold on.

~~*~~

Dr. Vin Ellis, Wheels' uncle, worked on Johnny, deeply concerned about his patient's chances of survival. He'd lost a lot of blood and, even though the bullet hadn't hit his heart or lungs, it had still caused a lot of damage. After removing the bullet, Dr. Ellis closed both of Johnny's wounds and bandaged him up.

He had an orderly assist him in getting Johnny into a bed in the men's ward of the small hospital. After giving instructions on caring for Johnny to a nurse, he cleaned up and went to talk with Johnny's family.

Daphne had insisted on coming to the hospital with Cy and Daniel while Leigh had stayed at home with Dory. She spotted Dr. Ellis first as he came into the waiting room.

"How is he? Please tell us that he's still ..."

Dr. Ellis regarded her with kind, dark eyes. "Yes, Johnny is alive, but I must be honest with you. It's touch and go right now. But, he's young and strong, so hopefully he can hang on."

Cy put an arm around Daphne. "Can we see him?"

"Yes, but only for a few minutes. He's unconscious at the moment, but if he wakes up, please don't excite him," Dr. Ellis replied.

"Of course," Daphne said.

Dr. Ellis nodded and led them to Johnny.

Daphne's eyes flooded with tears as she took in Johnny's appearance. He was almost as pale as the pillowcase under his head and his lips were the color of blueberries. Going to his bed, she brushed his sweat-damp hair back from his forehead.

She loved Johnny like a little brother and the thought of losing him filled her with dread. Gently picking up his hand, she kissed his fingers. "Hang on, Johnny. We love you so much. You have to stay with us so you can bang the door and tease me and help Leigh with the ranch. Please don't leave us."

She kissed his hand again and laid it back down on the bed. Then she turned to Cy, startling him by grabbing his coat.

Tears trickled from her eyes. "You go find the coward who did this, brother," she said in Comanche. "Make him pay. Do you hear me?"

Cy's eyes were also damp. He nodded. "Yes. I hear you, and I will."

When Daphne released him, Cy briefly laid a hand on Johnny's shoulder. "You're a strong man, Johnny. Fight."

Cotton said a brief prayer over Johnny and then Dr. Ellis made them leave. They met Daniel and Sly outside the hospital. The twins hadn't wanted to come inside and potentially cause trouble if someone objected to their presence. They listened attentively as their cousins and uncle updated them on Johnny's condition.

Cy said, "I telephoned Rob from here and told him what happened. He knows I'll be leaving to go after Maynard."

Cotton said, "I'll go with you."

Cy nodded.

Cotton looked at Sly. "Will you look after Noreen and Dory while we're gone?"

"Yes. I'll stay with them in case Maynard comes back."

Their plans solidified, they departed from the hospital, going their separate ways.

CHAPTER TWELVE

Brock's heart went out to Daphne when he saw her the next morning at the hospital. Rob had told his staff what had happened and he'd come to visit Johnny as soon as he'd finished his morning patrol. Daphne sat in the waiting room, her head bowed, and her eyes closed. Brock sat down by her and took her hand.

She opened her eyes and looked at him. The sympathy in his blue gaze brought on tears and her breath caught on a sob.

Brock gathered her in his arms, rubbing her back consolingly. "It'll be all right, Daphne. He'll pull through. He's a tough kid. What did Doc Ellis say?"

Drawing back from Brock, Daphne pulled a handkerchief from her skirt pocket and wiped away her tears. "He said that it's encouraging since Johnny made it through the night and that he thinks he'll make it. Poor Johnny. He was so excited about taking Dory to dinner. He looked so handsome. I just can't believe this."

Brock rubbed her arms. "It's a big shock, but you're a strong woman."

"Yes, I am. I won't fall apart. Johnny needs me, needs all of us. I'm going to see if they'll let me stay and help take care of him," Daphne said.

Tipping her chin up, Brock said, "With you as his nurse, he'll definitely get better. If I ever get shot will you be my nurse?"

She laughed, grateful to him for adding some much needed levity to the situation. "You'd better not get shot. Thank you for coming."

"Of course I'd come. I can get you back there. Come with me," Brock said, taking her hand.

Daphne followed him over to the nurses' desk.

"Morning, Sadie," Brock said. "I need to see Johnny Decker. Official business. Ms. Decker is going with me."

Daphne blinked at his no nonsense tone and the steely expression on his strong-jawed face. Sadie didn't argue with him.

"Go on ahead, Deputy."

He gave her a curt nod. "Much obliged."

Once they were through the door that opened onto the hallway leading to the men's ward, Brock grinned at Daphne. "There are perks to the job. That's one of them. Getting into places no one else can."

Daphne chuckled. "Thank you."

They met Dr. Ellis as he came out of an office.

"Oh, Miss Decker. I was just coming to get you. Johnny's awake and asking for you."

Daphne said, "I'd like to help take care of Johnny, Doctor. I can change bandages and things like that."

Dr. Ellis nodded. "If you like. I'm sure he'd feel better with you here. He's hopped up on laudanum, just so you know. I'll be around after a little bit."

"Thank you so much."

Daphne was so happy to see that Johnny was awake that she had to blink back tears. He gave her a lopsided smile.

"There she is," he said hoarsely. "I been waiting to see you for days."

She sat down in the chair next to his bed and took the

hand he weakly held out to her. "You just got here last night, honey."

"Oh. I guess I'm a little mixed up," he said, still smiling.

His voice was weak and his eyes glassy from the laudanum, but he was alive.

Daphne giggled. "Just a little."

His smile widened, then he suddenly sobered. "What about Dory? Is she okay? He knocked her down and I was mad so I told him none of that. Well, he didn't listen, so I was gonna get that gun from him, but he shot me and now here I am."

Brock smothered a smile over his convoluted story. He understood what Johnny meant, though.

Daphne said, "Dory is fine. She's a strong girl."

"Pretty as a picker, too. No, that ain't right. Picture. Pretty as a picture. I'm gonna marry that woman," Johnny said. "You wait and see if I don't."

Daphne laughed softly. "How about we worry about that once you're better?"

He rolled his eyes. "Well, I certainly can't marry her like this. Will you bring her to see me? We didn't get to go to dinner. That damn father of hers messed it all up." He yawned.

Daphne said, "Why don't you go to sleep, Johnny. You need your rest. I'll be right here."

"Okay. Thanks for coming to see me, Brock. I knew you were there. You're too big to miss. Pardon my rudeness."

Brock said, "Don't worry about it, buddy. You do what Daphne says and get some sleep. You don't want to make her mad."

Johnny's expression turned solemn. "You're not kidding. She's tough."

Brock nodded. "I know."

Johnny's eyes drifted shut and Brock winked at Daphne. "I gotta go, but I'll stop by later on. Just call over to the office if you need anything."

Daphne said, "Thanks again."

Brock looked around to make sure no one was looking and then gave her a brief kiss. "See you then."

Daphne watched him walk away, admiring his broad shoulders and nice rear end. Once he was out of sight, Daphne pulled out a book from her bag and settled in to read until Johnny needed something.

~~*~~

Brock was glad that his shift that day was mainly uneventful, allowing him to leave work on time for a change. He went to La Fontana's, a modest restaurant that made excellent food, and picked up the food he'd ordered earlier that day. Entering the hospital, he greeted a few people he knew before going back to the men's ward.

Daphne sat in her chair, her head leaning back against the wall, eyes closed. Brock's gaze moved over her beautiful face, noting the faint smudges under her eyes. A feeling of such tenderness stole over him that it made it hard to catch his breath for a moment. He almost hated to wake her, but figured that bringing her good food would make up for it.

Going over to her, he brushed the back of his fingers over her soft cheek.

Her eyes fluttered open and she gave him a drowsy smile. He imagined that it was how she looked in the morning after a night of lovemaking. Stifling the spear of longing that pierced his stomach, he smiled back at her.

"How's the patient?"

"He's doing well. The laudanum makes him even funnier than normal. He still insists that he's going to marry Dory. He wouldn't go to sleep this last time until I promised to bring her to see him tomorrow," Daphne told him.

Brock's jaw clenched. "He's such a sweet kid. I hope

when Cy and Cotton find Maynard that they make him suffer before they haul him in. Johnny didn't deserve this."

Daphne nodded and stretched. "I know I shouldn't, but I've been thinking the same thing."

"I don't blame you a bit. Now, what do you say to dinner? Look what I brought," Brock said.

He showed her the pan of lasagna and Daphne's mouth watered.

"I say yes! I'm starving," she said.

"I thought you might be. Come with me. There's a little cafeteria downstairs." Brock saw her glance at Johnny. "He'll be all right for a while. That's what they have nurses for."

Daphne smiled. "I know I'm acting like a mother hen, but I can't help it."

"I understand. C'mon. Let's go eat," Brock said.

Once they were seated, Brock took out plates and silverware from the basket he carried. Daphne's stomach ached as she watched him put the lasagna on a plate and hand it to her.

"That looks wonderful."

Brock served himself. "Dig in."

It was so strange to sit in a hospital cafeteria to eat, she thought.

Brock grew concerned when he saw her try to blink away tears. "Hey, what's wrong?"

"Johnny always says grace. He says such nice blessings."

Brock reached for her hand. "Don't worry. He'll be back to saying them real soon."

His touch comforted her. "Thank you."

To distract her from the tense situation, he said, "Did you know that Ellie went out with Walt Gaines a couple of times?"

"No. Cy didn't mention it. Walt. That was the name of Leigh's first husband."

"Oh. I didn't know that. Well, she says that he's an odd

duck. Mysterious. He doesn't talk about anything serious," Brock said.

Daphne's brows drew together. "I've met him a couple of times, but I don't really know anything about him."

"That's the thing. No one really does. He had her over for dinner with a married couple he knows, but she said that they didn't talk about anything serious, either. You know, not a lot of personal information," Brock told her.

"Is she going to keep seeing him?"

Brock frowned. "I think she is, but only because she's curious. She hasn't mentioned if there's any chemistry."

Daphne said, "Now *I'm* curious."

"Me, too. It'll be interesting to see what happens. I know Ellie, and she won't let him get away with this too much longer."

"Good for her. Keep me informed."

Brock smiled at the mischievous gleam in her eyes. "Why, Miss Decker, are you a busybody?"

She gave him a saucy smile. "I like gossip as much as anyone else, Deputy. Especially the kind involving mysterious lawyers."

He laughed. "Once again I'm reminded that you're related to Cy. You can't resist a mystery any more than he can."

She wiped her mouth on a napkin. "We get that from Ma. She was curious about anything and everything and she loved reading mysteries, too. She used to tell us stories and read them to us. That's when Cy decided that he wanted to be a detective and solve crime."

Brock said, "I'm sure she was a wonderful woman."

"I miss her so much. She was so much fun," Daphne said.

"You must have inherited that from her. Cy must be more like your father," Brock said. "I'm not being smart, just trying to figure him out, that's all."

Daphne said, "You're right. Pa was more serious. Fun in his own way, but not like Ma. She used to be able to get

Pa to do silly stuff, though. And he gave us horsey rides when we were little, too. I've noticed a difference in Cy since he married Leigh. She's such a good woman and a good friend. I'm glad they make each other happy."

Brock grinned. "Something tells me that it won't be long until you hear the pitter-patter of little feet around the house."

Daphne said, "I hope so. I can't wait to be an aunt."

She didn't say it, but Brock knew that she was thinking about becoming a mother. She'd said as much the day she'd confronted him in the sheriff's office. He'd love to have kids, too. Brock let his mind wander a little, trying to picture what his and Daphne's kids might look like.

Would they have her dark hair and his blue eyes or would they more strongly favor one or the other? He thought about how different Daniel and Sly looked, yet if he let himself admit it, both were handsome men, each in his own way. Looking at Daphne, he thought that he'd love to have a little girl who looked just like her.

Daphne wondered at the smile on Brock's face and the faraway look in his eyes. "Brock?"

With a start, he came back to himself. "Hmm? What?"

She chuckled. "You were in a world of your own."

He colored a little. "Sorry. Woolgathering, I guess."

"About what?"

Brock searched for something plausible so that he didn't have to tell her that he was thinking about having children with her. "Well, I was just picturing how cute you must have been as a little girl."

Daphne smiled. "Thank you. I have some pictures if you'd like to see them sometime."

"Love to," he said.

"That can be arranged. Thanks for bringing such delicious food. It was very thoughtful of you." She gave him a speculative smile. "I think that you're a lot sweeter than you let on."

He gave her a heart-stopping grin. "Not with just

anyone, though. Only a certain beautiful woman I just had supper with."

His praise brought a blush to her cheeks. "Charmer. I'm sure you've told plenty of women that same thing. I have to get back to Johnny."

"About that," Brock said. "Daphne, they have a staff here. He'll be all right. You really should go home and rest, honey. You're bushed. Besides, I'm sure that Leigh would like an update. Let me take you home."

Daphne wanted to stay with Johnny in the worst way, but Brock was right.

Seeing her indecision, Brock said, "We have a telephone. I'll tell the nurses to call me if anything happens and I'll come get you. I'm sure he'll be fine, but just in case."

"Oh, Brock, I couldn't ask you to do that," she said, rising from the table.

He put a hand on her shoulder. "You didn't. I offered. I don't mind at all."

She thanked him and they gathered up all their supper things.

"I just want to check on him before we go," Daphne said.

"Of course."

Johnny was still sound asleep when they went to see him. Daphne kissed his forehead and then they left after Brock gave the head nurse his telephone exchange and instructions to call if there was any change in Johnny's condition.

As they walked out of the hospital, Brock took Daphne's hand. Holding it felt as natural as breathing, and looking into her eyes, he saw that she felt the same way.

CHAPTER THIRTEEN

When they reached Sundance Ranch, Brock went inside with Daphne to warm up a little before heading back home and to see if there was any news about Cy and Cotton.

Leigh said, "They're not back yet. I don't think it'll take them long to find Maynard. I'd like a piece of him when they do, though."

"Me, too," Daphne said, putting coffee on. "Johnny is holding his own. I just hope that infection doesn't set in."

Leigh said, "Sounds like they're taking good care of him. I'll go with you tomorrow after breakfast and harass him about getting shot when we have all this work to do."

It hadn't occurred to Brock that without Johnny around, the workload fell mainly to Leigh because Cy worked during the day.

"You need to hire a ranch hand," Brock said.

Leigh said, "We can't afford to pay someone a decent wage right now. We'll be fine. Once they get back, Cotton will help me. David sent over one of their ranch hands today and said that he'd come back tomorrow, too."

"That's good," Brock said. "You know, you've got another bunkhouse."

"Yeah. I'm aware."

Brock rubbed his chin a little. "Maybe you could find someone who'd be willing to work for room and board and a little money for now. You could put an ad in the paper and I'd be happy to ask around for you."

Leigh's eyes lit up. "That's a great idea. I keep tellin' Cy that you're not as bad as he thinks you are. I'd really appreciate it."

"Happy to help."

Brock only stayed long enough to drink one cup of coffee, wanting to get home just in case the hospital called. Daphne walked him out.

"I can't thank you enough," she said.

He took her face in his hands. "Daphne, I don't think there's anything I wouldn't do for you. I care about you and I'll help you with anything you need me to."

Moving closer, he lowered his head, pressing his lips to hers in a kiss that quickly grew hungry. Daphne wound her arms around his neck and kissed him back, twining her tongue with his and playing with the hair at the nape of his neck. He growled as he held her tighter, and Daphne reveled in his strength.

His mouth was hot and demanding and Daphne ached for him. She wanted him so much that she felt faint with need. She also had the mad urge to rip his clothes off and feast her eyes on him. Suddenly his hands were underneath the shawl she'd thrown on, caressing her back, creating an even hotter fire inside.

Brazenly, she guided his hand to her breast, wanting to feel his touch. He resisted at first, but she was insistent. He groaned as he gently squeezed it. His thumb grazed her nipple and she jerked as a current of desire shot through her.

Abruptly, Brock pulled away. "I'm sorry," he said hoarsely.

"What the hell are you sorry for? Why did you stop?"

He arched an eyebrow. "You jumped."

"Only because it felt so good."

Brock grinned. "Oh. I'm glad. It sure felt good to me, too."

Daphne was still dazed by the passion that hummed through her body. "Take me to the barn and make love to me. We can't in the house, but we can out there."

His eyebrows shot up. "What?"

"Don't you want to? I do."

She took his hand and tugged, but he didn't move.

Brock bit back his mirth, knowing that he'd greatly offend her if he laughed. "Honey, I want to make love to you more than you know, but I don't want our first time to be in a barn. Besides, we're not married."

Daphne forced herself to be reasonable. "I know. You're right. I have to go to bed. Without you."

He wanted to kiss her again, but she warded off his hands.

"No, no. I can't touch you and you can't touch me because, well, I'm not to be trusted right now. I'm too hot and bothered and you'll only make it worse. Goodnight, Brock."

He sighed as she went inside the house. "You're not the only one who's hot and bothered."

It was a couple of minutes before he got into his buggy and drove away.

~~*~~

Aaron Howard looked up from the book he'd been reading when the door of the sheriff's office slammed open. A man came flying through the doorway, falling to the floor. Aaron shot to his feet as Cy and Cotton stomped into the office after him.

Cy grabbed the man by the back of his threadbare coat and hauled him to his feet.

"Get up, you worthless piece of shit." Cy's eyes blazed with rage. "This is the drunk coward who shot Johnny.

Aaron, you better take him because if you don't, I'm gonna kill him. I shoulda just done it, but—just take him."

Cy might not have killed him, he hadn't treated Maynard any too kindly, Aaron saw. He took Maynard without a word to Cy, pushing him back to the cell room.

Wheezer still sat calmly with his feet up on his desk. "You got him. Good. You okay?"

Cy nodded. "How's Johnny?"

He was afraid that Wheezer was going to tell him that his cousin had died.

"Hanging in there." Wheezer chuckled. "I saw him this afternoon a little and he was funny as heck. Laudanum."

Cy blinked back tears of relief. "I'm glad to hear that. Poor kid. He just wanted to take a pretty girl out. He never did that before." He sat down in Ellie's chair. "Hell, I don't think he's even kissed a girl. If he'd have died without even doing that—"

Wheezer pulled open a desk drawer and pulled out a bottle of bourbon. "Here, son. You'll feel better when you get a little of that in you."

Cy took it and downed a couple of gulps before handing the bottle to Cotton, who took a pull from it.

Cy said, "Maynard will need a doctor. Burt got him pretty good on the leg."

Wheezer grunted as he took the bourbon back from Cotton. "Good."

"Is it all right if I leave the dogs here? I want to go to the hospital to see Johnny. I don't think they'd appreciate me bringing them in there," Cy said.

"Sure."

Cotton opened the door and the three pooches trotted inside, going right over to Wheezer, who pet them.

Wheezer smiled. "So I hear that you got some cats, Cy."

Cy growled as he got up and marched out the door. Wheezer and Cotton laughed before he followed his nephew out into the night.

~~*~~

A week later, Johnny was brought home and situated in the guest room in the main house despite his protests. He didn't want to be a bother to them. Daphne settled the matter by telling him that it would be more of a bother if she kept having to traipse out to his bunkhouse. He'd capitulated after that.

His wounds were healing, but he was still in a lot of pain. However, he was well enough to be bored. Used to being busy, lying in bed all day didn't sit well with him. Everyone had work to do so they couldn't constantly sit with him. He worked on some woodworking designs, but that just made him itch to get back out in his woodshop.

By the time he'd been home a week, he'd become cranky. He wanted to see Dory, too, and the fact that she hadn't come to see him made him even more irritable.

"Johnny, she's probably feeling guilty about what happened," Daphne said the Saturday after he'd come home.

"I don't know why. She ain't the one who shot me. It ain't her fault." He shifted where he sat up against the headboard.

"I know, but you can see how she'd feel badly," Daphne said.

"I guess so. You wait until I'm better, though. If she won't come to me, I'll go to her," he declared. "That woman ain't seen the last of me."

Daphne chuckled. "I didn't know you could be so stubborn."

He grinned. "I can be if I got something to be stubborn about."

"Do you need anything before I go downstairs?"

"No, ma'am."

"Okay. Ring your bell if you need something," Daphne said.

"Yes, ma'am," Johnny said glumly.

Daphne felt badly for leaving him, but she had laundry to wash. As she entered the kitchen, she heard a buggy pull up. Looking out the window, she blinked, thinking that she was seeing things. A handsome Standardbred horse stood outside the house, hitched to an odd looking vehicle.

"What the heck?"

She wrapped her shawl around her shoulders and went outside. Wheels grinned at her from inside the vehicle that looked distinctly like a chariot.

"Wheels? What are you riding in? Is that a chariot?" she asked.

"It sure is. Daddy and I just finished it last night and I wanted to try it out, so I thought I'd come see Johnny," Wheels said.

"But where's your chair?" Daphne wasn't bashful about asking because Wheels never shied away from anything related to his condition.

He motioned her closer to the stylish, black chariot. "Look," he said, pointing down.

Daphne gazed over the side of it and laughed when she saw that Wheels sat in his chair. The chariot walls weren't as high as a traditional chariot because he couldn't stand, but they were solid. His chair was held in place by a leather belt-like strap on either side of the chariot.

"I'm always amazed by what you and your father make," she said. "I guess it worked. How does it ride?"

"Like a dream, thanks to those bicycle tires. We just used the bigger size and put two on each side to give it more stability. See?"

Daphne had been so focused on the rest of the vehicle that she hadn't paid attention to the wheels. "How clever!"

"That way, I won't tip over if I go fast around turns," Wheels said, unhooking the chair.

"Oh, wait. Do you need help getting out?"

"Nope. Watch."

Wheels gauged his distance and backed up until he hit

the back of the chariot. He flipped up two eyehooks, releasing the back. When the wooden door fell, it formed a ramp, down which he easily rolled.

"That's incredible," Daphne said.

"I'll take you for a ride sometime," Wheels said.

"I'll take you up on that," Daphne said. "Come on in."

Since there was only one step up onto the back porch, Wheels navigated it with ease, his powerful muscles propelling him up onto the level surface. Daphne held the kitchen door open for him and he rolled through.

"He was awake when I came down just now," Daphne said.

"Don't matter. I'll get him up if he ain't. He'll want to see what me and Daddy came up with."

"Oh. Um, it's not good for him to do the stairs a whole lot right now," Daphne said.

Wheels' eyes sparkled. "No problem. Just point me in the direction of the stairs and I'll take it from there."

"How can you take your chair up the stairs?"

"I can't."

Doubtful about how this was going to work, Daphne nevertheless led him to the stairs. Wheels lifted his legs from the footrests and leaned forward, bracing his arms on the stairs. The next thing Daphne knew, he was rapidly hoisting himself up them, his legs dragging behind him.

"What are you going to do once you reach the top? You don't have a chair."

"Same thing I'm doing now. Don't worry, darlin'. I've got this handled," Wheels said. "I do it all the time."

"All right."

She followed him just in case he needed help, but he pulled himself down the hall easily.

"Hey, dumbass! Where are you?"

Johnny sat up a little straighter, wincing at the pain in his muscles. "Wheels? Is that you?"

"Yeah."

"I'm in here."

Wheels followed the sound of his voice. "There you are."

Johnny smiled. "Slithering around again, huh? Your nickname should be slither instead of Wheels."

"Shut up or I won't show you the schematics we came up with."

Daphne was amazed by the way Wheels pulled himself up into Johnny's bedside chair. If one didn't know any better, they would never know that he was paralyzed from the waist down. When not in his wheelchair, he looked just like any other man.

Wheels smiled at her. "Thanks for looking out for me, but I'm all right. You owe me, though."

"What for?"

His smiled broadened. "I just dusted your floor for you."

Daphne and Johnny laughed, the latter holding his chest as he did.

"You're terrible," Daphne said.

"No, I'm not. You gotta find humor wherever you can."

Shaking her head, she said, "I'll leave you men to your …whatever it is that you're doing."

They made sure that she'd gone downstairs before Wheels pulled a thick packet of papers from his inside coat pocket. They pored over the drawings and the list of equipment and supplies they would need to build Johnny's next special project.

"Do you think we can get it done in time for Christmas?" Johnny asked.

Wheels ran a hand through his dark hair. "I think so, especially if you get your rear out of this bed. You need to start walking around a little every day. Staying still for too long will make your other muscles weak. I know that from experience."

Johnny said, "That's what I keep telling Daphne, but she's scared that I'll reopen my wounds."

Wheels said, "Then you have to prove her—and everyone else—wrong. Nobody thought that I'd ever do even half the stuff I do. I showed them that even though my legs might not work that I've still got my arms and upper body to work with. The most important thing I have to work with though is my brain. If I put my mind to it enough, I'll figure out a way to do something. Speaking of which, you need to come over when you get feeling better. I have something to show you."

"What is it?"

Wheels broke into a grin. "I figured out a way to walk."

"What? You can't walk," Johnny said. "You just said your legs don't work."

Wheels tapped his temple. "Like I said, my brain and upper body. Well, I better get back to help Daddy, but I'll see you in a couple of days. In the meantime, work on getting your strength back."

"Okay," Johnny said. "See ya then."

Wheels made his way down the stairs and pulled himself into his chair. "I'll be seeing you, Daphne. Always a pleasure."

She'd been plucking a chicken for supper. "All right. It's always good to see you, too. I'll get the door for you."

"That's okay. I got it. Let's do this from now on: unless I ask you to do something, don't worry about trying to help me," Wheels said. "That's what we do at home. It might take me a little bit to get it done, but I'm stubborn and rarely give up."

Daphne nodded. "All right."

"So I understand that things are going well with you and Brock."

She blushed. "Yes, they are, thank you."

"About time he woke up and realized what a wonderful gal you are. I'm happy for you," Wheels said.

"Thanks."

He opened the door and backed up to get around it. "All right. Have a good day, sweetheart."

"You, too."

She closed the door behind him and then watched him bounce off the porch and roll over to his chariot. He pulled himself up into it and in a few moments, he drove away.

"Amazing," she muttered to herself and went back to plucking the chicken.

CHAPTER FOURTEEN

Cy looked up from his drawing when Brock came into his office.

"What?"

Brock sat down. "Come up with any new theories yet?"

They'd been working on solving a rash of cat burglaries.

"Nope. You?"

"Nope. These guys are professionals and it's gonna be hard to nab them."

Cy grunted in agreement. "You wanna come home for supper? Daphne's making a chicken. At least that's what she said this morning."

Brock was taken aback by his offer. "Did you just invite me to supper or did I imagine it?"

"Yeah, I invited you. Look, you make Daphne happy, so I figure that we should maybe try to get along better," Cy said. "We've been doing better lately, so that's encouraging."

Brock smiled. "We haven't smacked the crap out of each other for a while, so I'd call that an improvement. You also haven't been acting like a conceited jackass, so that might have something to do with it."

"Likewise. So what about supper?"

"I'll take you up on the offer."

Cy said, "Good."

Pudge jumped up on Brock's lap and the deputy said, "Let's go over everything again, just in case something jumps out at us."

Cy admired Brock's investigative skills and he was secretly happy that it seemed as though the barrier between them had been tentatively breached. It also made him glad that they shared the same dogged determination to solve a crime.

"Okay. Let's start at the beginning," Cy agreed.

~~*~~

Ellie had just put on a pot of coffee when Walt came into the office.

"Hi," she said, smiling. "Are you here to see Toby again?"

"Aye. I've finally convinced Reese to release him to me. He knows nothin' about his former associates' whereabouts, nor did he commit any crimes. So I'd be grateful if ye'd let him out."

Ellie took the sheaf of papers he handed to her, surprised by his fierce attitude. She wasn't used to seeing him like that. She looked over the papers and found everything in order.

"All right," Ellie said. "Are you upset with me?"

He arched an eyebrow at her. "What makes ya ask?"

She fingered the papers nervously. "Well, you haven't asked me to dinner lately."

"Ah, I see. I've wanted to, but you don't seem to enjoy my company very much," Walt said. *The spider shall draw the fly into his web.*

Ellie's eyes widened. "Yes, I did. It's just that you're … strange. Secretive. It makes it hard to get to know you when you don't really talk about yourself."

He smiled, his gaze softening. "Curious, then? Good. I'll pick you up tonight. Dress for a picnic."

"A picnic? It's winter. Where the heck would we have a picnic?"

He took her face in his hand. "I know a very special place. You'll see. Six-thirty?"

Ellie nodded. His touch did funny things to her. "That'll be fine."

"Good. Now, about young Toby." He dropped his hand.

"Right. I'll bring him out," Ellie said.

~~*~~

When Ellie answered Walt's knock, she was surprised to see him wearing jeans and a denim coat over a white wool sweater. He looked casual yet handsome.

"Hello, Ellie."

"Hello. You look nice."

"Thanks. So do you. Shall we?"

Walt enjoyed the uncertainty and curiosity in Ellie's beautiful blue eyes. He wanted to keep her guessing, just itching to know more about him. It had taken a while to wear her down and now that he had her attention, he planned to keep it.

Ellie liked that Walt assisted her into the buggy even though she was perfectly capable of getting in herself. He didn't treat her like a lawwoman, just a woman, which she appreciated in a man she was seeing socially.

"How's Toby?" she asked.

Walt clicked to his horse, getting them underway. "He's confused, but glad to be out of jail. He'll be out of sorts for a while, but I'll help him."

"I think it's very nice of you to want to help him, but why do you want to?"

He smiled wryly. "Let's just say I have a fondness for helpin' the underdog, those who can't help themselves."

"I see. What are you going to do with him?"

He gave her a questioning look. "Do with him? He'll stay with me until he can make his own way in this world. He'll also go to school. I want him to have an education."

Ellie shook her head. "I can't figure you out. Being kind is one thing, but taking a boy who's a complete stranger into your home is another."

Walt gave her an understanding smile. "Most people would say the same thing. It's simple, really. He needs help and I can give it to him."

Ellie took in their surrounds as they left town. Walt didn't live right in town, but still close enough that he was able to have telephone service. They passed the driveway to his house.

"You missed the turn."

"I didn't. We're goin' around the front way."

Ellie's brow furrowed. "The front way?"

"Aye."

"So that's the back way?"

"It is."

She shook her head and fell silent. Walt smiled as he regarded her pretty profile. Intense longing for her flowed through him as he watched her. He tore his eyes from her before she caught him staring at her. She was gorgeous, sweet, and feisty, and he intended to make her his, and very soon.

~~*~~

The drive they turned down was much wider than what Walt had said was the back way to his house. As they drove, Ellie saw huge creatures rise up on either side of the drive.

When she gasped at seeing Pegasus looming near the road, Walt put a comforting hand on her arm.

"'Tis all right, lass. Nothing but topiary figures."

Even though she now understood that they weren't

alive, the moonlight-gilded animals still appeared threatening. She'd never seen anything like them. They were beautiful and frightening at the same time.

"I think I like the back way better."

Walt chuckled as they pulled up in front of the house. A porch ran the whole length of it, and light shone in the windows. It was a very nice house, but it seemed as though the impressive topiary and long drive should've led to a huge mansion instead of such a modest residence.

"It's a pretty place," she said. "Of course, so is the back of it. Why do you have two ways in and out of it?"

He helped her down from the buggy, standing closer than was necessary. "Because sometimes it's quicker to go out the back and sometimes out the front. Come."

He led her in the front, which opened into a foyer. Ellie stopped cold, closed her eyes, and shook her head. She reopened her eyes, but the foyer was still there.

"This looks just like the foyer and stairs at the back of the house."

Walt's eyes gleamed. "Does it?"

Ellie stepped through the doorway on the left into the parlor and stopped again. "This is the exact same parlor, too."

"Is it?"

"I don't understand. What kind of game are you playing? Did you drug me?" she asked.

"No, love, I didn't. I take it ya don't like games."

"Yes, but not life-sized ones."

"Well, that's a shame. I have a fondness for carnival games. A friend of mine dared me to renovate my house like this, so I did. I won quite a tidy sum of money from him, too," Walt said.

Ellie smiled. "You did this on a dare?"

"I take dares very seriously."

"Is the whole house like this?"

"Aye. I call it Mirror House," Walt replied. "Would ya like to see?"

Curiosity got the best of her again. "Yeah."

"The dining room is the connector, so you can always find your way back and forth between the two halves."

"I wasn't past the dining room."

"Right," Walt said, leading her through it. "Here we are in the other parlor."

Ellie stared around it, marveling that even the furnishings were exactly the same. It was bizarre, but it delighted her the same way a fun house did a child. From there, she crossed the duplicate foyer and stepped into the formal sitting room.

"I didn't look. The other sitting room is like this?"

"Right."

Her pretty laugh rang out and she came back to him. "May I see the upstairs, too?"

"If ye like."

Walt was thrilled that she'd responded positively to the odd house. He laughed at the way she kept running back and forth across the hallway to see each "mirrored" room. The only two rooms he didn't let her go in were his and Toby's rooms, which she completely understood.

"So that's the whole place," he said as she rejoined him in the hallway.

"It's wonderful! I'd love to live here! And can you imagine what fun it would be for kids?"

"Would ya, now?"

Ellie blushed. "Don't be getting any wild ideas."

Too late, Walt thought. "I'll try not to. How about that picnic now?"

"I still don't understand why we're having a picnic outside in the middle of November."

They exited out the back way and she tucked her hand in the crook of his arm as they walked along a brick pathway and around the side of the house. What looked like a large greenhouse stood a short distance away.

"We're eating in a greenhouse?"

"Aye, but not just any greenhouse."

Walt had her stand just inside the doorway of the dark interior. "Close yer eyes while I light some lanterns."

Willing to play along, Ellie closed them. She felt giddy with anticipation. What would she see when she opened her eyes again? More funhouse games?

"All right. Open those lovely eyes of yers."

She did and her jaw dropped open. The brick walkway ended and lush, green grass carpeted the floor of the whole interior. A vast array of flowers and tall green plants almost obliterated the glass walls. In the center sat a bright red checkered blanket and picnic basket. Eight lanterns provided plenty of light for them to see by.

Watching Ellie's face light up filled Walt with happiness. "Do ya like it?"

"No. I love it. It's warm in here," she said.

"Let me take yer coat, Miss Ellie."

She let him slide it down her arms and watched him hang it on a brass coatrack.

"We'll take our shoes off so we don't damage the grass."

Ellie slipped off her boots and socks without a qualm. Once they were both barefoot, he motioned to the blanket. Her feet sank into the spongy grass.

"This has to be the softest grass in the world," she said, laughing.

"Aye. Ma was a plant and nature lover. Da built her a greenhouse like this in the country outside New York City and we had many a party in it. So, when I moved here, I built one, too. Sort of in honor of her memory," he said.

As they sat down, Ellie said, "I didn't know that she'd passed."

"Both my parents did. They were older when they had me. I was a complete surprise," Walt said. "I miss them. They were great people."

"I'm sure they were," Ellie said.

"Well, enough of that. Let's eat."

CHAPTER FIFTEEN

During their meal, Ellie learned more about Walt. He told her how his family had come to the United States to meet with some of his father's business partners. It was supposed to have been a month long stay, but Lawrence and Margaret Gaines had fallen in love with America and had decided to move there permanently.

As they ate pieces of black walnut cake, Ellie asked, "So you come from some pretty rich people, huh?"

"I do. All of my grandparents were wealthy and, since my parents were only children, they inherited all of the money. So I'm a very wealthy man," Walt replied.

"It's a shame that you don't have any brothers or sisters."

He nodded. "It was sometimes lonely growing up, which is why when I marry, I hope to have a whole passel of wee ones."

"I can understand that," Ellie said. "Don't take this the wrong way, but your house doesn't seem like the type that someone rich would live in."

"I don't like to throw my money around. Too many people come to ya with their hands out. I prefer to donate anonymously, which I do. Being wealthy lets me do what I love doin'. Helpin' people who are truly innocent."

Ellie said, "But you defend a lot of people. They can't all be innocent."

He cocked his head. "Can I tell ya somethin' in confidence?"

The suddenly hard glint in his eyes set her stomach fluttering with fear and curiosity. She wasn't sure that she wanted to know what he was going to say, but couldn't stop herself from saying, "Yes."

"I'm a prosecutor in disguise."

Her eyes widened. "What do you mean?"

"Well, ya see, I used to be a prosecutor in New York, but when I moved here, there were no criminal prosecutor positions. So, I became a defense attorney, but not exactly."

"I still don't understand."

"All right. Take that pickpocket. He was guilty as sin, so I perhaps didn't try as hard to keep him out of jail as I did Toby. The lad is innocent. Do ya see now?"

Ellie gasped. "You deliberately throw cases? Isn't that against the law?"

He grinned. "Not against the law, but it's unethical in some people's minds. Just not mine. Chance City is safer without that pickpocket, just as it is without other criminals on the loose."

Conflicting emotions on the matter swirled in Ellie's mind. "Does anyone else know about this?"

"No one."

"Why did you tell me?"

Walt took a steadying breath. "Because I trust you. I have feelin's for ya, Ellie. Ya know that's why I kept askin' ya out. But, if this is somethin' ya can't accept about me, then there's no point pursuin' anything. I'll understand, but if ya decide ya don't wanna see me, please keep this to yerself. If ya say we're done, I won't bother ya when I come to the sheriff's office, either. So don't worry about that."

Their gazes met and Ellie couldn't look away. There was something enigmatic, charismatic, and dangerous about Walt. Why hadn't she seen that before? Or had she and that was the reason she'd refused his advances? She could no longer deny that he was very attractive.

His hazel eyes captivated her and she wanted to kiss him. She had the first time she'd gone to dinner with him, but he hadn't then or the last couple of times they'd been together. His gaze grew heated and she knew that he could see her thoughts in her expression.

Her heart beat in triple-time as he hooked a hand around the back of her neck and leaned in to kiss her. Ellie found herself swept away by his hot, demanding kiss. Wrapping his free arm around her waist, he pulled her against his chest, and threaded his fingers through her hair.

Ellie held onto his sweater, bunching it in her fists, and responding in kind. Their tongues met and dueled as their breathing grew ragged. The way Walt's chest rose and fell under her hands fascinated her and she traced the contours of his muscles through it. His growl of pleasure made her feel feminine and powerful and she wanted more.

When she abruptly pulled away from him, Walt felt off-kilter. She took off his glasses and set them off to the side. He was glad that he didn't need them to see up close so that he didn't miss the desire shimmering in her eyes. The next thing he knew, she pulled his sweater up.

"I want you, Walt. You're weird, and quirky, and mysterious, and sort of dark, but you're also handsome, fun, and wonderful. I shouldn't want you like this, but I do," she said.

Walt wasn't going to argue with her. He'd wanted her for so long and if she was willing, so was he. It was wicked and wrong in some people's minds, but not in his. What two mature adults did was no one else's business.

He yanked the sweater the rest of the way off and took her in his arms again. She ran her hands over his toned, muscular chest, reveling in the way his chest hair felt against her palms. His lips reclaimed hers and he pressed her harder against his body, stirring her ardor even more.

She couldn't stop touching him and he seemed to have the same problem. He pulled her blouse from her jeans and spread his hands over her back, skimming his fingers along her spine. She shivered against him as ripples of desire washed over her.

A noise from outside made her jerk and she pulled back from him.

Walt heard it, too. "It's just an animal. Don't worry about it."

He reached for the buttons of her blouse, but her hand closed over his, stopping him. Looking in her eyes, he saw her uncertainty and his shoulders sagged.

"This isn't gonna happen, is it? Ye've changed yer mind."

"Not about you, just about this. And not exactly this."

She would have run a hand over his chest, but he intercepted it. He kissed it before moving away from her.

"I don't understand," he said, putting his sweater back on.

Ellie almost groaned when he covered up his fine torso again. "It's just that I don't want Toby to walk in on us."

Walt squashed his frustration. "He has strict instructions not to unless disaster strikes, but boys aren't always reliable about following orders. Yer right. I'll take ya home. Just give me a few minutes."

Ellie couldn't contain the giggle that bubbled up in her throat as she gathered their picnic things. His aroused condition was quite apparent.

"It's not funny. You women have it easy regarding this. Ya can't tell when yer excited and if ya are, ya can still move around just like normal."

It was the first time she'd seen him cross about something and it both excited and amused her. She chuckled again and his expression darkened.

She pulled herself together. "You're right. I'm sorry."

Letting out a long breath, Walt got to his feet and helped her. Once they had everything ready and they'd put their shoes and outerwear back on, Walt doused all of the lanterns. There was enough moonlight for them to see by as they walked along the path to the back of the house. They deposited their things in the kitchen, Walt telling her that he would take care of them later.

Walt was quiet for a little bit as he drove her home. Ellie knew that he was disappointed and so was she, but the thought of Toby interrupting them made it impossible for her to have made love with him in the greenhouse.

"Walt, I'm sorry, it's just—"

"Don't worry about it, Ellie. I understand." He gave her a smile. "So do all of those things ya said about me mean that ya want to keep seein' me?"

"Yes. I meant it when I said that I didn't change my mind about you."

Happiness spread through him. "I'm glad to hear it."

Ellie snuggled up to him. "You know, there's no one at my house to interrupt us."

Walt groaned. "Ellie, don't tempt me like that. It's gettin' late and I shouldn't leave Toby to his own devices on his first night out of jail."

She let out a sigh as she rested her head on his shoulder. "You're right."

To distract them from the desire that still thrummed through them, Ellie started talking about work. Grateful to her, Walt followed her example, eagerly picking up the conversation. When they arrived at her house, he walked her to the door, but only kissed her cheek. He knew that if he kissed those sweet lips of hers they would wind up in bed.

Ellie waited until he drove off to go inside. With deep regret, she went to bed, but her thoughts were filled with the handsome Irishman for quite some time.

~~*~~

Brock and Daphne sat snuggled together on the sofa a few nights before Thanksgiving. Cy and Leigh had gone out to dinner and Johnny had moved back over to his bunkhouse. He'd taken Wheels' advice and was moving around more. Daphne hadn't been able to sway him from his decision and in the end she'd given in.

Brock kissed the side of her head and gave her a squeeze. "I know you're cooking here for Thanksgiving, but what about coming over to our house in the evening? We're not eating until later in the day."

Facing him, she asked, "What about your parents and sisters? Won't they object?"

"Don't worry about that. If Cy is starting to get used to idea of me being around, then it's time for my family to do the same with you. I want them to get to know the wonderful woman I've fallen in love with."

Daphne jerked a little. "What did you just say?"

Holding her gaze, Brock said, "I said that I've fallen in love with you. Hell, I knew it after the day you kissed me. I've had my eye on you for a while and I couldn't get you out of my mind. And after that, I couldn't deny what I felt for you. During these past few weeks, it's only gotten stronger. I thought it was time that you know how I feel."

Daphne closed her eyes against the tears that burned her eyes, but a couple escaped them anyway. Brock took her face in his hands and wiped them away with his thumbs.

"Why are you crying?"

Opening her eyes, she said, "I've loved you for so long, but I gave up hope that I'd ever hear you say that to me. I feel like I'm dreaming and any minute, I'll wake up and none of this will have been real."

Guilt threaded its way through his body. "I'm sorry it took me so long to come to my senses, but it's not a dream. I'm here and I'm not going anywhere. I love you, Daphne, and I'm not going to let anyone or anything come between us. Not your family or mine, either."

He had to bite back the words that wanted to spill forth. It wasn't the right time. The next moment, he was pleasantly distracted from his thoughts by Daphne's kiss. It was sweet and filled with gentle fire. Lingering over her lips, he nibbled them before kissing his way along her jawline to her neck.

Daphne wound her arms around his neck and laid her head on his chest, listening to his slightly rapid heartbeat. "I love you."

Brock tightened his arms around her, holding her closer. "I love you, too."

They sat that way for a long time, just enjoying being close, and savoring the moment.

~~*~~

Cotton stood outside Johnny's bunkhouse, steadying himself for the coming conversation. Finally, he knocked.

Johnny looked up from the plans he'd been drawing. "C'mon in."

Cotton smiled at him when he entered the dwelling. Although orderly, the place was more design shop than residence. In the small parlor area, a design table took up one whole corner by the fireplace. A tool bench stood in another corner and tools hung on the wall over it.

Johnny sat at the design table, working on something.

"Should you be doing that?" Cotton asked.

"I'm all right. I need to start moving around more and get my strength back. Besides, I'm bored just lying and sitting around," he said.

Cotton nodded. "I have something for you."

Johnny took the envelope Cotton held out to him, reading his name on it. He gave Cotton a curious look and then unfolded the paper inside.

Dear Johnny,

I know I should have come to see you, but I just couldn't. It's cowardly of me, but I feel so bad about what happened, and I'm so sorry about it all. It's my fault. If you hadn't been coming to pick me up, he wouldn't have shot you.

Ma and I are moving to Nebraska to live with her cousin. I can't stay in Chance City. Everyone knows about what happened and Ma and I would always be looked down on. We need to start our lives fresh some place where no one knows us. For what it's worth, I really liked you and I was looking forward to seeing you.

You're a good man and I hope you find someone who makes you happy. I hope you can understand why we have to do this and that you can forgive me someday.

Regretfully,
Dory

Johnny's eyes were stormy with emotion as he raised them to meet Cotton's gaze.

"They left three days ago," Cotton said.

Johnny's chest ached, but it had nothing to do with his injury. Anger and disappointment surged through him and he crushed the letter, flinging it across the room. He ignored the pain the movement caused.

Pounding a fist down on the design table, he said, "You shoulda told me right away, Cotton. I would have stopped them. I would've married Dory and taken care of her and her ma."

"I'm sorry, Johnny. I didn't know until I got the letter in the mail today. Yours was inside of it. Mine said that they left on Friday," Cotton said.

Johnny nodded his understanding, unable to speak around the lump in his throat.

"I know you don't want to hear this, but Dory is right. You know how people are. They would've been judged by Maynard's actions and he was their only source of income. I am sad that they left, too, but I think they made the right decision," Cotton said.

"You're right. I don't want to hear it. It's easy for you to say that because you weren't in love with them. People think I'm nuts, but I love Dory." He shook his head. "It doesn't matter now. Please just leave."

Cotton understood his need to be alone and respected Johnny's wishes. He walked home, his heart heavy with sadness for all involved in the situation.

~~*~~

With concern, Daphne watched Johnny pick at his breakfast the next morning.

"What's wrong, Johnny? Is your pain worse again?" she asked.

He rubbed his chest a little. "Yeah, but it's on the inside."

"What do you mean?"

Letting out a sigh, he said, "Dory and Noreen moved to Nebraska to live with their cousin. She's gone. They left last Friday."

"Oh, Johnny, I'm so sorry." Daphne laid a hand on his arm.

Leigh and Cy echoed her sentiments.

Johnny's jaw worked as he tried to rein in his emotions. "None of you believed me, but I loved her."

His grief was too much to contain. Dropping his fork onto his plate, he pulled his arm away from Daphne, and went out the kitchen door.

"Poor kid," Cy said. "His first broken heart. The whole damn thing's a shame."

"I know it won't be any comfort to him, but it's better it happened now instead of later on when he was even more attached to her," Leigh said. "That doesn't help him right now, though."

Daphne got up and put her coat on. She grabbed Johnny's from its hook and left, heading for the barn where she'd seen Johnny go from out of one of the windows. She found him in the tack room. He sat in one of the chairs, just starting to clean a bridle. A couple of tears fell from his eyes and he wiped more away with his shirt sleeve.

He looked up as she came in and scowled at her.

"You forgot your coat. You're going to catch your death being out here in the cold without it."

He took it from her and put it on. "Thanks."

"I know you're hurting, Johnny, and I'm so sorry."

Johnny tried to swallow the lump in his throat. "I should've gone to see her, even if I had to crawl to get there. I shouldn't have let her get away."

Daphne said, "There was no way for you to know that they were leaving and you were in no condition to go to their house."

"Daphne, I know you mean well, but I don't want to talk about it. I just want to be alone. Please?"

She kissed his cheek. "Okay, but you know that I'll always listen to you and help however I can."

He gave her a tiny smile. "I appreciate it."

Relieved when she left, Johnny went back to cleaning the bridle, trying to put everything else out of his mind, but his heartache wouldn't leave him alone.

CHAPTER SIXTEEN

On Thanksgiving, Daphne was so nervous about going to meet Brock's family that she could hardly concentrate on cooking. However, she reprimanded herself and put her mind to her task again. Leigh was competent in the kitchen and helped with the meal preparations. Cy helped by putting in the extra leaves in the table and then making himself scarce since he would have only slowed them down if he'd tried to assist the women.

After a while, the Lone Wolfs showed up, bringing a couple of dishes with them. Bonnie pitched in as did Sly, who liked to cook. After suffering the loss of his secret girlfriend, Catherine Branson, in September, he'd been withdrawn and even quieter than usual. He was just getting to a point where he felt like socializing a little more.

David joined the other men in the parlor, sitting down by Cotton on the sofa.

Daniel lounged in one of the wingback chairs, a long leg thrown over one arm.

"Sit up straight," David said. "What's the matter with you?"

Daniel frowned but did as he was told. "Better? Why are you so cranky?"

Cotton said, "Maybe Bonnie hasn't felt very frisky lately."

David punched him in the leg. "She's been plenty frisky."

Groaning, Daniel said, "If you're going to discuss that, I'm leaving."

The rest of them laughed.

Daniel looked at Cy. "Did you name the cats yet?"

"Just the inside ones."

"Well?" David asked.

Bashfully, Cy said, "The big one is Cuddles and the kitten is Buttons because she likes to play with buttons when Daphne's sewing them on stuff. You have to watch her because she'll steal them."

Daniel said, "Look at him smile. For a cat-hater, he sure seems to like them."

Cy gave him an annoyed look. "I like it that they helped with the mice, but that's all."

David grinned. "So who named them?"

Leigh came into the parlor. "He did. I heard him in here one night sayin', 'You're so cuddly-wuddly, aren't you? Your name is Cuddles.' I couldn't believe it, but that's how it happened."

Cy's face turned pink as the room rocked with laughter, but he eventually joined in the fun. Then Leigh announced that dinner was ready and the men eagerly followed her to the kitchen.

Once they were all seated, Johnny said a nice blessing, even though it was short. He was doing his best to get through the day without being short tempered or wallowing. Sly wasn't as angry, but he had trouble keeping his grief at bay. He and Catherine would have been celebrating their first Thanksgiving together.

Yanking his mind from those thoughts, he concentrated on the conversation that flowed around the table. He commented or asked questions here and there, but for the most part, he just absorbed what was said.

Cy looked at Daphne. "Where's Brock?"

"I didn't invite him," she said.

"Why the heck not?"

"Because I was nervous enough about meeting his family without worrying about him being here with ours," she replied. "Besides, he's helping his mother cook."

David said, "Daphne, don't be afraid to invite him to things. If he's respectful of us, we'll be respectful in return. How will we get to know each other if we don't socialize?"

Daniel snorted and Cotton cuffed him.

"Stop it right now," he warned his nephew.

Bonnie and David nodded in agreement.

Cy smiled. "Yeah, Daniel. If I have to play nice, so do you. I have to admit that things are better between Brock and me. I doubt we'll ever be best friends, but I'll settle for mostly civil."

Daniel made a face, but refrained from saying anything more on the subject. They heard a horse trot up to the house. Cy turned around and looked out the window.

"It's Ray. Must've got kicked out of somewhere."

Bonnie said, "I'm not surprised. They're all getting tired of his lifestyle, according to his Aunt Charlotte."

Johnny said, "He's not as bad as everyone makes out. He might hop around from place to place, but he helps out wherever he goes. Watches kids, does chores, and when he has money, he gives people some for room and board."

Bonnie said, "Oh, I didn't know that."

Leigh said, "Well, you know how it is. Sometimes it's hard to get the full story from people."

When Ray knocked, Cy told him to come in.

"Happy Thanksgiving, everyone," he said, smiling.

After his greeting was returned, Daphne said, "There's a stool in the pantry, Ray. Come have some dinner."

Ray put a hand on his stomach. "Thanks, Daphne, but I'm stuffed from dinner at Uncle Boyd's."

Cy asked, "Did you get kicked out?"

Ray laughed. "No, I left of my own free will, believe it or not. Twenty kids in their small house isn't my idea of fun. I can still hear their squealing."

He went into the pantry and brought back the stool, sitting it by Bonnie. "Hi, Mrs. Lone Wolf. Aunt Charlotte said to tell you all Happy Thanksgiving if I saw you."

"I'll thank her when I see her on Saturday. We're working on costume repairs for the Christmas pageant," she said.

Ray rolled his eyes. "She's worrying herself sick over it. I told her that she always does a great job with it, but it doesn't make a difference. I even helped sew on buttons to give her a little free time the other day, but she just started sewing on something else."

Bonnie gave him a surprised look. "You sew?"

"Mmm hmm. Sew, cook, clean—hell, I do so much of that stuff that I've been accused of being light in the loafers." He shrugged. "I'm good at it and it's actually relaxing. I can do field work, groom horses, brand cattle, all of that, but I don't mind pitching in with other stuff, too."

Johnny looked around the table with an I-told-you-so look.

"I don't mean to be rude or nosy, Ray, but why don't you stay in one place? Get a job and rent or buy somewhere to live?" Bonnie asked.

Ray shrugged. "That's easy to answer. I got used to being passed around when I was growing up, and I prefer it now. Pa ran off and Ma was drunk so much that she couldn't take care of me right. So, someone would take me for a while and then I'd go live with someone else. So forth and so on. When I need money, I do some odd jobs. I usually take part of that and play poker and make more money to last me a while."

Cotton clenched his teeth together to keep from laughing. Ray's idea of odd jobs differed greatly from what most people considered odd jobs, but he kept that information to himself. Not even Johnny was aware and Cotton wasn't about to enlighten him. He almost lost the battle when Ray caught his eye across the table. He took a drink to break eye contact and keep his control intact.

"I had no idea that you possessed so many skills," Bonnie remarked.

"A lot of people don't," Johnny said.

Cotton and Ray exchanged another glance and then Ray started teasing Cy about the cats, changing the subject. When the meal concluded, Johnny and Ray went to his bunkhouse while the women cleaned up from dinner.

Cy hitched up the buggy so he could drop Daphne over to Brock's. The deputy would bring her home. As they rode, Daphne was glad that she'd already eaten because the closer they got to Brock's, the worse her stomach ached.

Cy noticed her fidgeting with her coat and gloves. "It's gonna be all right, Daphne. Brock will be with you and you know Aaron."

"I know. I can't avoid them forever. Things are serious between us and if things are going to work out, then we have to make people understand that we're not going to let our families come between us," Daphne said, giving him a pointed look.

"Don't look at me like that. I've been cooperating," Cy said. "As long as he treats you well and makes you happy, there won't be an issue."

She smiled at him. "Make sure it stays that way."

He grinned. "I'll do my best."

~~*~~

Brock had anxiously waited for Daphne to arrive, so as soon as he saw Cy drive up to their house with her, he rushed out to the buggy. He'd made his father promise to behave, telling him that they would leave the moment he acted up, even if it was during dinner.

141

"Hello, beautiful lady," Brock said.

Daphne returned his smile as he helped her out of the buggy. She noted his nice suit. "Hello, yourself. You're looking quite spiffy."

"Thanks. Ma makes us dress for dinner. Happy Thanksgiving, Cy," Brock said.

"Same to you. I drove her over so that you didn't get another lecture from Johnny," Cy said.

Brock chuckled. "Thanks. How's he doing?"

"Well, I think his heart will take longer to heal than his body," Cy said.

"I think that's true in a lot of cases. Tell everyone I wished them a happy holiday. Let's get in out of the cold, honey," Brock said.

"Have a nice dinner," Cy said before clicking to the horse.

He watched the couple walk up on Brock's porch, noting that the deputy had his arm around his sister. Sighing, he hoped that her dinner with Brock's family went well. As he drove away, he knew that he'd be anxious until she came home and he knew that she was all right.

~~*~~

Daphne laughed so hard that she snorted as Brock's sister, Nora, related a tale about how Brock had gotten so much honey in his hair one summer that their mother had had to shave his head.

Amelia said, "And it was such slow going because I couldn't cut it. It kept making the scissor blades stick together. I finally gave up and shaved it."

Brock said, "But I was the most handsome eight-year-old boy with a shaved head this world has ever seen. Right, Ma?"

"Well, I had to tell you something to make you feel better after you cried for a good hour—"

"So, did I tell you that Cy named their new cats?"

Brock asked loudly to drown out his mother.

He laughed as much as the others, though, seeming not to mind being the butt of a joke.

"What did he name them?" Doug asked. He loved cats as much as Cy loved dogs.

Brock smiled. "The mama cat he named Cuddles and he named the kitten Buttons."

Doug nodded approvingly. "Cute. Good names. Brock says that your dogs like the cats, Daphne."

She giggled. "Like might not be quite accurate. Pudge and Queenie love them, Burt hates them, and Slink is scared to death of Buttons, but he likes Cuddles."

Doug laughed. "Sounds about right. Cats can be intimidating to dogs, but that's only because they're smarter."

Daphne arched an eyebrow at him. "Really? Maybe they're smarter than some dogs, but not ours."

Aaron said, "Oh, boy."

Doug said, "Cats are smarter than all dogs, just the same way that women are smarter than men."

Daphne said, "I'll agree with you on the last half of that statement, but not the first."

"Most dogs are loyal, loving, obedient, and will protect their family until the end. Cats on the other hand, make you chase them for attention, are able to get you to pet them while you yell at the dog, and will almost always run from danger. Almost. There are exceptions, but the vast majority of them are interested more in self-preservation than being an attack cat. Unless they're a lion. That's different," Doug said. "Men and women are the same way. Who usually chases who? Men chase women, trying to gain their affection, trying to show that they're worthy of the lady. Not usually the other way around. Men are the dogs and women are the cats."

Daphne grinned. "Wait until I tell Cy that. He'll have a conniption."

"Don't tell him in the morning right before he comes

to work," Brock said. "I'll have to send him out to the Dog House so I don't have to hear a lecture about why dogs are better than cats."

She said, "All right. I'll tell him after supper tomorrow night."

Brock groaned. "Can you get him drunk first? Then maybe he won't remember it."

Aaron grinned. "Just have Leigh distract him. She's a beautiful woman."

Amelia swatted his arm. "Behave."

Daphne said, "Actually, those are both good ideas. Between both things, he wouldn't remember."

Doug tapped his head. "See? Women are smarter."

They chuckled and then Amelia served dessert. Brock took Daphne's hand under the table, giving it a squeeze. She looked at him and he gave her a smile. When she returned it, Brock winked and released her hand again.

Doug saw, but he gave no notice. His son had been right. Daphne reminded him a lot of Cotton: very likable and easy to get along with. She might be part Comanche, but after spending a little time with her, he'd forgotten that fact. It was clear that she made Brock happy.

He came to a decision. If Brock and Daphne got married, he'd try to get along with Daphne's other family members. He'd been doing some thinking of his own and maybe Brock was right that the time had come to change his thinking on some things.

~~*~~

As he took Daphne home later, he wished that it wasn't so cold out. He'd have loved to find a nice field somewhere and spread out a blanket for them to lie on so they could watch the stars together. However, the fields were covered by a heavy frost and the temperature hovered around twenty-five degrees. Much too cold for doing that.

Brock reflected back with relief on how well dinner had gone. Daphne had won his family over, even his father. So far, so good. Riding with Daphne snuggled up against him, Brock was the happiest he'd ever been. He couldn't believe how much his life was changing.

Daphne's thoughts ran in much the same vein. Her stomach didn't hurt anymore and she'd liked Brock's family very much. It had been fun helping with cleanup and poking fun at the men along with the other women. Brock and Nora took more after their father in looks while Aaron looked like Amelia.

She grinned as she imagined Cy's reaction to Doug's comments about dogs and cats. It would most likely set off a tirade.

"What are you smiling at?" Brock asked.

"Just looking forward to agitating my brother about cats."

Brock laughed. "You're gonna tell him tonight, aren't you?"

"If he's still up, yes. I won't be able to resist." She rubbed her mittens together in anticipation.

Brock nudged her. "Women really are like cats. They like tormenting the dogs."

Daphne gave him a wicked look and meowed. Brock laughed at her playfulness, which encouraged her to further silly behavior. She ducked under his arm and crawled into his lap, purring as she did so. Grinning, Brock helped her get settled. She fit so perfectly against him and he would have ridden around with her all night if it meant that he got to hold her.

However, they were almost to her ranch. Brock held back a sigh of dismay. Daphne rose up so she could kiss his cheek. He smiled and she did it again and then he jerked when she bit his earlobe.

"Stop the buggy, Brock. I want to say goodnight to you here instead of up at the house."

He quickly complied and wrapped his arms around her,

bringing his mouth down on hers in an urgent kiss. She matched him, hanging on to his coat as best she could with her mittens. Her lips were sweet and pliant under his and he loved that she never hesitated to grant him access, touching his tongue with hers.

Resisting his intense physical hunger for her was getting harder all the time. She came alive in his arms and he knew that she wanted him just as badly. Every time he brought her home, they parted unfulfilled, and he didn't know how much longer he could hold off.

When he moved to draw away from her, she protested, holding onto him. He chuckled against her mouth and she smiled as they broke apart. Slowly, she moved off his lap, sitting on the seat again.

"Now you'll be all toasty going home," she said.

Brock said, "You're evil."

"You always say that, but you're the one stopping us," Daphne said. "I want you so much, but sometimes I don't think you want me as much."

Brock stopped the buggy again and turned his passion-filled eyes on her. "Take off your mitten."

"What? Why?"

He reached over, pulled off her mitten, and then brought her hand to his lap, pressing it against the bulge in his pants. "Don't ever doubt how much I want you, Daphne, and if I didn't respect you so much, I'd take you over there in that barn and make love to you until dawn."

Daphne's mouth stood partway open, her eyes wide. She wanted to go on touching him, but he pulled her hand away and started up the drive again. Since she didn't know what to say, she kept silent.

When they reached the house, Brock helped her down and caught her look at his pants.

He laughed. "You really are a wicked woman. Get in the house."

She giggled, kissed his cheek, and trotted inside.

CHAPTER SEVENTEEN

Johnny woke up to searing pain in his chest and a pounding head. Groaning, he cracked one eye open. Faint light filled the room, but after a few moments, he discerned that it wasn't his room. Then he felt a hand run over his back, making him stiffen in surprise.

"You all right?" A female voice asked.

As fast as he physically could, Johnny rolled over, bringing a very pretty blonde girl into his line of sight.

"Who are you?"

Sliding a hand up over his arm, she said, "You don't remember?"

Her movement revealed the fact that she was naked under the covers. Immediately, he pulled the covers over her. "No, ma'am. Where am I?"

She giggled. "In my room, where you've been since last night."

Looking at the window, Johnny asked, "I've been here all night? Where is *here*?"

"The Chowhound, silly. I knew you were drunk, but I didn't think you were *that* soused," she said.

Johnny sat up slowly, his chest hurting so badly that he couldn't breathe for a few moments. Lifting the covers, he saw that he was naked, too.

"Oh, no. Did we … did me and you … oh, my God." His words dissolved into another groan.

She sat up and kissed his back. "Well, we tried, but things didn't cooperate. You were too drunk."

Johnny closed his eyes in relief. "Thank God."

She pouted. "Well, that's not the reaction I usually get."

"Oh, I didn't mean anything about you, ma'am. It's just that I'd prefer to remember my first time and I'd prefer that first time to be with my wife whenever I get married," he said.

She laughed and pressed a kiss to his shoulder. "We could pretend I'm your wife if you want."

Johnny blushed scarlet. "Uh, thanks for the offer, but I don't think I could right now even if I did want to, which I don't. I'm in too much pain. I was shot about three weeks ago and I'm still healing."

"I saw your bandages and I kept asking you if you were all right, but you said you were. Of course, drunk men say all sorts of things," she said.

"Yeah. Where's Ray? Do you know him?" Johnny asked.

Gingerly, he got out of bed, trying to find his clothes. He hurt too badly to worry about being naked in front of her. She'd seen it all anyway.

"Ray was busy last night himself."

"Oh. He was with one of the girls, huh?"

"Oh, yeah. He had a couple different customers last night," the girl told him.

Johnny gave her a sharp glance. "Don't you mean he was with a couple of your, uh, coworkers?"

She laughed. "No. The only time Ray ever sleeps with one of us is when he hasn't had any customers for a while. Otherwise, he likes to save himself for them."

Johnny stared at her for several moments, trying to comprehend what she was saying.

"Oh, you poor thing," she said, getting out of the bed.

"Let me help you."

Johnny closed his eyes. "Can you please put something on."

She smiled. "Most men want me to take my clothes off."

After slipping on a negligée, she helped Johnny find his clothes and get dressed. The whole time, Johnny thought about what she'd said about Ray. Someone knocked on her door and she opened it.

"Is he up yet, Mandy?" Ray asked, coming in the room. "I guess he is. You ready to go?"

Johnny nodded.

Ray looked him over. "You don't look too good. You overdid it. I told you to take it easy on him, Mandy."

"We didn't even do anything. His equipment didn't work and he passed out," Mandy said, crawling back into the bed. "Johnny, you're a very sweet man. Don't change. Now, both of you get out of here. I need some more sleep."

Ray guided Johnny out the back door to Johnny's buggy.

"Let me help you in," Ray said.

Johnny brushed Ray's hands away. "I can do it."

With great effort, he pulled himself onto the buggy seat. Pressing a hand to his chest, he pulled a little bottle of laudanum out of his coat pocket and took a small sip of it. Ray climbed in beside him and took up the reins.

"I know you're hung over and in pain, but what else is wrong?"

Johnny said, "I'm embarrassed."

"Aw, don't be. It happens to a lot of guys when they get drunk," Ray said.

"Not by that. I'm glad that I couldn't … perform. I don't want my first time to be with a whore. I'm embarrassed by you."

Ray glanced at him. "By me? Why?"

"Mandy said that you had customers last night. I

thought maybe I'd heard her wrong, but I didn't, did I?"

"Damn her big mouth," Ray muttered. "No, you didn't hear wrong."

Johnny's stomach rolled and he gagged. "I can't believe you're sleeping with men."

Ray burst into laughter. The loud noise made Johnny's head throb harder. "Not men, dummy. I'm no rent boy. I'm a hustler. I sleep with *women*, who pay me to have sex with them."

Johnny met his eyes. "You sleep with women for money?"

"Yeah. It pays real good, too. You'd make a killing with that good guy personality of yours. There are women who'd like to corrupt you," Ray said, his gray eyes shining.

"You're a whore or whatever they call men like you."

"I'm a hustler, not a whore," Ray corrected him.

Johnny couldn't believe his cavalier attitude. "You can call it whatever you want, but it's still wrong."

Ray said, "I disagree. It's an honest profession. The women I see know that there's no romance attached to our time together and I make a lot more than I ever would working a regular job."

Johnny fought another wave of nausea. When it passed, he asked, "Does Sandy know about this?"

Ray grinned. "Yeah. I rent a room from her, just like the girls do. However, unlike the girls, I usually have standing appointments since not many women come to the Chowhound."

Johnny was curious despite his disgust. "Why don't you live there?"

"Because it's not like it is for the girls. Men don't care if other men know that they're seeing whores. I have to be more discreet because women are a lot more timid about it. Plus, they're judged harsher than men, which is total bull crap."

Johnny rubbed his eyes. "Please tell me that they're not married women."

"I can't do that. I know this is all a shock to you. Look, these women are lonely and unsatisfied by their husbands, who are some of the whores' biggest customers. They'd rather sleep with those girls than their wives. If their husbands paid them enough attention, their wives wouldn't seek out male companionship," Ray explained.

"It still isn't right."

Ray grew annoyed. "By your standards and most of society's, but a lot of those people are hypocrites. I know town council members who come there and other important people, too. You'd be surprised. So if you're gonna judge me, you gotta judge them, too."

Johnny said, "That may be, but those people aren't my friend. You are. I think you're headed down a dangerous path. What if you get one of those women pregnant?"

"That's what Mother's Little Helpers are for."

Johnny frowned. "What's that?"

"I keep forgetting how innocent you are about all of this." Ray guided the horse around a turn. "I'm talking about condoms."

"What?"

Ray groaned. "Didn't your pa explain to you about all of this? Cy? Cotton? Someone?"

Johnny felt stupid. "No."

"Do you know how sex works?"

"Sort of."

"Well, when you're feeling better, I'll explain it to you."

Johnny shook his head and then grabbed it when his headache pounded harder. "No, you won't. I can't be friends with someone like you."

Ray's eyes widened in alarm. "You don't mean that. You're in too much pain to think straight."

Johnny fell silent.

"Johnny, tell me that you don't mean that."

Johnny refused to look at Ray. He was too angry and disgusted.

Ray said, "I thought we were best friends and could tell

each other anything, Johnny."

Johnny said, "I thought so, too. I could handle the fact that you were popular with women, but knowing that you're a whore and sleep with married women? I'm sorry, but I just can't stomach that."

Hurt and angry, Ray stopped the buggy and thrust the reins into Johnny's hands.

"What are you doing?" Johnny asked.

Ray jumped out of the buggy. "Get home yourself since I disgust you so much. I wouldn't want you to be embarrassed by your association with me. I know you have morals, but I never thought you'd turn on me. You need to go to church and make friends with some other fellas with a holier-than-thou outlook on life, Johnny. Then you'll have friends who are worthy of you instead of scum like me."

Stunned, Johnny couldn't say anything as Ray jogged back towards town. Eventually, he adjusted the reins and got the horse moving. His heart dropped even lower in his chest than it already was with the loss of his best friend. Tears stung his eyes as he made his way the rest of the way home.

~~*~~

Leigh left the barn with a pail of milk for breakfast. As she crossed the drive, Johnny came driving up the lane. From the absence of the buggy and horse, she'd known that he hadn't come home last night. He drove up to the house and pulled the horse to a stop, but he didn't get out.

Sensing that something was wrong, she quickened her step to reach the buggy faster.

"Johnny? Where's Ray? Why didn't he drive you home?"

Johnny mumbled, "We're not friends anymore. I can't get out on my own."

"What the hell happened?" she asked. "Never mind

that right now. Let me get Cy."

"Okay."

Leigh hurried into the kitchen and set the milk pail on the corner. Daphne was just putting on some coffee. Going to the bottom of the stairs, Leigh called up them for Cy.

"What's the matter?" he asked, coming downstairs.

"Johnny's out in the buggy and he's in bad shape. He didn't come home last night and he drove home alone," she said. "I need help getting him out of the buggy."

Cy's face tightened. "I'll kill Ray when I see him again. He should've driven Johnny home."

Daphne had heard Leigh and she'd hurried out to the buggy. Leigh and Cy joined her. By the look in Cy's eye, both women knew he was furious.

"You've looked better, buddy," Cy said. "Let's get you out of there. Lean towards me. I'll get you from there."

Johnny leaned over and Cy picked him up, setting him on his feet. Cy put an arm around Johnny's waist and helped him into the house. He led him into the parlor and had him sit on the sofa. Daphne pulled off his boots and helped him swing his legs up onto the sofa. She fixed a couple of pillows behind his back and covered him with an afghan.

She wrinkled her nose when she caught a whiff of him. "How much did you drink? You smell like someone poured whiskey all over you."

Johnny covered his eyes with a forearm. "I don't know. I had a couple of shots and it gets fuzzy after that. I remember a couple of the guys daring me to drink more. And then—" His voice cracked as shame gripped him. "I woke up in one of the girls' bed. She said nothing happened because I was too drunk, thank God."

Daphne shook her head. "Shame on Ray for getting you drunk like that and letting you go with one of those girls."

Leigh asked, "What about Ray? Why didn't he bring

you home?"

"He brought me partway home, but then we had a really bad argument and he took off back to town. I, uh, we're not going to be friends anymore," Johnny said.

The others exchanged surprised glances.

Cy crouched down by the sofa. "What could be so bad that you guys would stop being friends?"

"Daphne, Leigh, will you excuse me and Cy? I can't say it with you here. No offense, ladies."

"Sure," Leigh said.

She and Daphne went to the kitchen. Daphne put the tea kettle on to heat. A cup of tea with a little ginger would help Johnny's stomach.

Cy waited until he was sure the women were out of hearing range. "What happened, Johnny?"

Johnny took a deep breath and then told Cy what had transpired that morning. Cy was so surprised that he sat down on the floor.

"Ray is a hustler?"

"Yeah. I can't believe it. I thought I knew him. I thought he was a good guy even though he slept around. He just slept around more than I knew. I can't pretend to approve. He said that I was being holier-than-thou, and maybe I am, but I can't go against my beliefs, Cy."

"I understand," Cy said. "Wow."

Johnny asked, "Are you gonna arrest him?"

Cy said, "No. If I do that, then I have to arrest Sandy's girls. Despite the morality issue, he's not doing anything different than they do."

"Yeah. I guess you're right. I don't know how much more I can take. First, I'm shot, then Dory leaves, and now this with Ray. I lost my best friend and the woman I love."

Cy squeezed Johnny's shoulder. "Hang in there, kid. Things'll get better. One day at a time."

Johnny laid his head back and closed his eyes, not trusting himself to answer. There was nothing to say, anyway. Exhausted from all of the physical and emotional stress, he dropped off almost immediately.

When Johnny's breathing became deep and regular, Cy left the parlor. When he walked into the kitchen, Leigh and Daphne's expressions were filled with curiosity.

"This can't go any further than this room," he said.

Both women nodded and Cy began the story.

CHAPTER EIGHTEEN

Cy looked out the window of the Dog House, not really seeing the scene outside. He was worried about Johnny and wondered how he was doing. When Brock came in, Cy welcomed the distraction.

"What?"

Brock smiled. "I want to talk to you about something personal."

Cy leaned a hip on his desk. "Shoot."

"I'll get right to it. I love your sister. I admit that I was an idiot not to court her before I did. She's everything I could want in a woman. I respect her and I'll always treat her well. I'm asking for your permission to ask her to marry me," Brock said.

Cy crossed his arms over his chest. "So our Comanche heritage is no longer an issue?"

"No. I've really worked hard on that. I don't see Daphne as Comanche. She's just the woman I love who happens to have that heritage," he said.

"What about the rest of our family?"

Brock's expression turned hard. "I'm willing to try to get along with them, but I'd like them to meet me halfway."

Cy nodded. "Where would you live?"

Brock shook a finger at him. "That's the problem. I don't want to live with my family, but I don't know if you and I would survive living together."

"I agree." Cy rubbed his chin. "Daphne's not going to want to move out. She's too used to running the house."

"Right. Which complicates things. I have no problem buying a place, but I know how attached she is to that house," Brock said.

"But I'm not attached to it. It holds a lot of good memories for me, but I wouldn't have any problem moving. In fact, me and Leigh have been talking about building our own house on the property."

Brock held up his hands. "Okay, let's back up to my question. Does this mean that I have your permission or not?"

Cy appreciated Brock's respect for tradition. "Not that you really need it, but, yeah. You have my permission. Why she had to pick you of all men, I don't know, but I'm not gonna stand in your way."

Brock held out his hand and Cy shook it.

"Thanks. So you'd really move out?" Brock asked.

Cy said, "Yeah. Leigh and I would like to build a place together. Somewhere that's ours. Know what I mean?"

"Yeah. And I really don't care where Daphne and I live, as long as we're together," Brock said.

"Well, we won't be able to build until spring since we'll need to dig a cellar and lay the foundation."

Brock said, "I think it would be good to wait until after the holidays, but I'm not waiting until April to marry her."

Both men frowned.

Then Cy gave Brock a speculative look. "Think we can get along until then?"

Brock smiled. "I don't think we have a choice."

Cy grunted in agreement. "When are you gonna ask her?"

"Not sure yet. I want it to be special."

158

"Okay. I'm hungry. Let's go get lunch at the Chowhound. We'll see if Ellie and Rob want anything," Cy said.

Brock's eyes widened and he put a hand to his chest. "Is the sky gonna fall?"

"What do you mean?"

"You just asked me to go to lunch with you. I never thought I'd see the day that would ever happen," Brock said.

Cy laughed. "Shut up before I take the invite back. Let's go."

"Yeah. You're even crankier when you're hungry."

"I told you to shut up."

They left the Dog House, trading sarcastic remarks as they went.

~~*~~

"Where are we going?" Daphne asked Brock as they traveled along a trail that ran past Cotton's place.

That's where she'd originally thought they were going, but Brock had led her around her uncle's tipis.

"It's a surprise," Brock said, squeezing her hand.

Daphne's curiosity made her impatient. She was often impatient when it came to surprises and she had a nosy streak.

"How much farther?"

Her question made Brock grin. "Are you like this at Christmas, too? I can just picture you snooping around the house trying to find all the presents when you were a kid."

Daphne laughed. "Yes. I was terrible. Cy wasn't any better. We used to pretend to be detectives on the trail of criminals."

"Why am I not surprised?" Brock said, laughing. "He really was born to be a detective. Don't get me wrong, I love my job, but I'm not quite as driven as he is."

"Leigh's been working on that," Daphne said. "He's

always been so intense about everything. It's good that she's helping him loosen up some."

"Good. God knows he needs it," Brock said. "There's more to life than work. I'm glad he's learning that."

"Me, too."

Brock said, "Here we are."

Daphne was confused by the sight of a small tipi in an area that had been cleared of underbrush. "What is this?"

"It's a tipi."

She lightly punched his arm. "I know that. What's it doing here? Whose is it?"

"I put it here and it's ours."

Daphne met his gaze. "Ours?"

"Yeah. We don't have much privacy at my house or yours. It's too cold out to spend much time outside. I want us to be able to spend time together where we don't have to worry about people coming in and out," Brock said.

"So you built a tipi for us?" she asked.

"Yeah. I wanted to honor your heritage and show you that I don't harbor bad feelings against it anymore."

His statement gave her a warm feeling inside. "I'm so glad to hear you say that. You don't know how much that means to me."

He pressed a kiss to her lips. "Come on. Let's get in out of the cold."

"No argument here," Daphne said.

Brock held back the tipi flap for her and took off his hat before ducking in behind her. A fire burned in the center of the tipi. Over it hung a cooking pot and other cooking equipment.

"Please be seated, madam," Brock said in a British accent while he took off his coat.

Daphne giggled and sat down cross-legged, removing hers as well.

"You make that look so easy," Brock said, lowering himself down a little awkwardly.

"I've been doing it since I was a kid, so I've had a lot of

practice."

He smiled as he took the lid off the cooking pot. "I made us a traditional Indian meal. Cotton told me how, but I did it all by myself and I made a few alterations."

"It smells wonderful. Your sweet potatoes and cranberry sauce on Thanksgiving were delicious. I'm sure this will be, too," she responded.

Brock's thoughtful gestures touched Daphne. That he'd done all of this told her that his change of heart towards her heritage was real. Watching him fill a bowl with stew, she loved the way the firelight flickered in his blue eyes, turning them a little green.

He handed the bowl to her. "I killed and butchered the deer this meat came from. Not only that, I shot it with a bow and arrow. I had Cotton give me lessons and I'm pretty good now."

Daphne grinned. "You learned how to shoot a bow and arrow?"

He dipped himself a bowl of stew. "Yeah. It was rough going at first. I almost poked out my eye and I pinched my fingers a couple of times. Not to mention the fact that my aim stunk. It sure gave Cotton a lot of laughs, though. I figured that I needed to prove that I could provide for my maiden."

The image of Brock dressed in traditional Comanche garb made her laugh. "I wish I could've seen that."

"I'm glad you didn't. I was embarrassed enough as it was. Cotton just fired off shots like it was nothing. It made me work harder at it, though. I was determined to master it," Brock said.

Daphne took a sip of the hot stew. It was rich and hearty with a different flavor than she was used to. "Is that rosemary?"

"Yeah and a little parsley. The ground is too hard to dig up tubers, so I cheated a little and used potatoes and carrots. Onions, too."

"It's delicious. The venison is so tender. I'd say that

you'd make a fine brave, Deputy. We could call you Pokes Out His Eye."

Brock almost choked on his stew over the funny name. He swallowed and then let his laughter loose. She laughed with him.

"And your name would be Woman Too Nosy."

She narrowed her eyes at him. "I'll get you for that. Us Comanche have great ways to exact revenge."

His grin made her heart skip a couple of beats. "I'm sure you do."

When they'd finished their stew, Brock set about making fry bread. Daphne liked watching him cook it. She approved of the way he mixed and handled the dough. He was competent and sure as he went about shaping it. Then he dropped it in the hot oil and tended it until it turned a nice golden color.

He put a piece on a plate and drizzled a fruit dressing over it. "We don't have chokecherries, so I used some raspberry preserves we canned this summer."

When he handed the plate to her, she saw that he'd made her piece heart-shaped.

"Well, aren't you romantic?" she said.

"I have my moments," Brock said.

Balancing her plate on her lap, Daphne broke off a piece of the bread and popped it into her mouth. The sweet berry dressing and crispy bread created a heavenly combination.

"That's scrumptious, Brock."

He'd also taken a bite. "Thanks. Not bad for my first time making it. It's probably not as good as what you make, but it'll do."

She shook her head. "It's better than mine. I'm not especially good at making fry bread."

Brock was pleased with himself. "Really? I thought all Indian women could cook."

Daphne snorted. "No. Just like any other race, there are good and bad cooks. Women tried the best they could, but not all were skilled in making meals. Or sometimes they only had certain dishes they were good at, so that's what they made all the time."

"Really? I had no idea."

"It's the same for the men. Not all of them were good hunters and not all of them were ever meant to be leaders. But they used the abilities of each individual to make their tribe strong. Children are indulged and rarely spoken sharply to. They're gently guided into good behavior or shamed into it. They're praised for good behavior so much that they want to keep doing things the right way," Daphne said.

Brock could easily see all of this in his mind as he listened to her and looked around the tipi. "Did your parents yell at you and Cy?"

Daphne giggled. "Pa tried to, but Ma always scolded him about it, so he would leave a lot of the discipline up to her."

Brock said, "Pa didn't do it too much, but every once in a while Aaron and I got the switch."

Daphne said, "No child of mine will ever be hit like that."

The firm tone of her voice and the suddenly fierce light in her eyes made it clear that this was a serious warning.

"Well, it was only when we did something really bad. Like the time Aaron set the woods in back of our house on fire. It was a good thing that we'd had a lot of rain or else we'd have lost the house and a lot of other homes would have been burned down," Brock said. "He never played with matches out in the woods again."

Daphne still didn't like the idea, but she could see why Doug's punishment had been so severe. Her father probably would have done the same thing to Cy.

"I'm glad that no one lost their home," she said.

Brock was glad that they were having this sort of discussion. It gave him a glimpse into what kind of mother Daphne would be. As they finished their dessert, Brock grew nervous about what he was about to do.

Shifting closer to Daphne, he took her hand and kissed it. "You make me so happy, honey. Since we started seeing each other, I've come to see even more what a special woman you are. You make me laugh and you're kind and caring.

"But you're tough, too. I love all of the different sides of you. No one has ever made me feel the things you do. I love you so much and I can't imagine my life without you. Daphne Running Doe Decker, will you become my wife so I can spend the rest of my life loving you?"

Daphne froze in place, her eyes growing larger.

"Did you just ask me to marry you?" Her voice was barely more than a whisper.

Fear tripped its way down Brock's spine. "Yes, I did."

Daphne launched herself at him, wrapping her arms around his neck. Her momentum knocked him over. She landed on top of him, smothering his face and neck with kisses before pressing her lips to his. Then she smiled down into his startled eyes.

"Yes, Brock. I'll marry you. I'd marry you tomorrow if I could," she said.

She couldn't contain her happiness as her heart swelled inside her chest. He'd finally said the words she'd longed to hear for so long, the ones she'd dreamt about. He flashed a grin at her and laughed, the rumbling sound vibrating against her palms where they rested on his chest.

"You scared me to death. I thought you were gonna turn me down at first," he said.

"Don't be stupid. Why would I turn down a proposal from the man I've loved for so long?"

Her kiss took the sting out her words. Brock reached into his jeans pocket and withdrew a ring box from it.

Breaking the kiss, he asked, "Would you like your engagement ring?"

Daphne sat up and Brock sucked in a breath because the movement caused her to straddle him. Wickedly, he didn't make her move away.

"Hurry," she said, holding out her hand.

He laughed. "Yep. Nosy and impatient."

She glared at him as he took the ring out of the box and then gasped at the sight of the lovely ruby.

"This was my grandmother's. She gave it to me before she passed and made me promise to give it to the woman who captured my heart." He slid it on her finger. "And you have certainly captured my heart, Daphne. *Uh kah-muh-kuh-tuh nuh.*"

Hearing Brock say that he loved her in Comanche was so shocking and sweet that it made her eyes fill with tears. Holding her hand over her heart, she repeated it back to him. Brock broke out in gooseflesh as she said the words. She'd never spoken Comanche around him before and he suddenly realized that she'd been holding back from doing so. She'd most likely been afraid that it would repulse him.

However, it had the opposite effect. He'd never had anyone speak to him in anything but English.

"Say it again," he said.

"*Uh kah-muh-kuh-tuh nuh.*"

It was the most erotic thing he'd ever heard. Sitting up, he wrapped his arms around her and kissed her with a passion that he couldn't hold back. He demanded entry and when it was granted, he delved his tongue into Daphne's mouth. The combination of berries and her own sweetness was intoxicating and he couldn't get enough.

Daphne's ardor matched his and she kissed him back fiercely, caught up in the sensual web he wove around her. This was what she'd wanted for what seemed like forever and she wanted more, needed more. She caressed his chest before moving her hands to his shirt buttons. When they were all undone, she opened the shirt, but she found that he wore an undershirt.

She gasped when Brock pulled her hips into harder contact with his. Even fully clothed it felt incredible and so intimate.

Breaking the kiss, she said, "Brock, I want to be with you. Please make love to me. Make me yours in every way."

"I want that so much, but are you sure you don't want to wait?" he asked.

She loved that he was so considerate of her, but she knew her own mind and this was what she wanted. Her gaze met his passion-filled eyes. "I want you, Brock, and I'm absolutely positive about this." She caressed his strong jaw and brushed her lips against his. "Make love with me."

With a growl, Brock captured her mouth again, kissing her until their breathing was ragged and desire raged through them. Pulling back from Daphne, Brock quickly unbuttoned her blouse and spread it open. He helped her get it off and, layer by layer, her beauty was revealed to his hot gaze.

They had to break apart to finish undressing. Brock's eyes traveled slowly over her lush curves and slightly copper skin. Moving closer to her, he kissed her and skimmed his fingers up her arms. His lips left hers to trail down her neck to her shoulder. He lightly scored her skin with his teeth and pulled her down to the soft blankets with him.

Stretching out by her, he caressed her shoulders before filling his palm with one of her full breasts. She arched into his hand and he teased her nipple, making her moan and squirm a little. Leaning over her, he took her other nipple into his mouth and created suction.

Daphne fisted her hand in his hair as sensation washed through her. Brock's growl of approval heightened her excitement. He glided the hand that had been playing with her breast down over her stomach to the junction between her legs. When he reached her core, she jerked and moaned. As he pleasured her, the rest of the world fell away. She yearned for something she couldn't name, but she trusted Brock to give it to her.

Brock kissed his way back up to her neck, murmuring

words of love and urging her on. He told her how beautiful she was and how much she excited him. Suddenly she wrapped her arms around his neck and shuddered against him. It was so satisfying to him that he could give her that kind of pleasure and he had more in store for her.

Daphne had never felt something so intoxicating, so consuming that she could think of nothing else but Brock and the sensations he created within her. She couldn't stop running her hands over his arms and shoulders as he covered her body with his. He was muscular and powerful and she liked the contrast in their skin tones. Her darker skin next to his paler complexion was beautiful to her.

Brock let her explore his body, loving the dark fire in her eyes and her quickened breathing. When she tentatively closed her hand around his erect manhood, Brock groaned and rested his forehead on her chest. He stayed that way for a few moments before his control broke and he had to have her.

Lovingly, he instructed her on what to do next. As they become one and he broke the barrier, she cried out a little. Brock held her and kissed her until she was ready to continue. Controlling his urges, he made slow, gentle love to her, taking them on a sensual journey to a shimmering pinnacle of sheer joy.

When the last bliss-filled tremors ran through them and ebbed away, Brock slowly collapsed on Daphne. When he heard her sniff, he quickly looked at her, startled to see tears trailing from her eyes.

"Oh, God. Are you all right? Was I too rough?"

He went to move away, but she wouldn't let him.

"No, stay right here. You were perfect."

"Then why are you crying?"

She smiled even as more tears welled in her eyes. "It was so beautiful. I didn't know it would be like that. I love you and I'm so glad that we made love. When can we do it again?"

Brock grinned down at her. "Well, give me a little time and I'll be ready."

She hugged him and giggled. "I'm so glad. Just stay like this until then."

"I'm not crushing you?"

"No. It feels so good to hold you like this."

Brock capitulated, perfectly content to remain where he was. They talked about all sorts of things from wedding plans to cats and dogs. Then, as promised, Brock made love to her again, trying to show her how much he loved and needed her.

They spent the night loving and laughing together, creating a bond that went beyond the physical. Their hearts joined as one as much as their bodies did and it was those emotions that made everything else much sweeter, more meaningful. Their little tipi was a place of magic and love. When dawn approached, they reluctantly left their little oasis, not wanting to return to their everyday lives.

Looking back at the tipi as she and Brock walked hand in hand, Daphne asked, "You're not going to take that down are you?"

"Hell, no."

Her face broke out in a huge grin. "We're going to come back here?"

"Hell, yeah."

"Stop swearing," she said.

"Yes, ma'am." Brock put an arm around her shoulders. "That's our love tipi and I'll never take it down."

She giggled and leaned against him. "Our love tipi?"

"Yeah. Our love tipi."

They laughed over his sappy name, but that was how they would always think of it.

CHAPTER NINETEEN

Brock sat at his desk the next morning, trying to finish a report about a burglary, but his mind kept straying to the night he'd spent in Daphne's arms. Making love with her had been unlike anything he'd ever known. He'd expected her to be shy and scared, but after her initial hesitation, she'd been eager and passionate.

She was the most beautiful, sensual woman he'd ever been with and already he craved her again even though they'd spent all those hours together. He knew that his desire for her would never be satiated. The way she looked, the way she felt in his arms... Brock jerked his mind away from that and refocused his attention on his job. It wouldn't do to get all worked up in front of his coworkers.

He'd just finished with the report when someone came in the door. The young man looked around curiously.

"Can I help you?" Brock asked.

"I'm looking for Sheriff Anderson. Is he around?"

Brock shook his head and stood up. "No. He's not back from a meeting yet, but I expect him soon. You're welcome to wait. I'm Brock Guthrie, one of his deputies."

He extended a hand to the other man.

"I'm Hunter Stetson, the new deputy."

Brock grinned. "That's right. I forgot you were coming today. Welcome aboard."

Hunter smiled, his warm brown eyes shining with good humor. "Thanks. It's good to be here."

"So, Stetson, huh?"

Hunter laughed. "No relation, unfortunately. I get asked that all the time."

"Crap. I could use a new hat," Brock said. "I thought maybe you could get me a discount."

"Sorry."

Brock surreptitiously looked Hunter over as he started showing him around. He judged him to be around six-three and probably around a hundred and eighty pounds and muscular with it. He wore black washmaker pants, a white shirt and a black, leather vest under a black duster.

"You *are* wearing a Stetson, though." Brock indicated Hunter's nice black cowboy hat. "And that's a pretty fancy gun, too."

Hunter took the pearl-handled silver revolver out of the holster and handed it to Brock. "Daddy gave me that for my birthday this year. Mama gave me the hat."

Brock looked the fine firearm over and then handed it back to Hunter. "I know what a gun and hat like that cost. You must not be hurting for money."

Hunter put his gun away. "Well, we own a pharmacy and don't do too bad. I'm an only child and I'll admit that they sort of spoil me."

Brock grunted. "Well, don't expect that sort of treatment around here."

Hunter turned serious. "No, sir. I don't want any special treatment. I'm here to do a job and I'll pull my own weight."

"Glad to hear it. This is the kitchen. Rob makes the coffee because he's fussy about how it's made. And out here we have the Dog House."

Hunter's forehead wrinkled. "The what?"

Brock smiled as they exited the kitchen door that opened onto the yard. "It's actually Det. Decker's office. He claimed the shed as his office and he has three dogs that work with us. So I started calling it the Dog House and it stuck."

"Better than calling it the Cat House," Hunter remarked, grinning.

Brock laughed. "You're right about that."

Cy was out in the yard working with Burt. He'd set up a small obstacle course at the one end of the yard and was putting the big dog through his paces. When he saw Brock and Hunter, he stopped and made Burt sit as they walked over to him.

"Cyrus Decker, meet our new deputy, Hunter Stetson. No relation to the hat company," Brock said.

Cy looked the boy over. "Even if I didn't already know you're from Texas, I'd have been able to tell right away."

"How?" Hunter asked, thinking it a strange greeting.

"It's in the way you hold yourself. You can't help it. You learned it by emulating the other men in your family who do it, too," Cy said. "Nothing wrong with it. It's just distinctive. German Shepherd."

Hunter shook his head. "German Shepherd? Is that code for something?"

Brock chuckled. "No. Cy is dog crazy and thinks about people in dog breeds. Ellie is a Jack Russell terrier, Rob is a blood hound, and now you're a German Shepherd."

Hunter had never heard anything so strange and he wasn't sure that he liked being equated with a canine, but he didn't say so. "Oh. I see. So what are you, Brock?"

"I'm not anything. He hasn't come up with a breed for me yet."

Cy said, "I finally figured out why. It's because you're not a dog at all. You're a cat. A big yellow tabby who walks up and down an alley, yowling his head off and annoying the hell out of everyone in hearing distance."

Hunter guffawed while Brock scowled at Cy whose

grin gave way to laughter. Brock was getting used to Cy's dry sense of humor. However, Cy's expressions were so fierce most of the time that it seemed impossible for him to grin or laugh, so it was always a little shocking when he did.

Cy whistled and his office door opened. Slink and Pudge came trotting over to meet the newcomer. He gave Burt permission to do the same.

Hunter said, "I can see why you'd have the two big ones working with you, but why the little one? Doesn't seem like he can do much to help bring someone down."

"Pudge is a Japanese Pug, a very expensive breed. He's also very smart. Annoyingly smart, sometimes. He's also solid muscle and can bite harder than you'd think he can. He rarely gives up on something he starts, either. He's chewed me out of a few ropes before and he can get in tight places the other two can't."

Cy gave Pudge the signal to start his repertoire of tricks. Hunter laughed as Pudge pirouetted, rolled over, and sat up on his hind legs. The next thing he knew he was flat on his back on the ground with Cy's forearm across his throat.

"He's also real good at providing a distraction so I can get the drop on crooks," Cy said.

Cy released Hunter and helped him up.

Hunter said, "I stand corrected." He looked warily at Cy as he dusted himself off.

Brock said, "Don't feel bad, Hunter. He did the same thing to me and Ellie."

Hunter frowned at Cy. "You did that to a woman? That's not right. You oughta be more respectful of her."

Cy and Brock laughed.

"Don't let her hear you say that," Brock said. "She hates it when we treat her any differently than a male deputy. And you don't want her to hit you. She's small but mighty and fast with her fists. That's why we call her Jabs."

"Really? Hmm. Rob said that he had a woman deputy,

but I thought maybe she did mainly secretarial type stuff," Hunter said.

"Nope. In fact, she's out on patrol right now. When she gets back, I'll take you and show you around town," Cy said.

Hunter would've rather gone with Brock, but he wasn't about to argue. There was something unsettling about Cy, never mind the fact that he'd just put him on his ass. Cy had a predatory air about him that reminded him of …

"A wolf," he said. "You remind me of a wolf."

Cy smiled. "Very good, kid. You catch on fast. Assigning dog breeds to someone is actually useful."

"How so?"

"It gives you insight into their personality. What their strengths and weaknesses are. My cousin Johnny is a golden retriever; loyal, friendly, and eager to please, especially where women are concerned."

"So what does me being a German Shepherd say about my personality?" Hunter asked.

"You like a lot of physical activity and you're dangerous when provoked. You're good-natured for the most part, but when you're threatened or someone you love is, you'll rip your foe apart or die trying in order to protect those you care about. You're also highly intelligent and have a good work ethic. Plus, they're a handsome animal. That about right?" Cy asked.

Hunter shook his head. "Yeah. That's spot on. Especially the handsome part."

"See, Brock. Doing that is useful. You should try it sometime," Cy said.

"Nah, I'll leave that to you," Brock said. "Well, I better get back in there so no one breaks our prisoner out. I'll get you set up at the other desk, Hunter."

Cy smiled to himself as the new deputy followed Brock. This was going to be fun.

CHAPTER TWENTY

A few nights after Daphne and Brock had become engaged, Johnny went over to Wheels' place to talk to him about starting work on his next special project. His wounds weren't as painful and his restlessness was getting worse.

After his friendship with Ray had disintegrated, he'd fallen into a funk, but that day he'd decided that it was time to get on with things. Dory wasn't coming back. It was time he faced it and moved on. The same with what had happened with Ray. He needed something else to focus on and beginning to work on his project was something positive he could do.

Arriving at the Ellis residence, Johnny rode around the main house to the carriage house in the back where Wheels lived. He dismounted slowly and went to the door, ringing the doorbell. He heard it chime inside. In response, the little bell beside the door on the outside jingled, indicating that Wheels was either busy or not in his chair and unable to answer the door.

Wheels and his father had rigged up an intricate bell system and there was a string in every room in the carriage house that was connected to the little bell. There was also a bell system connected to the main house in case Wheels needed help and couldn't get to his telephone to call over on his extension. He tried to be as independent as possible and the fact that he and his father were excellent engineers and inventors helped in that area.

Going inside, Johnny received a huge shock at seeing Wheels standing by the sink in the little kitchen. There appeared to be some sort of apparatus around Wheels' legs and hips.

"What the heck?"

"Hey, Johnny."

"Hi. How are you doing that?"

"Very carefully."

"Ha ha. Very funny."

Joining Wheels at the sink, Johnny looked him over. "You kinda look like you're in a cage. What's all that made of?"

"Well, part of it is from an old suit of armor that Skeeter had out at her place. Daddy found it and brought it home. When he saw it, he got the idea to use it to kinda give me legs. The fella who must've worn the outfit must have been a scrawny little guy, though. We couldn't get my legs in them. That was funny to see. We laughed the whole time we tried," Wheels said.

Johnny laughed just picturing it. "I would have, too. So how'd you put it all together?"

Wheels went on to explain how they'd used rivets, bolts, and leather belts to essentially make a support system for his whole lower body. They'd used a lot of the material from the suit of armor, but they'd had to supplement it with other metal and immobilize the knee joint to keep them strait. The strange equipment came up slightly higher than his waist, immobilizing his hips so that they didn't buckle.

Johnny scratched his head. "You look like something from the future."

"Funny you should mention that. Daddy and I are

gonna work on perfecting it and he filed for a patent. Can you imagine how much something like this could help people like me? Getting the patent will be easy, but getting someone to manufacture it will be tough. We're gonna try like hell, though."

Johnny nodded. "It would be a great help to them, but how are you actually walking? I can see how they help you stand, but how can you move your legs if you can't feel them?"

Wheels pointed to a leather loop on the outside of each thigh. "Allow me to demonstrate. I've been practicing hard. I've landed on my face a lot, but I'm getting better. The problem is that once I'm down, getting back up is almost impossible unless I'm near something I can use to flip myself over with so I can unstrap it. Don't be alarmed if I get off kilter. If I get in real trouble I'll let you know."

"Okay. Where's Ollie?"

Wheels pointed to the space above the kitchen cupboards. "He won't come near me when I'm in this."

Johnny saw the Capuchin monkey crammed between the cupboards and the ceiling. "Aw, he's scared. C'mere, Ollie. It's okay. Nothing to be afraid of."

Ollie's amber eyes flicked back and forth rapidly from Wheels to Johnny. He grimaced at Wheels and let out a grunt of disapproval. Johnny pulled a piece of wasna out of his coat pocket.

"Look what I got, Ollie."

The handsome, furry primate dropped down onto the counter for a couple of seconds, but as soon as Wheels moved, he jumped back on top of the cupboards.

"Boy, he really doesn't like that thing, does he?" Johnny said.

"Nope. I'll show you how this works and then take it off. I've been in it for a couple of hours and I'm starting to get tired. You have no idea how good it feels to stand, though. And to be able to take a leak like this. That's something most guys take for granted. Anyway, here goes."

Using the straps on his thighs, Wheels was able to shuffle forward a little at a time. He pulled up on the strap, lifting his leg and repositioning it a little ahead of him. Then he repeated the process with the other leg. It was slow going, but Wheels didn't care. He was walking and that was all that mattered. He'd take shuffling while upright over not being able to do it at all.

Johnny watched him closely, but not because he was worried about Wheels. He studied how the apparatus worked, thinking about how to improve it.

Once they made it to the parlor, Johnny said, "Your real problem is balance. The structure is sound as far as support, but if you had better balance, you could walk faster with less effort."

Wheels was sweating by this point. "Yeah. We're trying to figure it out, but haven't come up with anything yet. If you do, let us know."

"Will do. Now, how do you get out of it? Do you need help?"

"No."

Wheels backed up to his wheelchair and unstrapped the hip section of the equipment. When his thighs bent at the hip, Wheels caught himself on the arms of the chair and lowered himself the rest of the way onto the seat. Then he unstrapped the rest of it and let it fall to the floor. With his arms, he lifted his legs onto the foot pedals and sat back in his chair, slightly out of breath.

Johnny picked up the strange "suit" and looked it over thoroughly. "Amazing. You guys are geniuses."

"We try. You can just put it over in the corner," Wheels said. "C'mon, Ollie. I'm in my chair."

Ollie ran into the room and jumped up onto Wheels' lap to be cuddled.

"We have to do this every time after I've had that on. I don't think he's used to me being that tall or maybe he just doesn't like all the metal. I don't know."

He pet Ollie, smoothing down the handsome gray and black fur that covered him. Ollie made happy little chattering sounds, indicating his contentment. Once he was soothed, Ollie stood up on Wheels' legs and faced Johnny, who patted his shoulder.

Ollie jumped over onto Johnny's shoulder and then started playing with Johnny's ear.

"Stop that," Johnny said, chuckling. He pulled the wasna out of his coat pocket and Ollie chattered. "Give me a kiss first."

Ollie wrapped his arms around Johnny's neck and kissed his cheek hard. Johnny gave him half of the wasna and Ollie nicely took it before jumping down and hopping up on a hassock to eat it.

Wheels smiled. "He loves that stuff. I appreciate Cotton making it for him with just fruit."

"He likes doing stuff like that. I like it that way, too," Johnny said, sitting on the sofa.

"You guys can all have my share," Wheels said. "I'd rather eat liver than that stuff and I hate liver."

Johnny laughed.

"How's everyone at home?"

"Good. I guess you know about Brock and Daphne getting engaged."

Wheels nodded. "Yep. We got Brock a little drunk the other night buying him celebratory drinks. Of course, Sandy had to give Ollie a shot. Have you ever seen a drunk monkey? You'd think it would slow him down, but he just gets more hyper, bouncing all over the place even more than usual. He played pretty good poker, too. Won twenty bucks."

Johnny laughed. "I can just imagine the faces of the fellas he beat."

"Priceless. Well, c'mon and I'll show you the drawings I came up with," Wheels said, rolling into another room.

A draft table at the right height for Wheels sat over near a window. A child-sized draft table and chair sat on the other side of the room. Wheels rolled over to his desk and took off the linen sheet that covered it. Ollie knew better than to mess with Wheels' desk, but just on the off chance that he got mischievous, Wheels always covered it to keep his work safe.

"I think your measurements for the scaffolding and framework are perfect. Here's where the problem is gonna come—"

Wheels broke off as Ollie climbed up on his shoulder and looked over the drawing. He chattered and grunted as his quick gaze took it all in.

"Do you approve?" Wheels asked him.

Ollie squeaked once, kissed Wheels, and hopped down. He scurried over to the little draft table and sat on the chair. He picked up one of the pencils lying on it and began making his own drawing on the large tablet of paper in front of him. Every so often he would look at Wheels and then go back to drawing.

Wheels sighed. "I'm gonna have enough pictures to wallpaper with pretty soon. He keeps wanting me to hang them up. Anyway, back to this."

They spent the next half hour finalizing the new plans before they were happy with them.

"I really appreciate all your help with this, Wheels," Johnny said.

"Sure. It's been fun and I can't wait to actually start the construction," Wheels said. "I was surprised that you weren't at the Chowhound the other night. You usually come down on Wednesdays. Not feeling well?"

Johnny cursed the blush that crept up his neck. "Uh, well, I sort of had enough of the Chowhound for a while."

Wheels said, "C'mon and have a beer while you explain it to me. I can tell that there's more to this story."

Ollie heard "beer" and ran out to the kitchen, hopping up on the icebox.

Wheels pointed a finger at him. "No. No drunk monkey tonight."

Ollie grimaced at him.

They settled in the parlor and Johnny recounted the events of his night of debauchery to Wheels, ending with his friendship-ending fight with Ray.

"He said I'm too innocent, too judgmental," Johnny said. "Am I?"

"Here's what I think. I think you were mainly raised by your mother and she sort of sheltered you a little. Most likely because of your father. So you didn't get into the sort of trouble that most teenage boys get into. Drinking, women, fighting—all of that. I'm not saying that's a bad thing. You're a good man, Johnny."

Johnny blew out a breath as Ollie crawled onto his lap, curling up. "Are you tired?" he asked the monkey. "Is it your bedtime? Maybe I'm too good. Did you know about Ray?"

Wheels said, "Yeah. It's not something that I could ever do, but it's his life and if that's how he wants to make his money, it's none of my business."

"But he sleeps with married women."

"I know, but the girls sleep with married men. You know, Johnny, it's possible to love someone, but not like what they do," Wheels said. "I know that what Sandy's girls do isn't approved of by most of society, but some of those girls have had a hard life growing up. They don't have any family and no other way to make a living unless they want to scrub floors for the rest of their lives."

Johnny said, "They could get married and let their husbands take care of them."

Wheels said, "True, but my guess is that about half of them would rather not depend on a man to support them, most likely because a man let them down or hurt them in the past. You should talk to Sandy about that sometime. As for Ray, I'd talk to him and maybe try to understand why he's doing what he is. Don't judge him, just talk to him."

"Do you know why he's doing it?"

"No. I never asked, but, then again, I'm not his best friend, either," Wheels said.

"Neither am I anymore."

Wheels grinned. "Johnny, if you apologize to him and hear him out, I'm sure he'll come around."

Johnny laughed. "He told me that I could make good money doing what he does, that women would love to corrupt me because I'm so …"

"Innocent?"

Johnny tried to ward off the blush he felt coming on. "Yeah."

Wheels' shoulders shook with silent laughter.

"Shut up!" Johnny gave him a fierce scowl.

"I reckon Ray's right. You'd be surprised how much women think about sex," Wheels said. "And they like sweet guys such as yourself."

"I feel so stupid about all of this," Johnny said.

"You're not stupid, Johnny. Just uneducated, that's all. I'll tell you what, though. It takes a lot of strength not to give in to that particular urge. It's hard to walk away from a pretty woman instead of taking her to bed," Wheels said.

Johnny said, "I ain't even been tested. I don't know if I have that kind of strength or not."

"If ever a fella did, it's you, Johnny. I can tell that about you. You're a better man than I am about it."

Johnny was quiet for a few moments. "So you've been with women?"

"Yep."

"Recently?"

Wheels laughed. "You mean since I got paralyzed? Yeah. Sometimes things work and sometimes they don't, but I've learned to live with that. I'll take sometimes over never. Even if things don't go right, just holding and kissing a woman feels good. And I never leave her unsatisfied whether or not things work right."

Johnny had no idea what that entailed exactly, but he wasn't about to ask. "Don't you want to get married?"

"I'd love to get married and have kids, but only a very special woman would want to marry a man like me," Wheels said. "I hope to find one someday, but until then, I'm fine with things as they are. Besides, Ollie's like having a kid."

Hearing his name, Ollie raised his head and blinked sleepily at Wheels, chattering faintly.

"Well, I better get going and let you guys get some rest. So we'll start the day after tomorrow then?" Johnny said, getting up.

"That's right. Be careful going home."

Johnny hugged Ollie and deposited him gently onto Wheels' lap. "Thanks again. Goodnight."

Wheels watched Johnny leave and then looked at Ollie. "You'd like to have a mama wouldn't you? Maybe someday I'll find a pretty lady. Would you like that?"

Ollie grunted his assent and Wheels laughed.

"C'mon. Time for all good little monkeys to go to bed."

CHAPTER TWENTY-ONE

The next morning, Johnny made his family join him in back of the bathhouse. Then he handed Cy a packet of rolled up papers tied with a red ribbon.

"Merry Christmas to you all," he said, grinning.

The other three all glanced at each other before Cy untied the ribbon and opened the large papers to reveal blue prints. Daphne and Leigh stood on either side of him, trying to figure out what the drawings were of.

Leigh grinned. "If I'm looking at this right, you're gonna build a big hot water tank."

"Yes!" Johnny grinned. "That way, we won't have to haul hot water to the bathhouse when we want it and we can even use it for cooking. It'll cut down on the time it takes to boil water and save on wood."

Cy stared at him in wonder. "That's incredible. Don't take this the wrong way, but I didn't know you were so smart. I'm sorry for not giving you more credit, Johnny."

Johnny grinned. "That's okay. I know you don't mean nothing by it."

Daphne shook her head at the complex drawings. "I'm all for making cooking easier, but how are you going to get the water in the tank? It would take a long time to fill it with buckets."

"Follow me."

Johnny took them about twenty feet from where they'd been and launched into a complex explanation involving gravity, water pressure, and piping. Leigh nodded, fully understanding what Johnny had just said, but Daphne and Cy's eyes reflected their confusion.

Johnny finished with, "We might have to play with it once it's all built, but you always have to do that when you build experimental stuff. That creek doesn't freeze over, either, so we'll have water pressure year round," he explained.

Leigh took the drawings from Cy so she could look them over. "And this boiler would heat the water?"

"Right and we're gonna burn dried cow dung. It burns hot and long and God knows we have enough of that around here."

Cy frowned. "That's gonna stink to high heaven when it burns."

"Only when you first load the boiler," Johnny said. "Plus, we can keep the pastures clear of dung so there'll be more grazing land for the cattle since they won't eat where they poop."

Daphne shook her head. "You've thought all of this out thoroughly."

"Well, I had a lot of help from Sly, Wheels, and Mr. Ellis," Johnny said. "In fact, we're gonna start construction tomorrow morning."

"Tomorrow? I didn't think you'd be able to do anything until warmer weather," Daphne said.

Johnny tapped the drawings. "No need to wait. That's why I gave you these now. It's an early Christmas gift."

The women hugged him and Cy thumped him on the shoulder as they thanked him. As they went back inside to eat breakfast, Johnny felt better about things than he had since getting shot. Things were looking up.

~~*~~

Resting with Daphne in their tipi that night, Brock said, "New Year's Day."

"No."

"The day after?"

"No."

"Aw, c'mon. That's after the holidays."

Daphne giggled as she looked down into his eyes as she lay draped on top of him. "Boy, I guess you're really in a hurry to live with Cy."

His dark scowl made her laugh harder. "I'll be glad when spring comes and they can build their house. I'd dig the foundation myself if it would get it done faster." He closed his arms around her. "I'm just in a hurry to live with the woman I love."

"I still want to come to our love tipi."

Grinning, he asked, "You're not going to let me forget that, are you?"

She kissed him. "No, I'm not."

He put a hand over his eyes and groaned.

"Don't you know how much women like it when big, virile men are sweet like that?"

Looking into her luminous eyes, he said, "Is that a fact? I'll keep that in mind."

"Good. The last weekend in January?"

Brock considered it. "Yeah, I think that'll work. Hunter will definitely be settled in at work by then, so they won't be shorthanded while we're away on our honeymoon. He's already doing great."

Daphne said, "It helps that his uncle trained him so well."

"Yeah, we really got lucky finding someone who worked for a great sheriff like Shane Stetson," Brock agreed. "We've even heard of him up here. I didn't know that's who his uncle was until Rob mentioned it. Hunter's not a bragger. That's a good thing."

"Is he still trying to treat Ellie special?"

Brock chuckled. "He's getting better about it. At least he's not jumping up to hold the door for her every time she leaves. He wants to, though. You can see it in his eyes. Cy was walking through the office yesterday when Hunter started for the door. Cy snapped his fingers at him and told him to sit back down and stay. Hunter was so surprised that he did it. I thought Rob was gonna piss his pants laughing. Poor kid."

Daphne laughed despite feeling badly for Hunter. "You guys are so bad."

Brock said, "Don't worry. I'm sure before long, he'll be pulling his own pranks on all of us."

Daphne sighed and looked into the fire. "We have to go back soon."

Brock ran his hands along the smooth light copper skin of her back and sides. "I know. How shall we make use of our time, m'lady?"

Daphne was always amused when he used a British accent. She'd tried several times and couldn't pull it off. "Well, I have an idea."

"Care to share, madam?"

Daphne whispered in his ear and then let out a surprised yelp when he rolled her over and proceeded to carry out her idea.

~~*~~

"You gonna actually drink that coffee or just hold it?"

With a start, Daphne realized that Leigh had spoken to her. "I'm sorry. What was that?"

Leigh smiled as she sat down at the table. She'd been outside watching the water tank construction for a little while and had decided to come inside for some coffee before she went back to work out in the barn. It had only been a week, but the men were making excellent progress.

"Boy, you were a million miles away. Thinking about

your man?"

Daphne sat her cup down with a chuckle. "That obvious?"

"Yep. I'm real happy that you finally roped him and hauled him down from that fence he was on."

"Me, too. Of course, you gave me the advice to go after him, so I owe you. We've decided to get married on the last Saturday of the month. Thank you for being my maid of honor," Daphne said.

"You were mine, so I'm just returning the favor. You two aren't waiting long. That's good."

Daphne fiddled with her cup and glance shyly at Leigh. "We don't want to wait for several reasons. One being that it's hard being apart and we want to start out life together. But, um, we've been intimate."

Leigh's eyes rounded. "You have?"

Daphne bit her lip as she nodded. "I know we should've waited, but we just couldn't. And I don't regret it one bit."

Leigh's expression relaxed into a smile. "I remember how hard it was to wait, both for Walt, and Cy."

"But you did it. You must think that I don't have any morals."

Leigh patted her forearm. "I don't think that at all. I think that you waited long enough for your man and you got swept away. It's happened to plenty of people and it always will. I'm not judging you. It's just a good thing you're not waiting long in case you get in the family way."

Daphne nodded. "I know. I've already considered that. However, that doesn't seem to be the case as of today."

Leigh smiled tightly at her meaningful statement. "That's a good thing. I'm sure it won't be too long until there are a bunch of little Brocks running around here, though."

Her smile faded quickly and she blinked back tears.

"Leigh, what's wrong?" Daphne asked.

Unfilled longing flooded Leigh, painfully squeezing her

heart. She tried to rein in the hurt, but she couldn't quite manage it. "I'm fine. It's just that I can't have children. I'm barren and I want to give Cy a child so bad. Walt and I tried so hard, but I never conceived. I went to doctors and everything, but they didn't really have any answers for me. Most of the time I can deal with it, but once in a while it gets to me."

Daphne moved her chair closer and put her arm around Leigh. "I'm so sorry. I didn't know. Cy never mentioned anything."

"Well, you know how he is. He says that we'll just keep trying and if it doesn't happen we'll adopt," Leigh said. "I'm all right with that, but I want to feel his child grow inside me. I feel guilty because I keep hopin' that there was something wrong with Walt, but I can't help it."

Daphne gave her a squeeze. "It's perfectly understandable why you would feel that way. Don't give up hope, Leigh. You're young and there's plenty of time for you to have a baby."

Sighing, Leigh leaned her head against Daphne's shoulder. "I know. You're right."

Daphne hugged her. "You can always talk to me, Leigh. Cy isn't the only one who holds things inside."

Leigh laughed at her pointed remark and straightened again, wiping tears from her cheeks. "Maybe that's why we get along so well. Although, he does talk to me an awful lot."

Daphne gave her a doubtful look. "Really? Well, he should. He's not as bad as Sly, though. I feel so bad for him and I miss Catherine so much."

Leigh frowned. "I know. It was hard enough prying words out of him before her death, but now it's twice as hard. Although, being around these guys is makin' him talk and he even laughed a couple of times. He needs to smile more. He's a good-looking guy, but he's kinda scary when he doesn't smile."

Daphne cracked up. "That's a great assessment of him.

Even as a kid, Sly was like that. It was one reason that not many of the boys at school ever went after him without a couple of their buddies being along. They were scared to fight him one-on-one and they should've been."

"He's really tough. I know he's still hurting, but I've been praying for the pain to start to ease. I know what that kind of loss is like and it ain't easy to deal with," Leigh said.

Daphne took her hand. "I'm certainly not happy that Walt passed away, but I *am* glad that you're here. I hope you know how much you've come to mean to me. You're a wonderful friend and I think of you more like a sister now."

Leigh squeezed her hand in return. "Same here. You and I are gonna have to play peacemakers once Brock moves in here."

Daphne groaned and rubbed her forehead. "I know. I'm so impatient to marry Brock, but I'm dreading the two of them living under the same roof."

"Yeah. I expect there'll be some fireworks, but we'll keep them from killing each other," Leigh said, chuckling. She released Daphne's hand. "Thanks for the talk. I best get back to work."

"You're welcome. Anytime."

Daphne went upstairs to work on some sewing, her mind alternately filled with thoughts of Brock and Leigh's inability to have children. She prayed to the Great Creator to bless Leigh and Cy with a child before too long. Smiling, she sent the same prayer up for her and Brock.

~~*~~

The Chowhound was fairly quiet for a Thursday night, but Sandy Hopper, the proprietor, knew that the next night would a different story. Once men—and a few women—had gotten paid, they'd come in to spend their money, so she wasn't worried about one slow night.

Looking down the bar, she saw Ray sitting at the end of it, nursing a beer. She knew about the rift between him and Johnny and felt badly for Ray. Although Johnny was younger, he and Ray had become almost instant friends when Johnny had moved into town.

Ray had few good friends because of his chosen profession. He had to be careful about who knew because if word got around about what he did, he'd most likely be set upon by men wanting to know if he'd been with their wives or not.

That thought alone made Sandy protective toward Ray. She hated double standards, no matter which way they swung. Women were expected to be pure and chaste, but it was perfectly acceptable for men to visit whores and sew their wild oats. Who did society think they were sewing those oats with?

She shook her head at the ridiculousness of it. And then there was Ray. The man was better looking than any male had a right to be with his jet black hair and silver eyes. She'd seen him barely dressed several times and she knew that he possessed the kind of body that could literally make a woman swoon. Just as society judged women so harshly for their indiscretions, so did it judge male prostitutes. Another double standard.

As she was about to pour a drink for a farmer she knew, Ollie swung up onto the bar and hopped over onto her shoulder.

"Oh, God, you again," she said, chuckling. "That must mean that your daddy is here."

Ollie bobbed his head a little, wrapped his arms around her neck, and kissed her.

"No booze for you. I got in trouble last time I gave you beer," Sandy said.

The farmer grimaced. "I can't believe you let that thing kiss you."

"Oh, yeah, Butch? I'd sooner Ollie kiss me than you. He's a hell of a lot better looking than your ugly puss. If you don't like it, get out."

Butch glowered at her but shut his mouth.

Ollie plopped back down onto the bar and ran down to where Ray sat. His expressive eyes roamed over Ray, who smiled at him.

"What kind of trouble are you causing?" Ray asked, petting Ollie's head.

Ollie bit his wrist lightly, indicating that he wanted to play. Grinning, Ray picked him up and threw the monkey up in the air. Ollie chattered in delight as though laughing. When Ray caught him, Ollie used Ray's arm like a tree branch, swinging from it down onto the floor, only to climb back up onto Ray's shoulder.

Ray laughed as Ollie started picking through his hair.

"I don't have any bugs, buddy," Ray said. "I had two baths today."

Ollie grunted in disagreement and kept looking. A whistle cut through the noise in the place and Ollie took off, heeding Wheels' summons. Caught up in watching Ollie swing and jump over to Wheels' table, Ray failed to notice Johnny approach. He was surprised to find Johnny seated next to him.

Ray arched a brow at him. "What do you want?"

Johnny smiled tightly. "To apologize for being a jackass."

"Leave me alone, Johnny."

"Ray, just listen to me, okay?"

"Fine."

Johnny took a sip of his beer before saying, "I shouldn't have been so quick to judge you. You were right. I was hungover and I hurt so bad that I just couldn't think straight. I also felt stupid because I've known you all this time and didn't have a clue about what you did for a living."

"That's nice."

Johnny pursed his lips. "I'm trying to make amends, Ray. Can't you meet me halfway here?"

Ray met his gaze. "Why should I? You were the only person outside of Sandy and Cotton that I could ever really count on, and you turned your back on me. Why should I give a damn about your apology? I'm not gonna stop doing what I'm doing, so I don't think you want to be seen with me."

Johnny held up a hand. "I know that and I'm not askin' you to quit. I don't agree with it, but it's not for me to judge you. Why do you do it? Can you just tell me that much?"

Ray considered whether or not he was going to answer Johnny's question. Would it make a difference or would Johnny judge him again? Johnny's sincere gaze got to him and he sighed. "Not here. Come with me."

Johnny followed Ray from the barroom, down the hallway lined with the girls'—and Ray's—rooms. Ray unlocked the last door on the left that was right before the back door. Johnny looked around at the rather romantically furnished room.

"Uh, this is different," he said, looking at the canopy bed and red silk curtains.

Ray laughed as he shut and locked the door. "You can't get a woman in the mood if your room looks like a typical man's room. At least not when you're a hustler."

Johnny took a seat on an overstuffed chair and Ray sat on the bed.

"How did you get started doing this?" Johnny asked.

"About seven years ago, when I was eighteen, I had a woman proposition me. I thought she was kidding, but she was dead serious. I told her no, but she wouldn't let it go. She ended up offering me two hundred bucks. I was desperate for money, so I did it. She's a beautiful woman, so it wasn't a hardship to be with her.

"Well, she told one of her lady friends and the next thing I knew, I had women lining up for a piece of me." Ray grinned. "The problem was that it was dangerous for me to be seen going to their places and renting a room at one of the hotels wasn't much better."

Johnny shook his head. "So you rented a room from Sandy."

Ray chuckled. "She thought I was kidding at first when I said that I'd rent the room she had available. She thought that I just wanted to sleep with the girls, but I soon convinced her that I was a hustler and she let me have the room. It's perfect because it's right inside the back door and the ladies can slip in and out without being noticed."

Johnny was amazed and intensely curious. "How many customers do you have every day?"

Ray shrugged. "Depends. I have regular appointments scheduled with a few women every week, but there are women who show up unannounced. We have a signal if they come into the barroom that lets me know that they're here for me. A slow day is two women, but I once had five."

"Five women in one day? How's that even possible?"

Ray laughed at Johnny's disbelief. "Well, it took a toll on me, I won't lie about that, but I made damn good money that day. Anymore, I don't usually make less than two hundred a day, but it's usually more like four. It depends on what they want."

Johnny shook his head. "Don't they want the same thing?"

Ray almost groaned at Johnny's lack of knowledge. "Some women want the fantasy that I care about them. They're lonely and they don't get any attention. Some are single, some not. So I have to seduce them and convince them that they're the most beautiful woman on Earth. Other women want it hot and fast and some like it sort of rough."

Johnny didn't know how to frame his next question so he had to figure it out. "I can see how a woman can have so many men a day, but how do you …keep going?"

Ray said, "It's a mental trick as much as it is physical. It took me a while to be able to do it. I'd have one customer every day and be done. The problem was that another woman would show up and offer me money. I couldn't turn it down, so I found the willpower and took care of business."

Johnny asked, "Do you like it?"

Ray smiled. "Yeah. I mean, there are a couple of women I'd rather not deal with but the money is just too good to turn down." He sobered. "The reason I'm doing this is because of Izzy."

Johnny frowned. "Your cousin? I thought she was going to college to be a doctor?"

"She is. I'm putting her through school. We've always been more like brother and sister and there ain't nothing I won't do for her. She's had her heart set on being a doctor since she was a kid and I wasn't about to let her dreams die. So when I saw the earning potential of being a hustler, I knew that I could help make that dream come true," Ray explained.

A new respect for Ray grew within Johnny. What he was doing was wrong, but it was for the right reasons, for the benefit of someone he loved. It made sense now and Johnny felt guilty all over again about the way he'd treated Ray.

"So that's where most of my money goes. I also save a little of it, too. I'm not gonna do this for the rest of my life. She only has two more years to go, so she won't need the money anymore. Then I'll be able to save it all for what I really want to do," Ray said.

Johnny grinned. "You're gonna open that bakery that you keep talking about."

Ray nodded. "That's right. This job is just a means to an end. Do you understand now?"

"Yeah, I do. I'm really sorry that I didn't listen to you, Ray. Can you forgive me?"

Smiling, Ray said, "Yeah. It's forgotten. Sure you don't want me to throw some customers your way to make a little extra cash towards your woodshop business. They'd eat you up."

Johnny blushed. "Thanks for the offer, but I couldn't do anything like that. No offense. Besides, I wouldn't have any idea what I'm doing."

Ray gave Johnny a teasing grin. "Showing you the ropes would be half the fun for them."

"I'm not cut out for that."

"Okay, but the offer still stands."

A knock sounded on the door and Ray looked at his alarm clock by the bed. "Crap! I didn't realize what time it was."

Johnny's heart jumped. "Is that a customer?"

"Yeah, and she can't know you're here. Uh, hide in the closet. I'll keep her busy on the bed and you can sneak out," Ray said, taking off his shirt.

"What are you doing?" Johnny asked.

"Distracting her." Ray undid a couple of buttons on his pants and pulled them a little lower on his trim, muscular hips. "A little window dressing so all of her attention is focused on me."

"Oh. Okay."

Johnny got in the closet, closing it until only a thin strip of light shone into the small space.

Once he'd made sure Johnny was out of sight, Ray opened the door, a seductive smile on his chiseled face.

"Well, hello, Mary, Mary Quite Contrary," he said.

The beautiful brunette laughed as she came inside and closed the door. "You look good enough to eat, Ray."

"We'll do that later."

He quickly undid her coat buttons and helped her off with the garment. Hauling her against him, he kissed her soundly, backing her over to the bed quickly and pushing her onto it playfully.

Mary laughed. "Goodness! You're in a mood."

"I'm in the mood for you. You've been on my mind all day. I hope you're well rested, woman, because this is gonna be a long ride."

Johnny gaped at Ray's statement and was surprised when Mary giggled.

"Oh, don't worry, honey. I'll keep up with you. Now get me naked."

Ray crawled on the bed and captured her mouth. He waved a hand towards the door, signaling for Johnny to make his escape. As quietly as he could, Johnny made his way out of the room, closing the door softly behind him.

In just those few minutes, Johnny had received a slight education about what might go on between men and women in the bedroom. Women liked playfulness and wanted to be wanted. He tucked that information away for future reference.

CHAPTER TWENTY-TWO

As December continued, the temperatures rose back up into the fifties during the day, which was normal for that time of year in Oklahoma. It helped Johnny's group finish the water tank quicker and the Saturday before Christmas, they were ready to test it out. Johnny was as nervous as if he was giving birth.

"Ok, Sly, go ahead and open the chute!" he shouted.

Sly waved a hand to let him know he'd heard Johnny. He smiled as he watched Johnny pace. Truth be told, he was just as excited to see how it all was going to work. He bore down on the lever that was affixed to the chute door, lifting the barrier upward. Water flooded perfectly into the pipe, rushing through it to the tank.

"Here it comes!" Johnny grinned as he followed the water's progress.

Vern stood on the ladder attached to the side of the tank, looking through the door in the roof of it to make sure the water entered the tank properly. When clear creek water burst from the pipe, rushing down into the tank, he let out a yell of victory and threw a fist in the air.

"We got water, y'all!"

The group gathered cheered and clapped. They all took

turns climbing up to watch the water spill into the tank. Ollie had climbed into the closest tree and his screeches of approval made them all laugh.

Daphne hugged Johnny tight. "I'm so proud of you! Proud of all of you!"

Johnny hugged her back. "Thanks. Now the real test comes. Let's go make sure it works inside before we start the boiler up."

"Okay."

Sly shut the water chute since the water level had reached the proper level and they all trooped inside to the bathhouse.

Johnny blew out a breath and rubbed his hands together nervously. "Well, here goes nothing."

He turned the handle on the newly installed spigot and stood back a little. Water spurted and sputtered from the faucet before settling into a strong, steady stream. Johnny shouted in joy and everyone joined him. Then he and Wheels watched the water go down the drain to make sure the tub emptied properly.

"We did it, fellas," Johnny said. "It took a lot of hard work, but we did it. I don't know how I'll ever repay you."

Vern said, "Oh, don't worry, son. Wheels and I will think of something."

Johnny turned off the spigot. "You just name it. I guess we can fire up that boiler and make sure it works right."

While they waited for the water to heat, they had a celebratory toast, even though it was only late morning. Daphne and Leigh served brunch and a party atmosphere ensued throughout the meal. Johnny kept running outside to make sure the boiler was still working properly, thrilled that there were no complications.

When brunch was over, they went back to the bathhouse. Johnny turned the tub faucet on again and hesitantly passed his fingers through the water. Elation flowed through him as he felt the lukewarm temperature.

"It'll be hot enough for a bath in a couple of hours," he

announced.

Cy clapped him on the back. "You get to take the first one since this was your invention."

Johnny grinned. "I can't believe it worked."

Cy said, "I can and I'm really glad it did because when our house is finished, you can build us one, too." He gave Brock a toothy grin. "Until then, we can still come use this one."

Brock rolled his eyes and laughed. "I can't get rid of you no-how."

Daphne watched them banter and was happy that the two men were coming to terms with each other. Cy hadn't complained much about Brock lately and vice versa. It made her less nervous about the two of them living under the same roof, even if it would be temporary. She and Leigh exchanged conspiratorial smiles as the party broke up and people left.

~~*~~

Christmas Day united Brock and Daphne's families for the first time and the couple was anxious over it. It was tense at first as everyone greeted each other when the Guthries arrived at Sundance Ranch, but Cotton, a master at putting people at ease, acted as a buffer. He cracked jokes and traded friendly insults with everyone, lightening the mood.

Cy stepped up to Doug and narrowed his eyes. "I understand that you think that cats are smarter than dogs."

Doug grinned. "As a matter of fact, I do."

Cy nodded. "I think you and I need to have a discussion about this over a drink."

"I'll take you up on that," Doug said, following Cy into the parlor.

Daphne could have kissed her brother right then for playing the good host. The house filled with conversation and laughter all that day. Like Brock and

Daphne, the two families found that the divide could be bridged with a little effort and respect. Surprisingly, the only real remaining animosity was between Brock and Daniel.

Daphne overheard David speaking to Daniel about it at one point.

"You must stop this! Brock is changing, as we all are. We have to learn to trust them as much as they do us," David said.

Daniel's blue eyes filled with fire. "It's hard after years of hearing him call us all kinds of horrible names and embarrass us. Hiding behind his badge if we got out of line. I still can't believe that Cy is becoming friends with him. Of course, he was gone for a long time and doesn't really know just how bad it was."

David put a hand on Daniel's shoulder. "I know, but it's obvious that Brock's heart and those of his family are changing. If you hang on to this bitterness, it will only cause trouble. No good will come of it. Do you want to cause a situation that would hurt Daphne?"

Daniel shook his head. "No. I love her and I want her to be happy. I just can't believe *he* makes her happy."

David gave him a stern look. "That's Daphne's business. Someday you'll understand. You can't control love, love controls you. Besides, the Great Spirit chose to put them together for a reason. I believe it's to show us that we can perhaps heal old wounds. Put this anger out of your heart."

Daniel inhaled deeply and let his breath out slowly. "I'll try. It's the best I can do."

David sighed and left the room, put out with his son. Daphne had pretended that she'd been busy with something in the kitchen, but her mind worried over the things she'd heard Daniel say. But when Brock came into the room and stole a kiss from her, the love in the blue eyes she loved so much reassured her and the joy of the day was restored for her.

~~*~~

Music and laughter filled Benny's on New Year's Eve. Brock, Aaron, and Wheels were joined by two other musicians. Wheels' sister, Maggie, aka Skeeter, who also owned a junkyard, played harmonica, and Lewis Flemming, played spoons.

Johnny pitched in tending bar so Benny could go dance off and on. Brock watched his fiancée dance with other men without much jealousy. His trust in her was complete, but he kept an eye on her in case someone got too familiar with her person.

He grinned as Rob spun her around on the dance floor, thinking that his tall, lanky boss looked a little like a crane as he moved in time to the fast song they played. Ellie was trying to learn some sort of dance from Walt, but she wasn't having much luck with it. Of course, she wasn't the most graceful dancer, so if Walt was trying to teach her anything complicated, her chances of success weren't very good.

Still, she laughed when she messed up and whatever Walt said to her in response only made her laugh harder. Looking over at the bar, Brock did a double-take at the look of pure dislike on Hunter's face as he watched the Irishman and Ellie. Hunter got the same expression whenever Walt came to the sheriff's office.

When he'd first noticed it, Brock had thought maybe Hunter had developed a crush on Ellie, but that wasn't the case at all. There was just something about the attorney that rubbed Hunter the wrong way and judging from the look on Hunter's face right then, that wasn't going to change anytime soon.

Loud laughter erupted over at a table and Brock saw a guy throw down his cards in anger. Ollie sat on the table across from him. Vern sat in one of the other chairs at the table, keeping an eye on Ollie for Wheels. Apparently Ollie was making a killing at poker. Brock leaned over and nudged Wheels' chair and then nodded in Ollie's direction. Wheels cracked up when he saw Ollie scooping up money from the table.

Turning back around, Brock smiled as Daphne crooked a finger at him. When the song ended, he informed the others that he was going to dance, and put his guitar to the side.

"You certainly sound in fine form tonight, Deputy. You look it, too," Daphne said as he took her in his arms.

Brock said close to her ear. "Why, thank you, Miss Decker. You're the most beautiful thing I've ever seen, and I've seen every gorgeous inch of you, so I should know."

Daphne laughed, loving his scandalous remark. "If you play your cards right, you might just get the chance to see it again."

"Then I'll be on my best behavior," he said.

Benny clanged the bell that hung behind the bar, gaining the crowd's attention. "Almost midnight folks! Get ready!"

He started off the countdown and everyone joined in. The clock struck midnight and the noise level rose tenfold as shouts of "Happy New Year" went up. Brock kissed Daphne soundly, properly ringing in the new year with the woman he loved more than anything in the world.

Parting, they raised their voices with all the others in signing Auld Lang Syne, but their gazes stayed locked. Even as their family and friends wished them Happy New Year's, they were acutely aware of each other. Desire shimmered between them, potent and raw.

Brock arched an eyebrow and gave her a small, wicked smile that she answered with one of her own, thereby giving him the answer to his unspoken question. He turned to go get their coats and came face to face with Daniel. A dangerous glint shone in Daphne's cousin's eyes.

"Where are you off to?" he asked. "Taking my cousin to your secret little spot?"

Brock's eyes widened and Daniel gave him a drunken sneer.

"That's right. I know about it. You took her—"

Grabbing Daniel's arm, Brock pulled him to the side. "Shut your mouth! You're drunk and you're gonna embarrass Daphne!"

Daniel yanked his arm away. "You really think you're something special, don't you? You think just because you wear a badge that you're untouchable. Well, you're not."

Brock reined in his temper. "Cy wears a badge, too."

"Yeah, but he knows what it means to be Comanche. At least he used to. Maybe he's forgotten, but I haven't! Just because you're marrying Daphne doesn't mean that you've really changed the way you think about us. We're just a bunch of dirty Injuns to you. Isn't that right?"

Brock's jaw clenched. "This isn't the place or time to discuss this. Come see me when you're sober and we'll talk then."

He tried to move past Daniel, but Daniel grabbed his shirt collar and hauled him back.

"Daniel! Let him go!" Daphne said. "What's the matter with you?"

"He's not good enough for you!" Daniel said.

Brock extricated his shirt from Daniel's fist. "He's drunk. Let's go."

"He was just telling me what a dirty, good-for-nothing Indian I am. Isn't that right?" Daniel let out harsh laugh. "He hasn't changed, cousin. He never will."

Daphne said, "Stop it, Daniel!"

"No! Not until you see what's right in front of your face. He doesn't care about you. He just thought it was fun to bed—"

Brock had had enough. He spun Daniel in his direction and socked Daniel's jaw. Daniel reeled back from the blow, but recovered quickly. He shook a finger at Brock and grinned.

"You're gonna wish you hadn't done that," Daniel said,

advancing on Brock.

Sly inserted himself between the two men. "Daniel, stop this. It's a holiday and you're upsetting Daphne, not to mention the rest of the place."

Daniel frowned at him. "So now *you're* siding with him? You can't stand him, either."

"I'm siding with you, but I'm not letting you start a fight tonight. Come home with me and sleep it off," Sly said, his dark eyes pleading with Daniel.

Daniel shoved him. "He's brainwashing you, too. Just like he did Daphne."

Daphne said, "No one brainwashed me, Daniel. Go home with Sly."

"You can't see it can you? Of course not. He seduced you and made you think he loves you."

Brock moved towards Daniel. "You need to shut that foul mouth of yours."

Cy arrived and put a restraining hand on Brock's shoulder. "You need to just leave, Brock."

Daniel snorted. "What happened to you, cousin?" he asked in Comanche. "You have forgotten who you are. Who *we* are. We used to stand and fight together, but not anymore. You left and forgot about us. You turned your back on your people."

Sly said, "No, he did not. He followed his dream. Everyone is entitled to do that."

Daniel was done talking. He shouldered his way around Sly, moving toward the door. At the last second, he rammed into Brock, taking him down in a swift wrestling move. Cotton pulled Daphne away from the bedlam that erupted as the two men fought in earnest, exchanging blows and hurling insults at each other.

Their fury burned so hot that it was hard to keep them apart, but finally both men were subdued.

Brock panted as Benny and Hunter held him back. "You know why people call you a filthy Injun? Because that's what you keep acting like! Your problems are you

206

own making, Daniel. If you started acting a little civilized instead of like one of the Comanche who killed my grandpa, people might actually like you and remember that you're part white, too."

With a sharp gasp, Daphne stiffened against Cotton.

Daniel let out a sarcastic laugh. "And there it is. How you truly feel. I told you all that he hasn't changed."

Daphne's stricken face came into Brock's line of sight and his stomach sunk. "That is not what I meant at all!"

Cy and Sly hauled Daniel out of the bar and Benny and Hunter released Brock. He immediately went to Daphne.

"Honey, I didn't mean that the way it sounded," he said. "You have to believe me."

Daphne wanted to, but the look on his face and the venom in his voice made her doubt him. "Cotton, please take me home."

Brock tried to put a hand on her shoulder, but she shrank away from him.

Cotton said, "Brock, let us pass, or Daniel won't be the only Indian to put you on your ass tonight."

Brock's temper flared until Cotton winked at him and shook his head slightly. His shoulders sagged as the fight left him and he stood aside.

"Daphne, I'll talk to you tomorrow," he said, as she passed by.

She looked at him, but didn't say anything as Cotton guided her toward the door. Someone nudged his arm and he looked to see Aaron holding out a shot to him.

"She'll come around. Drink this and let's go home," Aaron said. "She just needs a little time."

"This wasn't how I pictured this night going," Brock said. "I'm gonna kill Daniel."

"No, you're not. You're going to ignore him if he comes after you," Aaron said. "You have to rise above whatever he throws at you. Protect yourself if it comes to that, but no more. You'll only prove him right if you keep fighting with him."

Brock sighed and looked at the shot glass in his hand. The sight of his bloodied knuckles took away any desire for the drink and he handed it back to Aaron. "Yeah. You're right. See you in the morning."

"Careful going home."

Brock just nodded and walked out the door.

CHAPTER TWENTY-THREE

Cy had barely stepped into the kitchen the following morning before Daphne said, "I don't want to talk about it."

He looked at Leigh, who gave him a wide-eyed look and shook her head.

Taking his cue from his wife, he said, "Okay. Is the coffee ready?"

Daphne moved over to the sink to put water into a pot. "Yes."

In times like this, Cy was actually a little scared of his sister. "Okay. Leigh, do you want some?"

"I have, thanks."

Cy quickly poured a cup and sat down by Leigh.

He thought it best to try to act normal, but he suddenly couldn't come up with a topic of conversation. Leigh opened her mouth to say something, thought better of it and closed it again. The kitchen door banged open and Johnny bounded in as usual.

"Good morning, everyone. I brought the milk. Those cats followed me all the way over to the house, windin' around my feet and all. I spilled a little in the drive and they left me alone to clean it up."

Cy and Leigh were never so grateful for Johnny's rambling.

Johnny put the milk pail on the counter and kissed Daphne's cheek. "Don't you worry about Brock none. He didn't mean it. Daniel just likes to instigate."

Cy and Leigh cringed a little at his broaching of the topic.

Daphne shook her head and poured him a cup of coffee. "I'm not so sure about that, Johnny."

Cy and Leigh looked at each other, surprised when she didn't bite Johnny's head off.

Johnny said, "He's not like that anymore. I mean, he asked you to marry him. A fella just doesn't do that if he doesn't love the woman. Well, okay, some men might, but not Brock. He don't care if you're Indian or not."

Daphne wanted to agree with Johnny, but she kept hearing Brock's words in her head and seeing the look on his face. Questions crowded her heart and mind. What if they got married and his loathing for Indians returned? She couldn't take that.

She gave Johnny a small smile. "I appreciate what you're trying to do, Johnny, but I just can't talk about this right now."

He gave her a sideways hug. "All right. I understand."

"Thank you."

His blue eyes took on a devilish gleam. "You're not making us mice poop pancakes are you?"

Daphne laughed and the release felt good. "No. We're having oatmeal."

"Okay. You need help?"

"No, I'm fine. Just sit down and behave yourself."

Johnny grinned at her. "Yes, ma'am." He took a seat. "You know, I been thinkin'."

"That's never good," Leigh quipped.

"Be nice to me or I won't help build you guys a water tank," Johnny said. "I'm gonna talk to Vern and see how hard he thinks it would be to pipe hot water out here to the kitchen. Then we wouldn't even have to go to the bathhouse for hot water."

Daphne said, "That would be wonderful."

"I have to go into town later on. I'll stop by their place and ask him," Johnny said.

Daphne was grateful to Johnny for lightening the mood and helping to ease her stress. The knots in her stomach loosened enough so that she was able to eat a small breakfast. But once everyone went off to work, she was alone with her thoughts and the oatmeal felt like a heavy brick in her abdomen.

Doubt gnawed at her as she went listlessly about her work. Normally, she'd hum or whistle as she ironed and dusted, but not that day. With fortitude, she forged ahead, refusing to let her uncertainty and hurt interfere with her daily routine.

~~*~~

Brock tapped his pencil impatiently against his desk as he waited for Cy to arrive so he could find out how Daphne was. He hadn't been able to sleep, so he came into work early even though things were quiet and he really didn't have any paperwork to catch up on. He'd ended up cleaning the cells since they were empty, but that hadn't taken very long.

"Knock that off before I shove that where the sun don't shine, Brock."

Brock smiled at Wheezer. "Sorry. Why don't you and Aaron go home? I'm here and I'm sure you wouldn't mind knocking off a little early."

Aaron said, "You don't have to tell me twice." He rose and stretched. "Have a good day. Call me if you need help."

Wheezer also got up. "You'll have to send someone for me. I'm too far out of town to have a telephone."

Brock nodded. "Okay. Have a good day, gentlemen."

The other deputies bid him goodbye and headed out.

Brock decided to clean the kitchen to pass the time until Cy arrived. His shoulders ached from the tension he felt over the situation with Daphne. Had Cy also taken what he'd said last night the wrong way? They'd been making progress in bridging the divide and he was worried that what had happened would set them back again.

He was almost done cleaning the small kitchen when Cy came in, dogs in tow.

Cy came into the kitchen and gave Brock a hard look before going out into the yard. The dogs greeted Brock with their usual enthusiasm. Brock wasn't about to let the situation go on and followed Cy.

"Cy, stop. Let me explain," he said.

Cy turned and walked right up to Brock. "Talk."

Brock ignored the fact that Cy had issued an order. "What I said last night came out wrong. I never lied about my acceptance of your family's Comanche heritage. I've made my peace with that, I swear."

Cy crossed his arms over his chest. "What did you mean?"

Brock ran a hand through his hair. "Daniel keeps accusing everyone of treating him and Sly like dirty Indians. I meant that if he really wants people to treat him differently, then he needs to change the way he acts. I didn't mean that I had a problem with his heritage.

"I was trying to make him see that if he keeps acting uncivilized and causing trouble all the time, he can't expect people to see the good in him. I was mad about some of the stuff he was saying and it all came out wrong."

Eyeing Brock, Cy noted his sincere expression. Although anxious, Brock wasn't exhibiting any signs of deception. Cy nodded. "I believe you and, I hate to say it, but you're right about Daniel. I've told him and Sly the same sort of thing several times, but they don't listen to me. Of course, Daniel's the instigator most of the time. I'm worried that he's getting really out of control."

Brock sighed. "Yeah. I know I have differences with him, but I'd hate to see him seriously hurt if he ticks off the wrong person. How's Daphne?"

Cy's scowl said it all.

"Damn it! Do you think she'll listen to me if I go over there tonight?"

"Let it go for now. I'll talk to her and then you can come over tomorrow night. She should be cooled off by then," Cy said.

Waiting to talk to Daphne would be excruciating, but he thought Cy was right. "All right. What about you and me?"

Cy smiled. "We're fine as far as I'm concerned."

"Good. What are you working on?"

"Just some paperwork. It's been quiet the past few days, which is surprising. I'd have thought that some things would've gotten out of hand somewhere," Cy replied.

"I hope you didn't just jinx us. Rob and Ellie should be getting here soon. I'll let you know if something comes up," Brock said.

Cy grunted his assent and Brock went back to the office. Standing there, Cy thought that it was remarkable that him and Brock were in agreement on the situation with Daniel. With a smile and a shake of his head, Cy went to the Dog House and got started on his paperwork.

~~*~~

Daphne let out a groan of frustration when she looked out the kitchen window and saw Daniel ride up to the house and dismount. She didn't want to talk to him any more than she did Brock right at the moment.

She opened the door before he had a chance to knock. "Go away, Daniel. I don't want to talk to you."

He looked terrible and the spiteful part of Daphne was glad.

"I'm sorry about last night, Daphne. I shouldn't have started anything with Brock," he said sheepishly.

"You're damn right you shouldn't have! And the things you said to me about private matters was despicable!" Daphne shook her head. "None of that is any of your business."

"You're right. It's not. It's just that I don't want you to get hurt. I'm afraid that he'll change once you marry him. What if it's an act and he changes again? It'll be too late," Daniel responded. "And what about your kids? Is he really fine with them being part Comanche?"

Daphne gnawed on her bottom lip. She'd been having the same doubts.

Daniel said, "I really am sorry about the things I said about your private business, but not about Brock. You've never heard the kinds of things he's always said about us, about Indians. How God should've left us off the earth and that we're no better than scavengers and murderers. He's said a lot worse than that, but I won't repeat it. You can ask Sly if you don't believe me."

"You're just saying that because you don't like Brock."

Daniel understood why she didn't want to believe him. "Yeah, I don't like him, but I'm saying this because I'm worried about you. I love you and I want you to be happy. I know you love him, but do you really want to marry someone who might still harbor those kinds of feelings?"

Putting a hand to her forehead, Daphne said, "I don't know what to think. You say that he hasn't changed and tell me all these nasty things he's said in the past. He says he didn't mean the things he said last night." A dull ache throbbed in her temples. "I just need time to think. Please just let me be, Daniel."

Daniel's face fell as Daphne went back into the house and shut the door. Regret weighing him down like a boulder, he mounted and left for home.

~~*~~

Cy got home in time for supper that evening. He kissed Leigh and washed up.

"How was your day?" he asked.

"Fine. Busy," she said, sitting down at the table.

Cy tried Johnny's tactics with Daphne and kissed her cheek. "How about you?"

She smiled a little. "So-so. Daniel came to apologize, but I didn't want to talk to him. I'm so confused."

He took his usual seat by Leigh. "At the risk of you biting my head off, I'm going to tell you what I think about the situation and then you're gonna have to make your own decision."

Daphne pulled a roast pan out of the oven and put it on top of the stove. "Go ahead."

"I talked to Brock about it because I was mad, too. He explained to me that he just meant that Daniel needs to act differently if he wants people to treat him with more respect and I agree with Brock."

Leigh and Daphne exchanged a startled glance. Leigh put a hand on Cy's forehead.

"Are you feelin' okay?"

Smiling, he took her hand and held it. "I feel fine. Brock is right. I've talked to Daniel about it a few times, but he refuses to listen to reason. Do I like the things that Brock and others have said about us or done to us? Of course not, but I have to admit that I contributed to some of the bad feelings aimed at us when I was younger.

"And sometimes when I'd come home for a visit, I'd end up fighting right alongside of Daniel and Sly. Maybe it's because I'm older and I can look back on it with a new perspective that I see all of this. I'm not saying that the people who've been against us were in the right, but neither were we sometimes."

Daphne took the lid off the roast pan and put the meatloaf inside it onto a serving tray. "So you think that I should forgive Brock?"

"Yeah, I do," Cy said.

The savory aroma of the meatloaf wafted through the kitchen and Cy's stomach rumbled.

"That smells great, sis. I'm starving," he said.

He was startled when Leigh quickly pushed back from the table and ran out the kitchen door.

"What the hell?"

Running after Leigh, he found her retching in the driveway. Her stomach was empty, but the dry heaves left her breathless. Cy rubbed her back, trying to lend his support since there wasn't much else he could do to help her. After a bit, her nausea subsided and she straightened again.

Cy handed her his handkerchief, concern etched on his face. "You okay?"

She nodded. "Yeah. It was the smell of the meatloaf. It hit me and I just couldn't take it."

"I hope you're not catching the flu," Cy said. "It's still going around a little."

Leigh shook her head. "No. I felt fine all day. It was just the meatloaf. I don't know why. I love Daphne's meatloaf. Maybe it's just a little stomach bug."

"I hope not." Cy put an arm around Leigh as they walked back to the house. "Maybe you should go lie down. I'll bring you some tea."

"I'm not tired. I just felt so sick."

The fresh air had helped settle her stomach and she felt better. However, as soon as they stepped into the kitchen, her queasiness returned. She broke away from Cy and ran upstairs.

Cy said, "She said the smell of the meatloaf is making her sick. I don't know why. It's never bothered her before. I hope she's not getting the flu or something. She didn't eat all that much for breakfast, either."

Excitement gripped Daphne, but she didn't want to say anything in case she was wrong. Might Leigh be pregnant? It would explain her sudden symptoms, but it might be a stomach bug going around. Erring on the side of caution, she didn't voice her suspicions to Cy.

"I'm sure it'll pass. We'll just keep an eye on her. I'll put on some water for tea."

"Thanks," Cy said. "I'll go check on her."

When he'd gone, Daphne allowed the grin she'd suppressed to spread across her face and she did a little dance. "Oh, Great Spirit, I pray that you've blessed them with the baby they want so much," she whispered. "Please let it be so."

CHAPTER TWENTY-FOUR

Once again crime picked up and the sheriff's staff was busy, which prevented Brock from going to see Daphne the next night. His frustration level rose as the evening wore on. There were a couple of domestic disturbances to break up, an armed robbery at one of the hardware stores, and a small house fire to help put out. By the time things quieted down, it was too late to go out to Sundance Ranch.

As he and Hunter were about to leave, Walt came in the door.

Hunter openly scowled at him. "What do you want?"

Walt's eyebrows rose. "I've come to see if Ellie is all right. We were supposed to have dinner, but when she didn't show up, I figured that she got caught up in somethin'. Not that it's any of your business."

Brock had never heard such a cold tone in Walt's voice before or seen the slightly malevolent gleam in his eyes.

Hunter said, "It's my business because Ellie is my coworker and friend. I don't like you."

Brock put a hand on Hunter's shoulder. "Walt's a good guy, Hunter. No reason not to like him."

Hunter moved away from Brock, glaring angrily at Walt. "He's a snake in the grass, Brock. He'll show his true colors someday and you'll see that I was right. See you in the morning."

With a last scathing look at Walt, he went out the door.

Brock shook his head. "Sorry about that. Pay him no mind."

Walt smiled, once again the affable attorney. "I won't. Where is our fair Ellie?"

"She should be back any minute now. I'm heading home. See you later," Brock said.

"Right. Goodnight."

Walt greeted Wheezer and sat down at Ellie's desk. "Busy day, eh?"

"Yep. We knew that it was too quiet for too long," Wheezer agreed. "Now we'll be run ragged with all kinds of stuff for a while."

Walt was about to respond when Ellie came in the door. He stood up. "There ya are."

Ellie smiled tiredly at him. "I'm sorry I missed our dinner."

"Think nothin' of it," Walt said. "Ya had more important things to do. Are ya hungry, though?"

"Not really. Can we change our plans until tomorrow night?"

Walt hid his disappointment. "Certainly. Would ya like a ride home?"

"I have my horse."

"Right. Shall I walk ya to yer horse?"

She knew that he was just being sweet, but his question sparked her temper. "I can walk to my horse by myself, Walt."

He lifted an eyebrow at her sharp tone. "I didn't mean that ya couldn't. I'll tell ya what. Let me take ya to breakfast tomorrow."

Wheezer knew when a fight was brewing and he didn't want to be present. He got up and went out to the yard.

"Walt, I'd have to rush around in the morning to make it before my shift starts."

He rubbed the back of his neck agitatedly. "Ellie, I just want to spend some time with ya. I understand that yer tired tonight, but I have the feelin' that even if I were to ask ya to dinner tomorrow night, ye'd refuse."

Ellie sighed. "No. Yes. Maybe. I don't know!"

"What is it that ya don't know about? Dinner or me? What are we doin' here?"

Her forehead puckered. "What do you mean?"

"I'm talkin' about us. Are we courtin' or not? I've asked ya that a couple of times and ya just change the subject. And right now, ya don't seem to want anything to do with me, but in a couple of days or so, ye'll want to have dinner or somethin'. Ya tease me, getting me all aroused and then stop. Are ye waiting for marriage? I doubt it because we both know ye're no virgin. Ya need to piss or get off the pot!" The words came out in a torrent, Walt's frustration and anger pouring forth.

Ellie gasped. Fury burned so hot that she felt slightly dizzy. Her fist shot out, catching him squarely on the jaw. The force of the blow made Walt stagger back a few steps. His foot hit the leg of her desk and he landed hard on his backside.

Ellie clapped a hand over her mouth, staring at Walt in shock. His hazel eyes blazed with anger as he got up and sat in her chair, needing a moment to clear his fuzzy brain.

"I'm so sorry, Walt. Are you all right?"

He glared at her. "I s'pose that's my answer. I'll be fine. I thank ya for not breakin' my glasses at least."

Remorse made her cheeks burn. "I'm so sorry."

"Ya said that, but what exactly is it that yer sorry about? Hittin' me or that ya don't want to see me anymore?"

Ellie said, "I didn't say that I don't."

His anger grew hotter and he pounded her desk. "But ya didn't say ya do, either! Ya can't have it both ways, Ellie! I can't take it. Why did ya want to go out to dinner with me that first time if ya weren't really interested in me? Was it a game? Is that what this has all been to ya?"

"I hit you because you basically called me a whore!"

He let out a short, sarcastic laugh. "See? Ya did it again. Ya can't even answer my questions, which tells me even more than ya hittin' me does. I guess ya got off the pot."

"Walt—"

He moved so swiftly that she didn't have time to react, grabbing her around the waist, and kissing her roughly. She resisted, but he didn't let her go until she'd just begun to respond. He pushed her back a little, abruptly ending the kiss. Her eyes were huge as she stared into his.

"It's such a shame we never made love. I know how to do things to a woman that will make her beg for mercy but leave her desperate for more."

His gaze raked over her and Ellie's body reacted as though she stood naked before him. Then he strode out of the office, leaving her dazed and confused.

Walt climbed up in his buggy and rubbed his jaw. He knew that he would have a bruise by the time he arrived home. That made him chuckle. Ellie was a woman of strong passions, and he'd figured that if he pushed her hard enough she'd react exactly the way she had.

As he drove off, he laughed to himself, knowing that he hadn't seen the last of her. Walt understood Ellie better than she understood herself. The simple fact was that she was afraid to fall in love. Every time she got close to where she might let herself, she became frightened and backed off again.

Yes, he'd been angry and frustrated with her, but he wasn't done with her by a long shot. He had plans for his Ellie, and one way or another, he was going to claim her for his own. And once he had, she'd never want to leave him. He'd make sure of that.

~~*~~

Should she or shouldn't she? Walking back and forth by her horse, which stood outside Silver's Store, Daphne

222

could decide if she should stop by the sheriff's office to see Brock or not. It had been several days since she'd seen him after the fiasco at Benny's and she missed him. However, as much as she wanted to see him, it wouldn't be the right place to talk to him.

Letting out a frustrated breath, she stashed her purchases in her saddlebags and mounted up. As she turned her horse around, Daphne heard someone call her name. The voice sent a shiver of awareness down her spine even before she looked at its source. It seemed as though fate had made her decision for her by bringing Brock around right at that moment. The sight of his broad shoulders and handsome face hit her like a strong wind and hunger for him made her stomach flutter.

Every instinct she possessed told her to jump into his arms and drown in his embrace as he rode up to her. His intense blue eyes slowly roamed over her, almost like a caress and she was glad that she sat on a horse instead of standing on her own two feet. She wasn't sure that her legs would have held her for the desire that coursed through her.

"God, I've missed you," he said. He hadn't meant for that to be the first thing he said to her, but it was out before he could stop it. "We have to talk, honey. I deserve a chance to explain."

"Yes. We do need to talk." *Stop looking at his mouth!*

"I'll come out tonight after work, no matter what time it is. I can't let this go on any longer," he said.

Daphne raised her chin a little. "That's fine." She couldn't let herself get carried away until she'd made sure of some things first.

Her slightly cool tone irked him, but the desire he saw in her eyes gave him hope. He couldn't stop looking at her and it didn't seem like she was in a hurry to go anywhere, either.

Finally, he made himself say, "Okay. I'll see you then. I gotta go back to the office, but I'll try to get done on time tonight."

Daphne nodded, keeping a tight hold on her reins so she didn't launch herself at him. "All right. I'll see you when you get there."

The wariness in her expression made him want to kick himself for his big mouth and kill Daniel for his. Tearing his gaze from her, he nodded and urged his horse into a trot. He barely resisted turning around to look at her.

All day long, his mind was only half on his work as he thought about how to convince Daphne of his sincerity and that his feelings regarding her heritage had changed. An idea finally came to him and he thanked the heavens that nothing came up for him to deal with before he needed to leave.

The situation with Daphne wasn't the only reason he was glad to go. Ellie had been morose and withdrawn, but didn't want to talk about whatever was bothering her. Hunter had also been irritable, which was unusual for him. Cy had been the only one on dayshift in a good mood, which had prompted Brock to spend more time than usual out in the Dog House. They'd laughed about the strange twist that had made them prefer being with each other instead of their other coworkers.

As soon as he mounted up that evening, he put his horse into a canter, in a hurry to put his plan into motion.

~~*~~

When Daniel answered the knock at their front door, he was startled to see Brock.

"What do you want?"

Brock didn't let his rude attitude get to him. "I've come to make restitution."

Daniel gave him a dubious look. "What? Are you drunk?"

"No. I've come to make restitution," Brock repeated. "May I come in?"

Curiosity got the better of Daniel and he stepped back, noting that Brock carried a sack. "Sure. You better not be here to make fun of us or I'll put your head through a wall."

"Duly noted," Brock said.

Daniel shut the door and led the way into an expansive parlor. Brock felt like he'd just entered the lion's den as he followed Daniel through the beautiful home. Several chairs and a long sofa were attractively arranged around a large fireplace.

Rich blue drapes hung over the windows and a huge woven rug in blue and gold covered most of the gleaming wooden floor. It seemed a strange place for people with Indian heritage to live, Brock mused. David and Bonnie rose from their chairs.

"Hello, David, Bonnie," Brock said. "How are you?"

"Confused," David shot back. "Did I hear you say something about making restitution?"

Daniel's mouth twisted in a wry smile. "Pa can hear the grass grow."

"That's right. I've come to make restitution to your family," Brock said.

Bonnie was as perplexed as David. "For what?"

"Well, first off for the way that I've treated you in the past and also for the way I spoke about you on New Year's Eve." He looked at Daniel. "I'm also sorry for hitting you, but you had it coming and you know why."

Daniel's nostrils flared in annoyance, but he couldn't deny that Brock's remark was true. He owned up to it. "Yeah, I did."

Brock gave him a curt nod. Reaching into his sack, Brock pulled out a fine knife in an intricately carved leather scabbard, which he handed to Daniel.

"That one is yours and this one is for Sly," Brock said, giving him a second knife.

Daniel was impressed by the quality of the weapons and gave Brock a surprised look.

"Those are from my personal collection," Brock said.

"I can't take these," Daniel said.

Brock wouldn't take them back. "I thought it was offensive to refuse gifts of restitution?"

"It is," David said. "This is strange for us because we've never had anyone pay restitution to us before."

Brock nodded. "I'm sure they haven't, but they should. I want you to know that I'm doing this out of respect and with a sincere heart, not because I'm poking fun at you."

Bonnie said, "We can see that, Brock."

"Good."

"What's going on?"

The quiet voice behind Brock made him jump. He'd never heard Sly approach. The laughter in Daniel's eyes said that he'd seen Brock's reaction. Sly came out from behind Brock to stand by his brother.

Bonnie said, "Brock is here to pay restitution to us."

Sly lifted an eyebrow but didn't comment.

Daniel handed him the knife Brock had brought for him. "This is your gift."

Sly looked over the scabbard and took the knife out of it, testing its balance and the blade before sheathing it again. "It's a fine knife. Thank you."

Brock smiled. "You have better manners than your brother. He tried to give it back."

Daniel scowled at him while David and Bonnie chuckled and Sly smiled a little.

Moving over to Bonnie, Brock gave her a bottle of French perfume and fine pair of silk gloves. "I didn't think you'd like a knife so I figured those would be better gifts for you."

Bonnie sniffed the perfume. "Both gifts are lovely. Thank you."

"You're welcome." Brock had to steady his nerves as he looked at David. "I have a knife for you, too, but it means more to me than all of my other ones combined. Since you're the head of this family, I felt that it should go to you."

He pulled the knife out of his sack and said, "This was my grandfather's hunting knife. He had it all his life and I can only imagine how many deer and other animals he field dressed with it. Not to mention a lot of other uses he had for it. He gave it to Pa to give to me when I was old enough to appreciate it.

"I've used it a lot myself, so there's a lot of power in this knife from hunters. I want you to have it so that you know that my apology for my past actions and words against your family is sincere. Please accept this final gift of restitution."

All of the Lone Wolfs knew what it cost Brock to give David such a beloved possession. It wasn't something done lightly and even though they saw the shimmer of tears in Brock's eyes, he was resolute in his decision to give it to them.

Reverently, David took the knife. The leather scabbard was indeed old and worn, as was the knife handle. David took the knife from the scabbard and found the blade shiny and very sharp. He could almost feel the power in the weapon. He put it away and rested a hand on Brock's shoulder.

"It is a good gift, worthy of a chief. Thank you."

Brock cleared his throat. "You're welcome. Now, I've also come about something else. I need your help…"

~~*~~

Sitting in the parlor, Daphne stared at the book she'd been trying to read. She couldn't concentrate on it, however. It was almost nine o'clock and she was starting to give up hope that Brock was coming. Cy was home and had said that they'd been able to leave on time, so unless something else had come up, Brock should be able to make it.

She snapped the book closed and sat it on the sofa

beside her. Cy and Leigh were over at Johnny's bunkhouse, going over some of the plans for their house. Cuddles laid on one of the chairs and Buttons was outside somewhere. Burt lie asleep on the floor in front of the fireplace, but the other two dogs had gone with Cy.

Looking around the parlor, she felt lonely and imagined that this was how it would be once Leigh and Cy moved out if things didn't work out between her and Brock. She didn't want to entertain that possibility in the slightest. What would she do with herself once her work was done? They would still come for meals sometimes, but it wouldn't be the same. She'd never lived by herself and she didn't want to, either.

Her thoughts were interrupted by the sound of a flute. It stopped and she thought that she'd been hearing things at first. It started again and she rose from the sofa, hurrying out to the kitchen. Yes, someone was playing an Indian flute—badly. Horribly, in fact.

Snatching her coat, she quickly donned it and went outside. Someone sat cross-legged a little way from the house. It was dark, but she thought they wore buckskin clothing. Daphne couldn't figure out who it could be. Then she noticed that a horse was tethered to the porch railing.

"What on Earth is going on?"

Suddenly it hit her. Someone was performing the traditional method of courting an Indian maiden. He'd brought a horse as a gift and was playing the flute to draw her out of the house to listen. She was definitely listening, but the poor playing was enough to make one's ears bleed.

Who was courting her? It came to her, but she rejected it. *It can't be Brock. He doesn't play flute or wear buckskin.* There was only one way to find out. Stepping off the porch, she strode towards the flute player.

"Brock? Is that you?" she called out.

The flute playing stopped. "Yeah, it's me. Thank God you stopped me. I was giving myself a headache."

She laughed. "You're not the only one. What are you doing?"

He got up and grinned at her. "I'm serenading my maiden. Well, courting you, anyway. I don't count all that screeching as serenading."

He looked both virile and awkward in the buckskin leggings, breechcloth and tunic. He certainly filled them out well, but his short blond hair just didn't go with the outfit. Laughter erupted from her and she was helpless to stop it.

Brock pretended to be offended at first, but he couldn't keep a straight face, either. Wrapping his arms around her, he kissed her forehead and laughed with her. When they sobered, he cupped her face.

"Honey, I'm so sorry about what I said, but it just came out all wrong. I did this so that you could see that I respect your Comanche heritage and that it doesn't bother me anymore. I also made restitution with your cousins and David and Bonnie to show just how serious I am about it."

Daphne's wounded heart began healing as he spoke. "So you brought me a horse?"

"Yeah. A brave is supposed to bring gifts for his maiden, so I did. That's not just any horse, though. She's one of your uncle's Arabian mares."

She jerked a little. "You bought a horse from Uncle David? That's an expensive horse, Brock."

"You're worth more than any amount of money, Daphne. I also paid restitution to your family for all of the horrible things I've said about them and the awful way I've treated them and other Indians in the past. I needed to show them that I no longer harbor any ill will toward them. I want peace between us so that nothing comes between me and you again," he explained.

All of the things that Brock had done restored her faith in him and she knew that he meant every word.

She tenderly laid a hand on his cheek. "I appreciate everything you've done so much. I can't believe you did it."

"Daphne, you're the most important person in my life. I love you more than I ever imagined I would. I want to marry you, have a family, and grow old with you. Building that tipi was the best thing I could've done. Now I understand why your people love them so much and I learned a lot from Cotton and you.

"I see now that just like any other race, there are good and bad Indians. Your family is nothing like the Indians that killed Grandpa. You're good people and you deserve to be treated with respect and decency."

Even in the dark she could read the sincerity in his expression. "Thank you, Brock. I'm so relieved to hear you say that. I worried that you'd regret marrying me and be angry when I taught our children about my heritage. I shouldn't have doubted you, but hearing you say these things is very reassuring."

Brock hugged her. "I understand. It just came out all wrong that night. I'm so sorry that I hurt you. I promise to never do that again. Will you forgive me and still marry me?"

Joy surged through Daphne and her eyes filled with tears. "On one condition."

"Which is?"

An impish smile curved her lips. "That you never play flute again."

Brock burst into laughter and she joined in.

Sobering, he said, "I promise not to play it again. I love you, honey."

"I love you, too."

The light kiss he gave her then quickly turned urgent, his arms tightening around her. Her soft lips and images of what lie beneath her coat and clothing made him burn with desire.

Pressing against him, Daphne gave herself up to the passion he stirred in her. His lips were warm and supple, his kiss demanding. Her hunger for him intensified. She pushed against his chest and pulled back from him.

"Let's go to our love tipi. I've missed you so much and I want to make love with you."

Her slightly husky voice and her heated gaze made his blood run even hotter through his body. "What about your family? They'll know."

Daphne shook her head. "I don't care. I need to be with you. In Comanche culture, we would just be eloping."

The idea of them eloping made him grin. "Okay. Let's go."

He took her hand and they jogged around the barn, hurrying along the path that led to their love tipi. Their happiness grew with each step as they ran through the night, their hearts filled with a love that would survive and doubts or hardships that came their way.

EPILOGUE

Daphne sat calmly in the church office, waiting for Cy to collect her and her bridesmaids when it was time for the ceremony to begin. Her serenity came from her certainty that Brock was the man she'd always been meant to marry. The Great Spirit had chosen him for her and now they were about to be forever joined.

Leigh sat down by Daphne and took her hand. "I'm so happy for you and Brock. You belong together."

Squeezing Leigh's hand, Daphne said, "I owe it to you. If you hadn't pushed me to confront him, I wouldn't be sitting here, getting ready to marry him. Thank you."

"Nah. I might have started the ball rolling, but you took it from there. I'm glad you worked things out."

"Me, too."

Brock's sister, Nora, said, "He's a handful to live with. Consider yourself warned. He's cranky in the morning and he likes to play pranks."

"I think I'll be able to handle him," Daphne said. "I have ways of keeping him in line."

Leigh chuckled. "I'll just bet you do."

Daphne blushed. "Shut up. It's going to be so strange when you and Cy move out. I'm going to miss you."

"Oh, don't worry. You'll still see a lot of us. I'll be working every day like normal, so we'll still have lunch together. Besides, I'm sure you and Brock will enjoy having the house to yourself," Leigh said, winking.

Nora giggled. "Who knows what you'll get up to."

"Stop it, you two," Daphne said, turning a darker shade of pink.

"You're so lucky," Nora said. "I hope I meet someone soon."

Leigh said, "I'm sure you will. There are a bunch of eligible bachelors around, you know."

Nora frowned a little. "I know, but none of them seem to be interested in me. Of course, I'm so shy that I can't hardly talk around them."

Daphne asked, "Is there anyone in particular you're interested in?"

Nora shook her head.

Leigh gave her a kind smile. "Don't get discouraged. It'll happen."

"She's right. And sometimes, you just have to take matters into your own hands and make it happen. So don't give in to your shyness. You're a beautiful young woman and someday soon, you'll find the man of your dreams," Daphne said.

Nora brightened. "Do you think so?"

"Absolutely," Leigh said.

Cy arrived at that point, ending the conversation.

"You look beautiful, Daphne," he said, taking in her winter white satin gown. "I know I'm not your father, but I don't want to give you away."

His statement brought tears to Daphne's eyes. "Quit saying things like that! I don't want to bawl and have red eyes."

Cy laughed and lightly embraced her. "Sorry, sis, but I mean it."

"I'll always be your sister. That isn't changing."

Nora said, "And just think, you get to live with my

234

brother now."

Cy's expression immediately darkened. "You just had to remind me, didn't you?"

Nora laughed. "I couldn't resist."

Cy heaved a sigh. "Well, are you ready to go get married?"

Daphne bounced a little. "Yes!"

Cy gave her his arm. "Let's go then."

~~*~~

"I can't believe Pastor Clem let Ollie in here," Aaron remarked as he stood up at the altar with Brock and Wheels.

Brock said, "I paid him a little extra. I love Ollie and I wanted him to be here."

Wheels grinned. "Almost everyone loves Ollie. I hope he behaves for Nora. Although, she does have a way with him."

Aaron nodded. "That she does." Patting Wheels' shoulder, he said, "You clean up pretty good, Wheels."

Wheels ran a hand over his tuxedo jacket. "Thanks. I do what I can."

Brock said, "Yeah. You cut your hair and everything. I'm honored that you would go to all that trouble for our wedding."

Wheels glared at him. "Shut up. I just get so busy that I forget to get it cut."

"Now, now, gentlemen," Aaron said. "It looks like things are going to start."

The organist sat down at his instrument and began the pretty piece of classical music that Daphne had picked out. Pastor Clem took his place at the altar.

At the entrance to the sanctuary, Nora bent down to pet Ollie, who looked handsome in his little tuxedo. She handed him the little pillow to which the wedding bands were affixed.

"Take to Daddy," she said. "Go. Take to Daddy."

Ollie nodded and grunted before he took off down the aisle. He spotted Vern and almost got distracted, but then Wheels whistled for him and he bounded the rest of the way, hopping up on Wheels' lap. The congregation chuckled at Ollie's good performance.

Wheels took the rings from Ollie and handed them to Aaron. He praised the monkey and made him sit down and remain quiet. The look of distaste on Pastor Clem's face made Wheels grin, but he pretended that he was smiling at Ollie so that he didn't offend the clergyman.

Nora walked to the altar, beautiful in her pale lavender gown. Leigh followed her and Cy's eyes never left his wife as she made her way up front. He loved her more every day and he knew how blessed he was to have found her. Then he turned to Daphne.

"Ready?" he asked.

She nodded. "Ready."

Cy led her down the aisle, proud to be standing in for their father and wishing that their parents could be there. He put that out of his mind, concentrating on the joyful occasion instead.

Daphne couldn't tear her gaze from Brock. He was freshly shaven and his tux fit him to perfection. His shoulders looked even broader and his impossibly blue eyes were filled with love.

Watching Daphne come down the aisle to him, Brock felt as though his heart had grown too full with love to fit inside his chest. Her high-necked, long sleeved dress molded to her curves and her mahogany hair, which she'd let grow out somewhat, had been secured back with combs. Nora had woven baby's breath through the dark tresses, and the effect gave Daphne an ethereal appearance.

His bride arrived at the altar and Pastor Clem asked, "Who gives this woman to be married?"

Cy proudly said, "I do."

For a few seconds, he hesitated to let Brock take her hand, giving the deputy a hard glare that spoke volumes. Brock just smiled a little and took Daphne's hand, which Cy slowly relinquished. Daphne rolled her eyes at them and Brock chuckled. Cy grinned and went to sit with Johnny.

Their vow exchange was filled with laughter thanks to Ollie, who chirruped after almost everything Pastor Clem said. Wheels finally tucked him under his tuxedo jacket, a trick that always quieted Ollie. Brock and Daphne didn't mind, however, so filled with happiness that the laughter felt appropriate to them.

Tears stung Brock's eyes as he said, "With this ring, I thee wed." Sliding Daphne's ring on her finger gave him such pride that he couldn't quite contain it and a couple of tears escaped his eyes.

Daphne had never seen him cry before and it made her become misty-eyed as she put his ring on his finger. The tears kept coming as Pastor Clem finished the ceremony and gave Brock permission to kiss his bride.

Sweeping her into his arms, Brock distracted them from the tears by kissing her soundly, much to the pastor's consternation.

"All right, son, that's enough," he said.

Slowly, the newlyweds released each other and turned to the congregation, who clapped when they'd been presented to them.

Brock had hired a photographer, but he itched to take the pictures himself. However, that wasn't possible since he was the groom and had to be in the pictures. As he looked at Ollie sitting on Wheels' lap, he thought that it wasn't everyone who had a monkey in their wedding photographs.

Daphne must have been thinking the same thing because she coaxed Ollie over onto her lap and hugged him. Ollie put his arms around her neck and gave her a noisy smooch, which the photographer caught. Brock thought that outside of the pictures of him and his wife, the one with Ollie might just be his favorite wedding photo.

~~*~~

Staring into Brock's eyes while they danced together, Daphne finally believed that her dreams had come true. He was truly hers forever and she'd never let him go. He'd proven himself to her and she'd never doubt him or his feelings for her again. She was safe in his arms and she knew that she always would be.

Brock waltzed with his wife, never looking away from her luminous, dark eyes. His mind flashed ahead to when she was pregnant with their first child and then to when they had four or maybe five kids. He wasn't sure how she felt about that many kids, but he'd take as many as came along. Hell, between Cy and Leigh and him and Daphne, they could have enough kids to create Chance City's next police force.

That thought made him laugh and Daphne gave him a quizzical look. He told her what he'd been thinking and she laughed with him so hard that they had to stop dancing. Clinging to him as she laughed, she hoped that her and Leigh's suspicions were right. Leigh had refused to go to the doctor, preferring to wait a little while to make sure all of the symptoms remained.

Daphne could understand Leigh's fear of disappointment, but she hoped that she wouldn't wait too much longer. Brock started dancing again and her mind was pulled back to the man who held her. The man of her heart, who would forever hold it.

~~*~~

"Go on and ask her."

Hunter shook his head a little. "It would be too

embarrassing to be turned down at a wedding reception."

Johnny turned Hunter to face him. He and the young deputy had become good friends since Hunter had arrived in town. "Now, listen to me. I don't know much about private things between men and women, but I know that you can't waste opportunities. I did and it cost me.

"But you have a chance, so don't lose something because you were too chicken. If she turns you down, so be it, but at least you tried. Now get yourself together and go ask her to dance."

Ray lounged back in his chair. "If you don't ask her, I will."

Hunter glared at Ray. "No, you won't. Don't you get enough attention from women working as a whore."

Despite the fact that they were on opposite sides of the law, the two men liked each other.

Ray crossed his legs at the ankles and gave Hunter a lazy grin. "I'm always looking for more business."

Hunter snorted with laughter. "It's a wonder that thing doesn't fall off."

Ray and Johnny laughed.

"No danger of that," Ray said.

The other two grinned.

"Look, Texas, get over there and ask her to dance," Ray said. "You're a good-looking guy and you're respectful. Women like that."

Johnny asked, "Then how come you have so much business?"

"Because after some men marry a woman, they figure that they don't have to keep trying to please their wife. If all men treated their women right, I'd be out of business in a heartbeat. I'm just fulfilling something they can't get at home," Ray said. He kicked Hunter's chair. "I swear if you don't get over there, I'm gonna ask her to dance and once I get a hold of her, she'll be ruined for anyone else."

Hunter smirked at Ray. "You're awful sure of yourself."

"That I am," Ray agreed. "There's not a single woman, and a lot of married women, I couldn't get to dance with me."

Johnny grinned. "Is that so?"

Ray nodded. "Yep."

"Care to make a wager on that?" Hunter asked.

Never one to back down from a bet, Ray sat up. "Yeah. How much?"

"I got ten dollars that says you can't get the mayor to dance with you. She's single," Hunter said.

Immediately, Ray pulled out his money clip and peeled off a ten dollar bill, which he handed to Johnny to hold. He stood up and made sure his tuxedo jacket was neat. "If you gentlemen will excuse me, I have a mayor to seduce."

Johnny and Hunter exchanged startled glances at his proclamation. Hunter hadn't expected Ray to take him up on the bet because of who he'd chosen.

Ray walked brazenly up to the table at which Carly Branson sat with several other women.

"Pardon me for interrupting, Mayor Branson, but I was hoping that you might do me the honor of dancing with me," he said, bowing to her.

Even though she'd never been formally introduced to Ray, Carly knew who he was through a couple of her friends who saw him. In a cool tone, she asked, "And just why would I do that?"

Undaunted, Ray said, "Because I have a business matter to discuss with you."

Her eyes widened as they met his silver gaze. "What kind of business could *you* possibly have to discuss with *me*?"

Holding out his hand to her, he said, "It's not the sort of business deal I want anyone to know about in case they'd steal the idea for themselves. Just one quick dance and then I'll leave you be."

Out of the corner of her eye, Carly spotted Archie Hamilton approaching. She despised the man who fawned over her whenever she was around. She made up her mind in one second. Dancing with Ray was far more preferable than dealing with Archie.

She grabbed Ray's hand so fast that it made him blink. Leading her out onto the floor, Ray chuckled as they began dancing.

"Boy, you sure don't like him if you were that quick to dance with me."

Carly gave him a cold stare. "What sort of business do you want to discuss?"

He grinned. "None at all, sweetheart. None at all. See, I bet my friends that I could get you to dance. Thank you for helping me win that bet."

Color rose in her cheeks. "I am not a pawn on a chessboard, Mr. Stratton."

"Oh, so you know who I am. I'll bet Lucy Abrams told you, hmm? She's a lot of fun. Very giggly at certain times."

"Shut up," Carly said through clenched teeth. "You're despicable."

"Oh, you're one of *those*. I've been dealing with your kind all my life. Some of my best customers. You hate me during the day, but at night? Well, that's a whole other story," Ray said.

"I am nothing like them, Mr. Stratton. And let me remind you who you're talking to."

Sliding his hand far enough down her back to be indecent, he said, "I don't care who you are because there's nothing you can do to me. I'm untouchable, except if you want to touch me. It'll cost you, but you've got money to burn."

Rage surged through Carly and she practically ripped her hand from his. "This dance is over. It's been very enlightening. You're even more detestable than I thought."

Ray chuckled as she walked away from him. He left the dance floor in search of a drink, thinking that this was going to be a very fun evening.

~~*~~

"Excuse me, ma'am. May I have this dance?" Hunter asked the gorgeous blue-eyed brunette.

She'd been bored, but with one look into his gorgeous dark eyes, the evening started looking up. Giving him a coquettish smile, she said, "I'll dance with you if you know my name."

"Georgia Silver."

His immediate answer surprised her. "My goodness, Deputy Stetson. How astute you are. How did you know?"

"I'll tell you if you dance with me."

Georgia gave him a sly look. "It's a good thing for you that I'm curious by nature and that I love men with Texan accents."

She took the hand he held out to her.

"Is that so?" Hunter tucked her hand in the crook of his elbow.

Georgia said, "Yes, it is. Lead on, Deputy."

"Yes, ma'am."

As they danced, Johnny caught Hunter's eye. He smiled and winked and Hunter grinned before turning his attention back to the beautiful young woman in his arms.

~~*~~

The day after Brock and Daphne's wedding, Cy arrived home late because duty had called, delaying his departure for the day. He was tired and hungry and he was looking forward to eating and relaxing with his wife. Entering the kitchen, he found Leigh at the stove.

"Hi, beautiful," he said.

"Hello, handsome. Busy day, hmm?"

"Yeah. Something smells good."

"Ham. I was so hungry for it," Leigh said. "Wash up and sit down. I'm just getting ready to make our plates."

Cy kissed her before he went to the sink and washed

his hands. "Where's Johnny?"

"He went over to Wheels' house. Said they were working on something."

Cy chuckled. "When aren't they? I can't wait to see what they have up their sleeves this time."

This was Cy's favorite time of day, when he could sit down with his family and hear what they'd been doing all day. There were times when he looked back on his time working with Pinkerton's and he wondered how he'd stayed in that life for so long. He'd thought it had been so exciting, but it couldn't hold a candle to how thrilling his life was now.

His beautiful, loving wife was the most exciting thing in his life. He still loved his job, but everything about Leigh thrilled him: her body, the things they talked about, but most of all her heart and how much she loved him.

After dinner, they did the dishes and cleaned up the kitchen.

Then Leigh took his hand. "Let's go take a bath."

He raised an eyebrow. "Together?"

"Yeah. We have the house all to ourselves and I'd love to take a bath with my handsome husband."

Cy scooped her up. "You don't have to tell me twice."

Leigh laughed as he carried her to the bathhouse.

Setting her down, he said, "Every time I go to get a bath I thank Johnny in my head. It saves so much time not having to heat the water. I still don't know how they figured out just the right temperature to heat the water so you don't have to add cold to it. He's so much smarter than I gave him credit for.

"And they rigged up a drain and all. He said that in the spring, they'll install a proper bathtub. I'm glad that we included one in the plans for our house. I asked him why they didn't just use the water from the well and heat it somehow. He said that this way it wouldn't pull too much on the well during a drought. So—"

He glanced up when he heard Leigh giggle. She stood

already naked, apparently undressing while he'd been rambling on and watching the tub fill with water.

He grinned. "Looks like I'm falling behind."

"You're so cute when you go on like that."

"So you tell me."

He quickly shed his clothes and turned off the water. Slipping into the tub, he laid back. "Come on in, Mrs. Decker. The water's fine."

She laughed and got in, Cy helping her to get situated in front of him. Leaning back against him, she sighed as he embraced her. Taking his hands, she slid them down low on her stomach.

"Does that feel a little bigger to you?"

"Uh oh. Is this a trick question?"

"No, I promise. Does it?"

Cy wanted to spare her feelings, but he had to be truthful. "Maybe a little. Not much. I wouldn't worry about it. You're beautiful no matter what. I think I gained a few pounds over the holidays. I can't stay away from pies and Daphne kept making them. Of course Johnny eats a whole one—"

"Cy, shut up. I'm trying to tell you something."

He frowned. "Okay. Go ahead."

Pressing his hands a little harder against her abdomen, she said, "This is our little miracle, Cy. We're gonna have a baby."

Words left Cy as he tried to process what she'd just said. "But, I mean, you said, and I thought." He snapped his mouth shut until he could think coherently again. "A baby. Are you sure?"

Leigh blinked back tears of joy. "Yeah. Doc Ellis confirmed it. Our baby will come along around late June or early July. We made a baby, Cy. I guess I'm not barren after all."

Cy's heart soared with elation. He wrapped his arms around her and kissed her as she half-turned toward him. "We're having a baby! I love you so much and I can't wait for our baby to get here. July is a long way off."

"I know, but the time will go fast with getting our house built and a nursery ready," Leigh said.

"A nursery!" Cy practically shouted. "That's right. We'll need that."

Cy couldn't remember being so excited about something and he felt drunk with happiness. Under most circumstances, he remained calm and collected, but he couldn't manage it right then.

Leigh couldn't help laughing at his ecstatic attitude. "Yes, we will. We're also gonna need another ranch hand since I won't be able to do a lot of the work later on."

"Okay. We'll find someone. No heavy lifting for you. No overdoing it and working long days. You have to make sure to rest and eat and, shut me up, for Pete's sake!"

Giggling, Leigh slid his hands up her body, closing them around her breasts.

Cy grinned. "I like your method of subduing me. Let me get the soap."

He wasn't quiet for long. As he soaped her up, he talked about the baby, making her laugh, even as they made funny, awkward love in the tub. And later, when they went to bed, they still talked about their plans for the baby, how they'd set up a college fund, and how excited everyone else would be.

Finally, Cy's words ran out and he held Leigh, completely content to hold her while she slept. Her and his baby. As his eyes closed in slumber, a smile settled on his face before he completely relaxed into a deep sleep.

~~*~~

Cy and Brock living and working together proved to be a trial until their women devised a plan to give them some space from each other. The couples took turns going to visit someone in the evenings or just for a walk after supper. Some nights, Daphne and Brock stayed at their love tipi, too.

On one such night, Daphne couldn't sleep as she lay curled up against Brock. Looking at his handsome face that was slack as he slept, such a feeling of joy welled up inside her that she almost laughed out loud from it. She fought it back, but grinned as she gazed at him.

From his golden locks to his toes, he was a beautiful man. His strong hands and nimble fingers that played guitar so effortlessly also brought her so much pleasure. His kisses stole her breath away sometimes and making love with him was the most amazing thing she'd ever experienced except for one thing: his unconditional love.

It was always there in his voice, his eyes, and his touch. He was thoughtful, bringing her little treats and taking her out for romantic dinners. They learned more about each other all the time and we're getting to know their families better, too.

Her thoughts were interrupted when Brock stirred and opened his eyes a little. "What are you doing?"

"Watching you sleep."

Brock rubbed his eyes. "Are you all right? How come you're not sleeping. Didn't I wear you out enough?"

Daphne grinned and bit his chest.

"Don't do that. You know what that does to me."

"I was just thinking how happy you make me," she said.

Gathering her close, he kissed her softly. "You make me happy, too. I hope you know that."

"You might have mentioned it once or twice."

He smiled. "Once or twice a day is more like it. I mean it, though. I always think that I couldn't be happier, and yet I am every day when I wake up."

She bit his chest again. "Aren't you glad that I pulled you down off that fence?"

He groaned. "You're not gonna let me forget that, huh?"

"No, but I promise not to bring it up all the time. Just

when I can use it against you," she said.

"You sound like a lawyer," Brock remarked.

"Speaking of lawyers, has Walt been around much?"

"Off and on. I can't figure Ellie out. Talk about being on a fence. She watches the guy when he comes in, but doesn't want him to know she does. I can tell that she still likes Walt. I tried a couple of times to get her to tell me what happened between them, but she won't.

"Hunter is thrilled that they broke up. He has it in for Walt. He keeps saying that there's something strange about him. I don't understand it because Hunter likes almost everyone, but he can't stomach Walt at all."

"It's definitely a strange situation," Daphne agreed, yawning.

Brock smiled because she was falling asleep and now he was wide awake. He might tease Daphne when she made the remark about dragging him off the fence, but she was absolutely right. If she hadn't, he might still be sitting up there, miserable and alone.

He was incredibly grateful that she'd had the courage to make the first move. Her bravery was one of the things he loved most about her. He'd decided to emulate her and never miss an opportunity for happiness again. If he hesitated, it might pass him by, and he couldn't allow that. Lying in the dark, holding his beautiful wife, he vowed that he would never sit on the fence about anything ever again.

The End

Dear Reader,

The main reason I write is to entertain my readers, and I hope that you enjoyed *On the Fence, Chance City Series Book Two*. Make sure to sign up at my website, www.robindeeter.com to receive email alerts about new releases, news about upcoming works, and special little treats. You can also contact me through:

Facebook https://www.facebook.com/authorrobindeeter/

Twitter at https://twitter.com/Deeterwrites

Email: robin@robindeeter.com

If you like my work, please share it with others. I would also greatly appreciate it if you would take a few moments to leave a review. They really do matter and I always listen to my readers. Stay tuned for more books in this series and, as always, thank you for reading!

Robin

ABOUT THE AUTHOR

Robin Deeter fell in love with the written word the day she picked up "The Black Stallion" by Walter Farley, and that love affair continues to this day. In high school, she realized she could do more than read good stories; she could learn to write them, too. She went on to hone her craft with the Creative Writing Program through Full Sail University.

But her first love was entertaining, so she tried her hand at singing and acting. But Motown and Nashville didn't call, and Hollywood and Broadway ignored her. So, she concentrated her creative juices on writing to entertain others. And she's been writing ever since.

In between writing her historical western and contemporary romance novels, she still pursues her love of music and theatrics with local performances. She currently writes two book series; the Chance City Series and the Paha Sapa Saga. She's also involved in several other multi-author series and has more novel ideas that she's exploring.

If you can't find her writing or performing locally in Pennsylvania, where she resides, you'll catch her sporting the Black and Gold and cheering on her Pittsburgh Steelers.

72020577R00156

Made in the USA
Middletown, DE
02 May 2018